Praise for CA

"Fluidly transitioning between past to present and back again, Gloria Mattioni pits the silent desire of one sister against the needs of the other in a story that is both breathtakingly beautiful yet fearless in flaunting the ugly realities of life and death. California Sister will force you to think hard about who has the right to choose."

BARBARA CONREY, USA Today Bestselling author of *Nowhere Near Goodbye*

"A powerful dual-narration of fierce love, loss, and redemption that addresses some of the most controversial issues of our contemporary society: the limits of medical intervention, the right to die according to one's terms, euthanasia, the value of universal health care, the responsibility and burden of caring for the disabled in a ruthless world where success doesn't contemplate any weakness."

ARIANNA DAGNINO, author of *The Afrikaner*

"In California Sister, Gloria Mattioni has given us a tender, angry, poetic, heartbreaking novel about the fragility of life, the miracle of sister-love and the potential of self-reflection and courage. You will be moved, and you will ask yourself the biggest questions life throws at us. Beautiful, haunting and ultimately life-affirming."

PETE MCCORMACK, writer and director

"Mattioni writes with emotional truth about what happens when one sister is plunged into the position of sudden caretaker while the other sister lies in a shadowland. Can the deepest bond between these two sisters survive the intensity of what lies ahead as the heartbreaking experience unfolds? Tender moments filled with smiles, tears, pain, fear, and extraordinary loyalty radiate across the pages. California Sister is a story of redemptive love."

DONNA KEEL ARMER, author of *Solo in Salento*

"Bells ring into our inner night: it is time to recalibrate our moral compass and depart. Two tears mark a new border between Italy and California, an intimate land where two sisters with a promise meet to face the ultimate life quest: love vs ego, freedom vs aggressive treatment. Mattioni takes us by hand in a free fall into the core of existentialism raising questions and doubts that cannot be ignored anymore."

ALEXO WANDAEL, director

CALIFORNIA SISTER

GLORIA MATTIONI

atmosphere press

Table of Contents

To Marina Mattioni, a sister like no other:
Because nothing will ever compare to you.

"I thought how unpleasant it is to be locked out; and I thought how it is worse, perhaps, to be locked in."

VIRGINIA WOOLF

The California Sister, whose Latin name is Adelpha Californica, is a species of butterfly common in California, unpalatable to predators thanks to its enhanced mimicry.

Prologue
CLAIRE

(dredging up a time when she was still CHIARA)

Lake Maggiore, Italy, September 10, 1972

"No way!" My father's fists hit the steering wheel. The Alfa Romeo swerved and my heart skittered. The Italian Grand Prix blasted from the radio, and Jacky Ickx, his favorite driver, was out of the race after his Ferrari died past the *curva grande*. I bit my lips to hold back my scream. Any noise, and I'd be the target of his anger.

The blaring noise of cars pushed to their whining limit swirled in my head like the buzzing of a monstrous beehive while the curves of the winding road made me want to hurl my lunch on the car's upholstery. And that would really put me in my father's sights. I distracted myself by drawing on the fogged car window with my finger, watching the still damp trees lining the road, their tops hovering in the absence of any wind.

Sundays were always Father's day in our broken family. Our parents were no longer together since before I was born.

Dad had run off with another woman and he and our mother had weaved their own custody arrangement, long before Italy passed a divorce law in 1974. We saw him only a few hours every Sunday, either in Milan where we lived with our mom or at the lake where we spent our summers.

This Sunday, we were on our way to visit our dad's aunt, Giuseppina, who'd suffered a bad car wreck. "She's lucky to be alive," he'd told us before getting in the car. "Her heart stopped, depriving her brain of oxygen for some minutes."

"And that's bad?" asked my older sister Ondina, who was ten and sat in the passenger seat, a privilege I wasn't given since, at seven, I could never sit still for more than two minutes.

"But she'll be happy to see you girls."

We were excited to go to the farm, not far from the lake. She had goats and sheep with adorable lambs, and she always made us a fresh berry pie. Besides, the visit interrupted the monotony we'd endured for the past week, forced indoors by the rain. In September, the weather turned and we became trouble. Or, truth be told, I was trouble. Ondina was books, let's make a cake and play dress-up, who cares if it's raining. I was a rowdy tomboy who couldn't stand to be cloistered, eager to break free and run out, explore and seek adventure. That evening, father would deliver us back to our grandmother's country house, where we'd stay until October 1st, when the school year resumed.

"We're here," Father announced as the car tires squealed into the driveway. "Remember to behave and be gentle with Auntie Giuseppina. She's like a big baby now." He exited the car and opened the doors for us. I frowned at Ondina. How could an *old* granny like our grandaunt, go back in time to be 'like a baby'?

Dad's uncle, Piero, blocked us before we could enter their bedroom. An eighty-six-year old, he was still a tall and lanky man. "Wait outside. Maria's changing her diaper."

Maria was their older daughter, about our father's age. I was shocked at the idea of an adult peeing and shitting herself. Ondina lowered her eyes and hid her face behind Dad's broad torso, but I caught her smirk. Did she think that was funny?

When we were finally admitted, the room smelled of stale air and urine. Auntie's gaze was unfocused, running over our faces without a sign of recognition. Her mouth hung low on the left, giving her a crooked smile, and without dentures it looked caved in. Her left hand kept lifting only to slap limp on the white bedspread, over and over. I couldn't make sense of the globe of white plastic deep in the hollow of her throat. I learned later that was a tracheostomy but at that time it was just another big scare.

Dad gestured us close to the bed. I moved two small steps forward, trying to hold my face neutral. Ondina kept her distance, staring at her shoes. He picked me up and held me, and I thought it was a reward for my courage. "Give a kiss to your grandaunt." He lowered my face close, but Auntie Giuseppina suddenly jerked her head to the side, revealing a cratered skull with a long red scar on her shaved scalp. Dad flinched and lost his balance. My dangling legs landed on the poor woman's stomach.

Aunt Giuseppina reacted at first with a low, sad grumble that increased to a prolonged screeching wail. My father pulled me back and I squirmed from his grasp and lurched across the room, seeking a place to hide while he tried to calm her. Her eerie howl pierced my ears even under my palms. Frantic, I ran out of the room, sobs rippling through my chest and fear propelling my shaky legs. I ran out of the house, across the pasture full of indifferent cows to the stables, my favorite hiding spot. The cows and sheep were out in the meadow but the animal smell lingered inside and comforted me. I climbed the wooden ladder to the loft two steps at a time, then plunged into the pile of hay.

Time went by. When I could no longer keep my eyes open, I closed them but to no avail. After a while, a sudden metallic sound pulled me out of my daydreaming. Somebody had just pushed the door open and a pitchfork leaning on the wall had fallen on the cement floor.

"Chiara? Dad is ready to go." My sister's voice sounded like a bubbling stream curving gently through the trees and dissipated my dread.

"Is he mad at me?"

I was scared around him, convinced it was my fault that he abandoned us. He was home before I was there, and then he wasn't.

"Don't be silly. I felt afraid, too. Now hurry up."

I still hesitated, reluctant to abandon my protective nest. "Why don't you come up here first?"

Ondina made her way up the ladder. "Here, here," she said, opening her arms. "It's alright and we are leaving."

I felt safe in her embrace, knowing I could tell her things I wouldn't anybody else. She had my back in so many ways. "I never want to come here again," I hiccupped on her shoulder, dampening the fabric of her sweater with my tears and inhaling the musty smell of wet wool. "I can't see Auntie Giuseppina like that. It's just... *wrong!*"

It was wrong for so many reasons. Wrong that she had to live like a mummy, bedridden and unable to speak or walk, maybe even understand. Wrong that our father took us there without warning. Wrong that such a terrible thing happened to a sweet lady like her.

"I know." She shifted wisps of tangled hair from my face, still holding me tight. "I wouldn't want to live like that either."

"Then, promise! Promise that we won't let each other live that way or... We'd be better off dead."

Ondina scanned the loft. "We need a knife. We'll each

make a cut on our palms and then we'll shake and our blood will mix with the handshake. Like in that movie about the Norsemen, remember? The blood oath will seal our pact."

"But I don't want to bleed!"

"Don't cry. We can spit on our hands then."

Gross. Still, it beat the pain from a cut.

"Spit!" She ordered, and I expelled a good chunk of saliva on my palm, while she did the same. "Now, shake. We promise that we will never, ever end up like Aunt Giuseppina. And if we do... you know what I mean."

I wasn't sure what she meant but I felt heartened that she went along with my plan.

We had a pact. An allegiance sealed with spit, which my sister assured me was as good as blood. We were stronger now, reinforced by our renewed sisterhood. Fierce Norsemen sisters. We'd never yield to a terrible fate. We had forbidden it.

Chapter 1
CLAIRE

Los Angeles, January 21, 2008

Bangalore, December 27, 2007

Dear Claire:

It's pouring cats, dogs, rats, elephants and anything else you can think of today. So much for the mild Indian winter! I should have stayed in Italy. Or capitulated and gone to Brazil to spend Christmas with Guilherme. But I'm so tired of being the one to tend to the man. And, I know, he didn't ask me to. He didn't consider coming with me on this trip either—way out of his budget. Plus, he has children and a drunken ex-wife who doesn't wish to be an ex, which might be part of the reason why he didn't ask me to accompany him.

Never date a penniless stud, lil' Sis. And if that means doing it solo, so be it. I can't stay put for too long in the same geography. Watching the same scenery, exchanging small talk, hearing the same language over and over... how boring! I'd lose my sparkle. And die.

Anyhow, I'm splurging on the Sita House. I sleep in a four-poster bed of carved rosewood, cocooned in cream-colored drapery that wraps my slumber. I sip my morning loose-leaf tea from a brass cup, regally ensconced in my new turquoise sari on an ivory silk arm-

chair, the scent of burning incense wafting under the door from the miniature shrines in the corridor.

I have this picture of me and you twenty years ago, drinking the local Kingfisher draft in a pub in front of the hotel. You with your eternally long hair, me with a new haircut. You said it was too short, that I looked like a cute lamb, all those tiny curls framing my face.

Back then, we could only afford the Sita House in our dreams. Remember the roses we stole from the table to put in our hair? Remember the boys, whispering 'nice flowers' to our backs, lowering their eyes as soon as we turned our heads? The scent of the gardens in bloom and that Royal English luxury that we needed so bad after all the chaos and misery of our adventures in Calcutta?

I can almost hear you now. "I don't care about memories. I'm living in the future." Ha! Or was that something Nails said in one of your early books? BTW, I finished reading your last on the plane. Dark Desert Nights, indeed! It helped to distract me from the bumpy flight. The slightest breeze feels like a gale on Indian Airlines. What was that tune that my long-lost bassist boyfriend used to sing? 'It's just a light breeze/ pulling all your hair out.'

I'm late to suggest a change, but why is it that Nails only fucks at the end of her missions? Give the poor woman a break. How about some random orgasms to relieve her stressful job? Or, if she has such a problem with fucking men, make her gay. Or better yet, bisexual, so she can double the fun.

I'm buying you some turmeric, cumin, coriander and cardamom in pretty, tiny tinplate cans at the market on MG Road. Also, the usual silver earrings. That is, if I can get through the panhandlers, always children and elders here in Bangalore. I hope the adults are out at work.

The other day, I almost jumped at the unmistakable smell of barbecued beef sold by a street vendor. Holy cow! Where did the worshippers of Aditi go? True, there are plenty of Muslims here. But I believe that religion goes down as the GDP goes up. Bangalore has become a consumer's orgy—one of the most productive cities in India. Who knew? Way different than when you were last here.

Yesterday, I hired a driver and toured the local temples. You were so in love with Tipu Sultan's Palace that I'd promised myself to *stop there again. I can assure you that all the flowers painted on teakwood are still there. Of course, the driver stopped at the HTM factory as well. I bought a watch twice as big as my wrist, gold-plated with a plastic strap. My tacky belated Xmas present to Guilherme for spending our vacation with his children.*

Why do I feel betrayed, competing even with his unsuspecting kids? Am I laying the groundwork to feel abandoned? Again? Why do I still need to lift the edges of this boring old wound, gnawing on it until I hit the bone? Fucking Cinderella syndrome?

I know you resent me whining about men, but you are my sister and confidant so too bad!

I can feel your irritation swelling like a tidal wave. I hear your dismissal: "Psycho-yoga babble, no doubt from the mouth of one of your self-proclaimed gurus." Well, yeah. It might be. But it's still the truth. One day we'll get to the bottom of all this.

Now, back to the real object of my obsession. Why the fuck do I need to fall in love while I was having so much fun being a single, kid-free, financially independent gal? Why him, when I could pick anyone?

Maybe I miss a committed relationship. Maybe I feel lonely when I'm not loved. The immediate gratification of casual open relationships is no longer rewarding. And I don't think I am PMS-ing or stressing about the big five-zero waiting for me with open jaws, just a few years away.

I want a man who will take me as I am, not try to change or limit my freedom through a bunch of shitty compromises. Somebody who can look at me and say: 20 percent fat, strong-headed but also with her head in the clouds; moody and confused sometimes, determined others. Affectionate. A cuddler. Not perfect, but she's just fine for me.

Guilherme thinks and says so but he carries enough baggage that it could take down a donkey. Still, I can't deny that thinking of him brings sweaty images to my mind. Not only that, Sis, Guilherme has a body with a capital B, but also a mind. I like the head on his shoulders as much as the one on his cock. Luckily, he thinks with the first one. And though it's inconvenient, I can't say that I don't respect the stand he's taking for his children. Lucky kids to have a father who refuses to let them be brought up only by their messed-up mother. Maybe I'm jealous because Dad never fought for us?

Anyhow, it could be worse. He could still be married to Beatriz, made me his Italian mistress and gone back to Brazil. Sure, it'd be nice to have him around more. Would be nice for him to have more money to do things with me. But distance also means more space for me. Do I still need space? Or am I ready to trade it in for a guy I can actually talk to on a regular basis, face to face, in the same room?

C'ést la vie. I was worse when I didn't have anybody fool for love about me. I craved a man's love more than I crave this Kingfisher beer, my evening treat. BTW, it will be warm as piss by now. Better stop writing, get to the drinking.

Be well, my little sister, and promise me. Never fall in love with penniless studs!

Your charming older sister,
Ondina

My sister was the only person I knew who still wrote handwritten letters on pretty stationery with a fountain pen. I admired her distinguished penmanship. Mine sucked, so I never wrote her back by snail mail. Sometimes, even *I* couldn't make sense of my own scribbles.

The day her letter arrived, the twenty-first of January, 2008, Los Angeles, smelled of dust and danger. I should have read the signs. Gusty winds had blown all night, rattling the windowpanes, jolting me awake. I hadn't emptied the mailbox in days. Buried among the usual junk, a Netflix DVD, an invite to a neighbor's birthday party and a few bills, was a light blue, square envelope marked as airmail. I noticed the postmark, and how many weeks it'd taken for that weightless envelope to reach me. Ondina would now be back in Bergamo after spending another week of her winter vacation in Tuscany, skiing on the Abetone with her beau, thanks to the generosity of his parents who offered their vacation house and the ski passes for his kids.

My day had started early. At 6:30 a.m. I'd had enough of

turning and tossing.

"Let's go," I whispered to the dog, Drago, who didn't need to be invited twice. I gathered my clothes as we stole out the bedroom, silent as falling leaves, making sure not to wake Xavier. I dressed in the entry hall, eager as Drago to escape the house. I didn't bother to check myself in the mirror.

There wasn't a trace of winter in the blue sky, only in the chill of the air.

I opened the hatch door of the Jeep in the driveway. "Get in."

Drago wasn't my dog but when he'd moved in with Xavier a few years earlier, we'd bonded on the spot. And Xavier wasn't my boyfriend. He was my roommate and friend. With benefits. *Lots* of benefits and none of the obligations I suffered in past relationships. It was an agreement that satisfied us both.

I stashed the envelope in the glove compartment, and we headed to Griffith Park. We often took our morning jog on a dirt trail on the stretch that runs above the pony rides and the little kids' train. Me, with that slight rhythmic pant I get when it's still early, the air is crispy. The dog happily trotting by my heel.

"Almost there, Drago," I said at the two-mile mark. Mostly to reassure myself. Drago would have gone for twenty if I'd keep up. His left ear was missing the upper part so that only the right pricked up on his large pitbull head, honoring his other half German Shepherd genes. There were old puncture wounds on his neck, random scars covering part of his shoulders but the shepherd fur hid most of them. When Xavier rescued him from the shelter, he was told he'd been used as bait in an underground dog fighting ring. His still-whole ear was up and cocked forward now—he'd stopped in his tracks, sniffing the air.

"What's up, bud?"

Then I spotted it. A fresh paw print, bigger than the width of my hand. It was still early but the wintery, lemony sun had risen so it was unlikely for a mountain lion to be out hunting. Still, the hair on the back of my neck prickled. Unlikely doesn't mean impossible. Adrenaline creeping up the finer nerves of my forearms gave my skin tiny flashes like a million pinches. They could have lit the Hollywood sign.

Despite my love for all kinds of animals, being caught by surprise by a wild cat wasn't on my bucket list.

I blinked, wiped sweat from my forehead and crouched, scanning the immediate surroundings to spot where a big cat might be lurking. The right leg of my jeans snared on the pads of a prickly pear cactus.

A gamey scent lingered with the hot, sour mix of tarry chaparral and pungent eucalyptus. Drago's nostrils flared, black fur raised along his spine.

I freed my leg and glanced at the bike path bordering the Los Angeles River on one side and Interstate 5 on the other. Maybe it had crossed the ridge and headed down the hillside in search of fresh water. A tan shadow moving through the myrtle undergrowth along the side of the trail gave me a jolt, but it was only a coyote scurrying away. Nevertheless, an unruly chill snaked up my spine.

The print looked fresh and huge. Predators react in different ways to dogs. They can think 'danger' or 'lunch,' depending.

I rolled Drago's leash onto my wrist to keep him closer and grabbed a good size rock from the side of the trail, gripping it in my sweaty palm. A rock could scare off a coyote. I wasn't sure if it would work with a mountain lion. But it was all I had. That, and hyper-vigilance.

Checking my back trail every few steps, Drago and I dashed down to the trailhead at the parking lot where I'd left the Jeep. The sky was bluer now. The city below looked half asleep despite the endless line of cars eating up all five lanes of the freeway in each direction. A slight movement between the branches of a box elder gave me another start. Luckily, it was only a raven taking flight, its black magician cape spread out to embrace the morning.

Soon we were back to the parking lot, inside the Jeep with the doors locked, safe again. I drank big gulps of water from my canteen, wishing for something stronger though I'd quit drinking years ago, when my previous dog was 'terminally' ill and I wanted to give more strength to my prayers: 'if the dog lives, I'll never touch a drop again.' That kind of childish gamble you offer when you wish for the impossible. But the dog lived and I'd been alcohol-free since.

I poured some water in Drago's bowl and he lapped at it. I drove away slowly with Drago's head out of the back window, still sniffing for danger.

Back in the carbon exhaust scented air of Los Feliz Boulevard, I closed the windows and put the A/C on. Almost the end of January and eighty degrees. Only a couple of weeks earlier, commuters had scraped ice off their windshields in Lancaster, barely seventy miles from downtown. Soon it would be rattlesnake dry, again. The Santa Ana winds would blow minds away. The Angeles National Forest would burn like a napalmed Vietnamese jungle from a careless cigarette butt or a spark from a power line.

I left the freeway and we climbed back home to Mount Washington, a neighborhood made of steep hills just upstream from where the Arroyo Seco and Los Angeles River merge. The downtowners spent the weekend here in their hunting cabins in the thirties and forties, when L.A. had a real city center and young families hadn't yet moved to the suburbs. I'd moved there in 2002, away from my amniotic ocean and the beach party-town of Venice, where I spent the same amount on monthly rent as a family of four in South Dakota spends on food for a year and buying was certainly not an option, given my budget and my desire not to join the National Debtors Association as a life member. My son had already graduated from college and was out on his own, so I went back to single life in my new neighborhood. And now I shared the house with Xavier.

"Home safe and sound, buddy." I shut the outside gate, grateful for my urban oasis where I didn't need to be constantly on guard or hear traffic all night. Mounds of leaves had collected on the brick path that led to the house, thanks to the dry inland winds. "We will have to rake them, Drago. But first let's go get some breakfast."

Xavier's car wasn't in the driveway; maybe he'd gone to the gym. Forced to sit for long hours, the nights of his live show at the radio station made him feel restless the morning after, eager to work out.

I bolted down coffee and made breakfast. I wore jeans and a t-shirt, was barefoot, my hair dripping all over my face after the hike. Or the mountain lion scare. Both had provided rivers of sweat. On the kitchen counter was a copy of *Dark Desert Nights*. On the cover, Nails, my detective hero, gun held in both hands, pointing toward an almost dark landscape with glimpses of Joshua Trees. Beside the book, a silver frame with the picture of a much younger me smiling and hugging a darker version of myself. The Dome cathedral of Milan in the background. Lots of pigeons flying around the two young women and in the foreground.

The phone rang in my pocket. I pulled and accepted the call.

"What are you up to on this fine day?" Ondina's silky singsong. I missed it. We'd not spoken in a month, thanks to her traveling.

"Not much." I skipped telling my morning adventure, not wishing to be reprimanded about my inclination for risk-taking. "Later I'll have to discuss next week's book launch with my publicist. How about you, back in your beloved, clean and orderly bachelorette's nest?" I chuckled, picturing my sister in the apartment she'd moved in six years earlier, after divorcing her husband. Walls plastered in delicate pastel hues, enhancing the colorful bounty brought back from her frequent travels. Sheer curtains made from the finest Chinese silk at each window, wool throws bought in Peru leaning on the designer sofa and the armchairs, Kilim rugs on the hardwood floor with Moroccan low cushions for additional seating, South American pottery on the shelves to space out the books and 'let them breathe.' Quite a difference from my minimalist, Zen style.

"You got my letter, didn't you, smartass?"

"I did, but don't get all the drama." I took the pan away from the range, holding the receiver between my shoulder and cheek while I slid my over-easy eggs onto the plate. "He has a messy house and it bothers you. Okay. Then, see him only when he comes to visit you."

I heard the door click open and close, and caught a glimpse of Xavier waving before disappearing in the hallway separating the day area from the bedrooms and bathroom. Discreet. One of his many qualities.

"Maybe I'm more impatient than usual because of the flu I caught from his son. Maria, my new next-door neighbor, keeps pressing. She thinks I'm too pale and pesters me about it when we see each other in the elevator. I finally asked my doctor to order some blood work, mainly to shut Maria up."

"It might be the leftovers from your flu. But getting back to your boyfriend dilemma: you two clicked only a few months ago. It's not like you're living together."

I'd not even met Guilherme yet, which said a lot about how young their relationship was. I made sure to visit my sister in Italy twice a year and Guilherme wasn't in the picture last time

I was there.

"But I've been thinking about it. Perhaps moving in together is the only way it could work. He'd asked me to, but that would mean moving to Florence with him. Leaving this house, leaving my job."

Huge. My talented sister had quit singing and embraced a career as a copywriter at an advertising agency because she couldn't handle the financial uncertainty artists face. Leaving her job to freelance? Tough choice. Leaving her home, that she so carefully put together to reflect her style? She spent a year visiting furniture stores and making a pros & cons list for each couch she saw before settling on the sofa she finally bought. She'd moved to Bergamo when she got married and she'd remained there even after leaving her husband because she'd fallen in love with the city.

"Are you really considering it?"

"I don't know, Claire." She was the only one in my family who'd call me by my author's name instead of my given, Chiara, which I'd dismissed for good when I published my first book. "I'm so confused! My head is pounding. I feel tired but I have friends coming over for dinner. I invited the whole group of yoga teachers. They've never come here before. I need to get off the phone and make the house presentable."

Like it was ever untidy.

"Pour yourself a glass of wine and put aside this man trouble. Your friends are coming over, and that will cheer you up." I tried to sound convincing but I had an uneasy feeling quivering in my stomach. I wasn't concerned about her love life. Just her health. She never had headaches that I knew about. And she was the opposite of pale, having inherited my dad's dark complexion. What if it wasn't just a flu?

We said goodbye, and I rolled with the idea that Ondina could be sick, not just under the weather. But she'd always been healthy and in great shape, taking good care of herself. I finished my breakfast, washed my cup and dish, then I sat back at the table to take in the glorious view out of the big picture window in the family room, facing the green hills on the other side of the river. I checked my emails, knowing there'd be many in need of a reply with the book launch date getting close and still lots of details to be finalized.

I worked for half an hour but my mind wasn't focused, Ondina's words still echoing. *Breathe and let go of your thoughts.* My sister's yoga mantra. It didn't always work for me. Instead, I decided to wash away my worries. Water on my head had the power to clear my mind. On my way to the bathroom, I bumped into Xavier coming out, a towel wrapped around his hips. I pulled him close, tugging at it, and kissed him on his soft, welcoming lips.

The telephone rang in the kitchen. The house landline, almost never used.

"I'll get it," he offered. "Why don't you take your shower and I'll tell them, whoever they are, that you'll call back later?"

The spray of hot water had started its magic when I heard the click of the door and felt a wisp of fresh air, steam escaping my warm sauna. I could feel him there behind the smudged shower glass. "Don't even think about it! I'm not going to let you in."

"That call was from Italy."

Something in his tone made me open the sliding door. I stood in the frame. Naked, dripping.

"My mom? Did something happen?" My mom had Parkinson's disease and was in fragile health.

"It's about your sister."

"My sister? I just talked to her!"

"They took her to the hospital. She suffered a massive brain hemorrhage and collapsed. She's in a coma."

I studied his face, trying to capture the meaning of those words. But they sounded distorted, like I was still under water.

And they didn't make any sense. It wasn't possible. Not my sister. Not her! I was the one who'd break bones and end up in hospitals when we were children. Ondina was my rock, my protector, the only one who could piece me together every time. She couldn't be sick. It couldn't happen to her. And how? Just like that? One minute I'm talking to her on the phone and ten later she's having a brain hemorrhage? And in a coma??

When I stopped being in denial, I dropped the soap bar I held in my hand together with my soul. I couldn't breathe. I gasped for air but I sprang into action, my usual way to get rid of uncomfortable feelings. I snatched a towel from the rack and moved to the bedroom. To get dressed, Xavier trailing behind.

"Did they say how? Did they give you a number? Who called? Who's with her?"

"Your stepmother called. She said Ondina had invited friends over to her house. They found her passed out on the entrance floor of her apartment building. She was in the vestibule before the elevator, keys already in its door. They called the ambulance and followed it to the hospital. They didn't want to scare your mom. But they couldn't sign the release for her surgery."

"Surgery? *What* surgery?"

"She is on the waiting list for the neurologic operating room. Your stepmom said you should call your brother. They'll be on the road as soon as he picks her up."

Fabio, my brother from another mother. He was driving to Bergamo from Milan to authorize this emergency surgery. How bad must it have been? I couldn't picture the scene of my sister, unresponsive, lying on a gurney parked outside a neuro OR, waiting for my brother to rush in to sign papers that could save her life. I couldn't, or I knew I'd break. All I could think about, all I wanted was to be with her. *Be with her.* She needed me there. And she needed me whole, as whole as I could be with my heart shattered in a zillion pieces.

"So will we!" I'd put on a clean pair of jeans, a fresh t-shirt and a hooded fleece jacket at lightning speed, despite my trembling fingers having trouble to zip up. Everything I tried to pick up fell out of my grasp and I could hear my heartbeat way too fast. I forced the images which tried to break in out of my mind and concentrated on getting things done.

"Pack your bag. I'm going to book you on the first flight out of LAX."

I never felt so thankful for Xavier as in that moment. Somebody who could keep his head on his shoulders while mine felt unscrewed like a champagne cork when there was nothing to celebrate, nothing to be happy about. Only fear.

Chapter 2
ONDINA

Bergamo, 9:40 p.m., Italian time

I fell fast like a stone on the marble floor of the lobby of my apartment building. I watched my legs bend under me and splay at an unlikely angle. A puppet with the strings snapped off. I'd tried to turn the key in the keyhole of the elevator door, tried to get back to my friends, but my legs gave out, escaped me. My hand not taking orders from my brain.

I panicked, horrified. Fear so thick I could taste it in my mouth. There was a disconnection there, all of a sudden. I was still me, Ondina, myself, up to then. But 'me' was limited to my mind. I could not think straight, though. A pounding headache, a burning ball of fire in the back of my head on the left side. Something bad had happened, was happening, that was all I knew. I tried to grasp the fact of it with all my force, knowing that I should fight. I clawed to that last shred of myself, but I lost it.

I could no longer see myself spread out on that floor. Or feel the cold marble under my back and limbs. I couldn't see or hear. I couldn't move one finger. I tried to scream, but I was slipping away. No sound! Like a nightmare, running, my voice missing, dying inside my throat.

It wasn't blank. It was dark red spreading through my cells. Red and black spirals twirling, pooling up in my mind, stealing me away. Then emptiness. Nothing. Suspended somewhere far away. But no discomfort inside that bubbly, whitish sheath. I could say it was bliss, peace in that spongy, cotton-like space far away from the world. And I thought, this is it, how it should be.

That peace didn't last. A horrible banging inside my body, down deep in the darkness of me, like a gunshot, huge and primordial. The awful clanging reverberated through my head, wave after wave of pain. I was a balloon about to explode.

Something choking me from the inside, in my nose and throat, snaking down to my lungs. I couldn't breathe. Words didn't make any sound. Was everyone gone? My friends? Didn't they see me fall? Everything smooth as an otter skin. Guilherme? Didn't you see me being dragged off by the orcs? Rescue me!

I don't know where I am now. Someplace where I'm all alone. And it's dark.

It's cold and I'm scared.

Don't leave me here on my own.

Please! Isn't anybody listening?

Please, bring me back to the land of living.

Chapter 3
CLAIRE

Los Angeles, 12:55 p.m.

Xavier, Drago and I were now in Xavier's Ram 2500 pickup truck, a bulky four-by-four with big tires and a crew cab, the same dull color of the asphalt rolling away under the wheels. Drago sat in the backseat but only his hind legs and hips were on the bench, his arms straight with his paws placed in the rear cup holders, checking the road, sensing concern in the air.

Xavier drove on the 110 South freeway. It snaked through the city center bordered by tall landmarks. The David Meyers' angular Wells Fargo Building. The iconic rounded U.S. Bank Tower standing one thousand and eighteen feet tall, the highest buildings west of the Mississippi River. The black and white Wedbush on the left. Tall and towering, thin or fat, glass and steel or stucco painted in neutral colors, they stood there scattered like sad Lego bricks fallen from a bucket, disorganized and guiltless. On the opposite side of the six-lane concrete ribbon, the Milano and the Medici, the faux Italian 'luxurious condo living' complexes. High-rise lofts with big glass walls that faced the freeway. Who cares about carbon dioxide? As long as we are the kings of cool!

We were jammed in the downtown traffic.

"I can't miss that plane."

"We'll get there in time."

Drago whined in the back. He could *smell* the tension, the variation in our scents. "Hush, Drago." Xavier turned his head and made eye contact for a second. He took my hand and gave it a squeeze. "He hates it when you leave."

I freed my hand to grab the phone, dialed my brother who had a new number scribbled by Xavier on a Post-it. My stepmom answered.

"Katarina? It's Chiara. What happened?"

I listened to the voice from the other side of the world, without interrupting. I could barely hold the phone with my trembling fingers. I gasped like a world-class runner after cutting the finish line but there was no record to break. When I got off, Xavier looked at me, inquisitive.

"They said that too much blood spread inside her brain."

I felt my own blood drain from my face. What did that mean? Was it an aneurysm? Katarina said a bubble exploded in her brain. But why was that bubble there in the first place? Where did it come from? And what were they trying to achieve with the surgery? A hundred questions spun in my mind but I'd been unable to voice them, knowing my stepmom couldn't answer them. And my sister was lying there, alone on a stretcher outside the neurologic OR, waiting for a surgery whose outcome was uncertain!

"Claire!" Xavier's voice brought me back where I was, in the truck with him, on my way to the airport. "Breathe. Making yourself sick won't help. Relax. Everything will be alright."

I looked at him sideways, slapping the air with my hand in rapid movements. "How can it be alright? How the fuck can I relax, not even knowing if I'll get to Bergamo in time to see my sister alive? How can you say such an idiotic thing?"

He didn't deserve it. Why did I snap? Taking it out on him was vile and unjustified, no matter if I hated the expression he used. Tell a person on edge to *calm down* and you'll get the opposite result. Tell somebody who's drowning to *breathe* and that *everything will be alright,* and she will neither listen nor believe you. Or, in my case, I'd get mad. *Anger.* My familiar reaction to anything I couldn't control. And I was back to being five years old, shutting down and refusing even an innocent rope to drag me out of my muddy concerns. *You don't understand!* When I was the one unable to sort out my emotions.

Drago stepped upright on the console in between our seats, a referee determined to dissolve the quarrel before it brewed into a storm. Xavier turned onto Century Boulevard and the Los Angeles International Airport soon came into sight.

He dropped me on the sidewalk, got off to hand me my luggage and wrapped me in a one-arm hug. "Take care of yourself when you get there. And text me, let me know how things are going."

He knew better than adding some other petty reassurance. He meant well, but my body remained rigid against his strong arm. Unable to apologize, I watched him leave fast, tires squealing like he was trying to erase our last interaction.

My plane had a forty-five minute delay. It'd take me eleven hours to get to Paris, since there wasn't a direct flight to Milan. Then a layover of another couple, then another hour and a half flight to Malpensa Airport. Add an hour cab ride to Bergamo, and nine hours difference from Pacific Time. I'd be at the hospital not earlier than twenty-five hours from departure.

"You're all set, Ms. Waters. Please, go through security and passport control and proceed to gate one hundred twenty-five." The Air France check-in agent smiled, handing me back my paperwork and wishing me a '*wonderful time in Italy.*'

I did as instructed, going through the motions like an automaton. But when I finally sat down in the waiting area of the gate, a surge of raw emotion made my hands shake. I spilled part of the coffee I'd just bought on my carry-on. Embarrassed, I slid both hands under my thighs, and chased away my anguish by focusing my thoughts on something else. *Xavier.* Why did I treat him that way, while he'd been nothing but good to me, accepting all my quirks? I thought about calling him, but phone conversation had never been our thing.

I'd met him in March 2002, as rare clear skies and snowcapped San Gabriel Mountains crowned the downtown skyline, the sun shimmered on the glass facades of the skyscrapers and photographers swarmed the city like locusts. Our 'first date' was arranged by my long-time friend, LAPD Lieutenant Ben Willis, a staple of Parker Center since 1997, on his way to retirement. "I got a guy straight from the Rez down in New Mexico. I have a hunch that he could work for you. Xavier Sanchez, Laguna Pueblo Indian. Did his four in the Navy, gave a shot at tribal police, then moved here. So far, so good. He made detective already. Quite impressive in such a short time."

I was looking for clues to flesh out the traits of a character in my upcoming new thriller. My novels moved along the lines of the Los Angeles hard-boil school, trailing in the footsteps of Raymond Chandler and Dashiell Hammett, or the likes of their successors Michael Connelly and Robert Crais. A very masculine universe. I'd decided to swim against the current from the start. A female detective as the hero? Never heard of that in hard boil, back in 1995, despite the fact there were women commanders of important divisions in the LAPD since a long time before.

I added a touch of mystery to my plots to tread even more off the beaten path. And I gave life to a hazardous mixture of determination, bravery and female intuition in the daughter of illegal immigrants who escaped the violence in El Salvador, the first of her family to be born in the U.S. She was a DACA recipient or 'dreamer.' My character was nicknamed "Nails" by her LAPD colleagues for her impossibly long, well-cared for, shiny polished nails. Quite a view when she was gripping her Glock 19 with both hands in a combat stance!

In the beginning, every agent and publisher discouraged me from following that route. But I didn't give in, and my timing was right on. Four novels since 1996, each driven by Nails to *The New York Times* bestseller list. The new book was going to pick up where the last one, *No Tomorrow,* ended. Nails' partner had been shot during the shutdown of a crack house in Venice. So, here was Nails, in desperate need of a new partner before the plot could begin to unfold. I needed a role model. My connection to Lieutenant Willis turned out to be platinum.

Speaking of metals, that day in March 2002, when I arrived on the scene, Xavier Sanchez was busy looking for clues in the Plumber Scavenger Yard located in an alley off of Cesar Chavez Boulevard, in East Los Angeles. A plate or a bumper, anything that could help trace the car of a hit-and-run that occurred a block from there almost seven hours earlier. The high-speed escape had gotten rocky, and the homeboys hit the corner pole. They made their way full force inside the yard, which they had mistaken for an alley. Backing up too late, they had lost bits and scraps of the car, an old beater according to the two witnesses' testimony.

"You need some of this?" He lifted his face toward me without wasting any time in greetings or other pleasantries. He stood tall at six-foot-two on top of a white porcelain mound of discarded toilets and sinks. I couldn't help notice that this guy didn't look like other cops I'd met, often overweight with a muffin top popping up from their belts. He was lean and fit, thanks to having been a Navy Seal. His longish hair was also unusual, with dark curls brushing his nape. He wore a gray cutout, sleeveless t-shirt, Levi's jeans, and work boots. Not exactly the uniform of LAPD investigators, which back then usually implied tweed jackets, pressed slacks, button-down shirts and laced patent leather shoes from Florsheim.

"Nah. Thank you but no thank you." I wondered how this Laguna Pueblo from New Mexico climbed the ladder in the LAPD and how he'd managed not to be kicked out. Roughness plays well in the ranks and on the field, but not so much in dealing with supervisors and bureaucrats.

"There is gold here that people like you cannot see." He picked up from the pile a biscuit elongated toilet bowl that had seen better days and hoisted it above his head. "These old toilets can still do good in the public restrooms of the Dancing Eagle Casino on my reservation. Our idea of recycling."

Irritation crawled up in my throat. What the hell did he know about what I could see? I wondered if his recycling concept included accepting federal nuclear waste to be discarded on tribal land, and if he'd voted for that on the ballot. I held my tongue, though. Why did this guy get on my nerves? At thirty, Officer Sanchez was seven years younger than I was. I'd never been attracted to younger guys. So why the tingle? Half amused, half embarrassed, I felt my nipples tighten, brush against the cotton of my t-shirt.

He looked sexy sorting through the discarded fixtures. He was good looking. Alright. So was I. Guys usually paid attention to me. Not this guy. This guy didn't give a damn. And that might have been a part of my attraction to him, the challenge. He seemed more interested in an old, rusty piece of cheap ceramic than in my presence. And I'd always liked people who could keep their mouth shut, but Xavier exceeded those standards. He'd only spoken a handful of words since I got there. I kept looking at him, busily sorting through the discarded items. Maybe he was aware of me watching him, but he wasn't interested in making conversation.

Twelve hours later, Xavier and I were in bed. The same bed. Xavier's bed in a nearby rental apartment. Naked. Both too independent to attach any romantic feeling to what just happened, we became best friends instead. A couple of years down the road, Xavier moved in with me, into the new house that I'd bought in Mount Washington. Officer Sanchez had already resigned from the LAPD then. "I wasn't meant to last as a cop in the City of Angels. One more year, and I'd have to spend most of my paychecks for psychiatric care, trying to cope with all the shit I got to see."

Another job? Not a problem for a thirty-two year-old, skilled and bursting with such passion for life that he could set the San Gabriels on fire. He embraced the opportunity to follow his heart, as his uncle, Bitten by The Snake, had encouraged him to do, back on the reservation in New Mexico. He turned the flames into fuel for a different career. No longer Officer Sanchez. Meet *Yellow Wolf*. He'd decided to go public with the charms of his Native name, reinventing himself as the disc-jockey host of a late night-show on public radio *Jam with the Yellow Wolf*. By 2008, he had two-hundred thousand listeners, jamming with him five nights a week. Only in L.A.!

"Air France flight 232 is ready for departure. Passengers, please approach the boarding area. First and business class and families with young children can embark now." The announcement rid me of my reminiscence. I gathered my luggage and the dark woolen coat Ondina gifted me on my last visit, grateful that the wait had finally ended. But my stomach was bound in a strangling knot. For the first time, I was flying out of Los Angeles not knowing when I'd be back.

Chapter 4
ONDINA

Bergamo, a few hours earlier

My first two guests and I laid the tablecloth, a batik that I bought in Bali, then we gathered in front of the antique English bureau that I used as a desk. The framed photo on the wall above it attracted Filippo's attention. "Who's this?" The photo portrayed an older woman carried by a young guy, in front of the Grand Canyon. "The mysterious California sister?" He lifted the frame to examine the image closer, then put it back on its picture hanger.

"That's her," I offered, a hint of irritation at his curiosity. He was here for *me*. But it was also true he'd never met Claire, nor seen any pictures of her before. When my sister came to visit, she never stayed long, and we'd so much to share that little time remained for us to spare for anybody else. And honestly—sadly—she never seemed interested in meeting my friends. So, the yoga collective didn't know much about my family. They knew me, and that should've been enough. "She'd just sprained her knee ligament jumping from a small cliff as we reached the bottom of the canyon," I explained while fluffing the pillows on the couch. "My nephew had to carry her for a mile before we could get any help."

"Nephew?" intervened Nicola. "I thought it was her boyfriend. They don't look that far apart in age."

"She had him when she was sixteen. Typical Claire, bold, brave and reckless. Compared to her, I'm a trembling fawn. Story of our childhood. I could beat her at a lot of other things. But being bold? Meet my sister."

"Why have we never met her?" inquired Filippo.

I rolled my eyes to the ceiling, casually draping a soft wool throw the color of wisteria on the sofa backrest. "She's lived in California since before I met you," I paused to check the visual effect and didn't like it, so I rearranged the throw in a different way. "And see those books? She's a mystery writer, pretty well-known in the U.S. Plus, I'm jealous. My boyfriends paid too much attention to her when we were young. Blondes have more fun, as they say."

Claire dyed her hair darker in her twenties, just to escape the stereotype. She didn't like the attention and would have appreciated my dark brown Strada curls more, but she'd taken after our mother instead.

"I love you guys too much to throw you into the praying mantis' embrace of my little sis," I added with a grin, moving around the living room, which was also the dining room and the home-office since the whole apartment consisted of about seven hundred square feet. Two rooms, a bathroom and a narrow rectangular kitchen with barely the space for one person to squeeze in between cabinets and appliances but to me, it felt like my personal art gallery: a colorful exhibit of the spoils from my treasure hunts around the world.

"Claire wears her new men for a while, while it's fun and exciting, and then disposes of them like last season fashion. A committed relationship to her feels like a trap. In fact, she can't even call the guy she's messing around with since the longest ever her 'boyfriend.' She pretends he's just her roommate." And I should have added, *Claire likes her men like her coffee, dark, hot and strong, as stereotypical as that can be, opposite to your gentle, soft look and demeanor.*

Nicola grabbed a book from the shelf. When I moved into this apartment, I'd placed the sofa with its back to a bookshelf so it could separate the conversation corner from the table I'd just lengthened with its middle panel extension. The walls were painted in soft apricot and pale marigold. They went well with the African masks carved in dark wood, the Kilim rug, the Indian pillows, the Guatemalan baskets and the pottery I bought in Ecuador.

"Why Claire Waters?" he asked. "Why doesn't she sign with her real name? Or was she married to an American?"

"Married? Claire? No! I guess she liked Claire Waters better than Chiara Strada. She thought changing her name would help her start her career after she moved to the U.S., fourteen years ago."

Family and friends in Italy didn't like Claire's reasoning. *Why? Is she ashamed of our family name?* commented our father. *Ashamed of the name I gave her?* echoed my mother. I was the only one who stopped calling her Chiara.

"First, she's a teen mom and then she leaves the country out of the blue," Nicola resumed. "She sounds like a piece of work! Any particular reason she ran away?"

"Claire is the only person I know who not only 'likes' change. She aches for it. Come on! The woman can't shop in the same grocery store twice or drive the same route every day. When she turned twenty-nine, she started to itch. She quit her well-paid job, packed her son who just finished 8th grade and left. So long! She's always been like that, chasing adventure any chance she has. She's a born wanderer, got the *pata de coyote.*"

I disappeared into the kitchen, returned with a pile of dishes. "Nicola, would you mind grabbing the silverware in the first drawer? And the paper napkins?" Disposable napkins were the only concession granted to my entertaining style. Disposable napkins are a step forward toward civilization. They avoid the disgusting habit of folding the food-stained cloth napkin of fellow diners to be reused at the next meal, a routine religiously followed in my childhood home.

I freed my hands from the china and pointed at another picture hung on the wall. Two little girls with matching velvet dresses for some kind of official occasion. The youngest showing off a cast on her right arm. Nicola and Filippo looked in that direction. "For as long as I can remember, Claire was always having some weird accident. She broke that arm when she was seven, jumping from the top of a ladder covered with a white sheet, the *Mont Blanc*! Broke her right leg when she was ten, skiing down the steep roof of a house in the mountains during our Christmas break. She was trying to land on a straw mound but it was too far. She crashed on the concrete driveway instead. Claire's a riot, can never be still. I'm surprised that she could stand Los Angeles for this long. But she explained it to me: 'I fit here. Just like everybody else. Nobody belongs in Los Angeles. It is the perfect home for the homeless.' She always felt misplaced here in Italy, like a comma on a page in the wrong spot."

"What about your mother?" asked Nicola who, in his forties, still lived with his widowed mom. "Did she leave when she was sick?"

"Mother was diagnosed with Parkinson's after she left. It took a few years to get truly serious." I owed Claire that. As much as I sometimes still felt a pang of abandonment, Claire didn't abandon our ill mother. "Mom's been in a wheelchair only for the past two years. In the summer of 2001, she was still able to fly to Los Angeles and spend a couple of months with Claire, as she did every summer since she moved. To my sister's credit, Mother always came back rejuvenated from the California sun."

In many ways, Claire was more patient than me with our difficult mother. They didn't clash. Probably because they fought like hyenas when she was an unruly teenager allergic to authority. And now, she didn't get as upset as I did with my mom's antics. I'd missed out on my teenage rebellion, putting up with too much of my mother's bullshit. In my defense, I was the one who dealt with her Sarah Bernhardt's pessimism and tantrums every fucking day!

Sometimes I wish I'd run away too. I tasted the thought in my mouth, rolling it inside with my tongue from one cheek to the other while I placed the fruit platter in the middle of the table. A hint of coffee and sweet tropical fruit. Colombia. Or Mexico, perhaps. But my strength only got me from Milan to Bergamo, barely fifty miles. Still, even that short distance from my mother saved my life.

A phone rang in the hallway. It was an old phone with an answering machine, connected to a landline. The LED light of the caller I.D. said 'MOTHER.'

"Speak of the devil," I uttered, and picked up the receiver from its cradle. The heavily accented voice of Wilma, Mother's Polish caregiver, thundered. Her Italian was already broken, now it was shredded.

"Ondina. It's me. Mama sleeps all afternoon. No wake up!"

I pictured it—my mom asleep in her big electric lift chair, her mouth slack. The chair in front of her old TV on a cupboard. The TV, bulky, the screen small, not plasma. The news on, our hideous premier Berlusconi blathering, but the audio too low to be heard. The room strangely put together. Some pieces of furniture were original sixteenth century and must have been quite glorious in better days, when they were polished on a regular basis. Others looked like poorly assembled Ikea cabinets with drawers and panels that didn't slide or close properly. One wall was painted a cheerful blue and hosted five decorative hand painted plates, each hung with its proper hardware. Capodimonte, Italy's finest porcelain.

"Maybe she's very tired. Did you go out with the wheelchair for a walk?"

"Mama no want."

Mother made us take pictures in front of those Capodimonte plates every year. Manufactured in Southern Italy, in this village close to Naples where artists and craftsmen specialized in artistic creations, exquisite centerpieces with delicate flowers and fruits, miniature figurines, plates, coffee sets for the best Italian espresso you can ever drink—served black, with a lemon peel and absolutely no sugar to destroy its strong flavor: 'because you're just as beautiful and I like to show my friends how you're growing,' she used to say to entice us.

"You've got to insist, Wilma. I told you!" I twirled the coiled rubbery cord of the phone, pissed to be interrupted on this rare evening when I'd invited friends over for dinner. "Mom would just stay there waiting to die if you leave it up to her. You've got to push her. I know she isn't easy. She's still a pretty stubborn lady." Silence on the other end. "Alright. Let's try and see if I can wake her up. Put the phone close to her ear."

Wilma told me she did, and I yelled. "MAMMA!!! MAMMA!!!" After a short silence, I heard my mother speak in a barely audible, fragile voice.

"What? Is it you? Are you here?"

"You've been sleeping for a really long time, Mamma. You need to eat some dinner before going to bed."

Mother grumbled. "Can I just go to bed? I'm not hungry. And I'm"—she yawned—"very... tired."

I softened my voice. "At least a snack. Then you can sleep."

Patience didn't have the effect I was hoping for. Mother became agitated. I heard her turning in her chair and slamming her hand hard. "O-kay, General!" and she hung up on me.

I put the phone back in its cradle, looked at Nicola and Filippo. I'd almost forgotten they were there. They'd been stunned silent. "She always makes me feel like shit. I know she's sick, but..."

Nicola came over and stroked my back in a circular motion to pacify me. "Come on, come on! They're all the same. My mom's like that too. Eighty-one and bossy, treating me like I'm still her baby. She's still convinced I need her to run my life. She thinks I'd die of starvation without her."

The clock flashed its LED digits: 7:00 p.m.

"Speaking of starvation," I told my friends, "I need to get a few more bottles of wine before the stores close." I wore a long gabardine skirt, taupe colored, and a lilac cashmere sweater with a printed shawl draped about my shoulders. I glanced at the already dark sky out of the window. The wind was blowing. Too cold to go out without a jacket.

"Should we come along and help you carry the bags?" asked Filippo while I grabbed my purse and my down coat, hat, and gloves.

"Oh, it's only a couple of things. And I need a few moments by myself in the fresh air. I'll cool down, or I might take my anger out on you all." I smirked, opening the door. I turned back toward my friends. "Thanks for the offer, though. Hey, by the way. Here!" I took a CD out of the rack from the bookshelf by the door. "Since you are so interested in my sister's life story, you can listen to this."

I dropped the CD in Nicola's hands. Nicola looked at the lyrics list.

"Wow. Is this from the time when you were a songwriter?"

"You bet! Scroll down to 'My Bougainvillea Sister.' That's her. I wrote it when Claire, still in high school, announced to my mom that she was pregnant."

I called the elevator and as I waited, I heard Nicola put the CD in the player. Music filled the air. Music, then words:

Flower ringlets down her shoulders
Purple truth sparkling in her eyes
Couldn't be any colder
What she got to say that night

Sixteen years, she was with child
Happy indeed to say goodbye
My little sister, oh so wild
Already grown, left us high and dry

I was nothing like her!
My bougainvillea sister
Climbing womanhood
Clinging hair to rosewood

Oh Sis, let me hold you tight
Let's go fly our kite
How can I let go of
Diving into your purple eyes?

Sixteen years and on her own
Reckless princess but not bride
Could not stand my mother's frown
I was weeping inside

I was nothing like her!
My bougainvillea sister
Climbing up the sky
No need for a knight

Let me hold you close
Let's go comb your hair
Lounging into your purple eyes
It's like breathing fresh air

I was nothing like her!
My bougainvillea sister
Climbing womanhood
Clinging hair to rosewood

Fourth... Third... Second... Ground floor, finally! I never liked elevators and usually I'd take the stairs, at least on my way down, but I was tired and my left leg seemed not to support me well. I'd bumped into the dishwasher door while I was in the kitchen before, a weird accident. I felt grateful for an excuse to be alone a few minutes before the others arrived. I adored Filippo and Nicola. They were so talkative tonight though, too interested in knowing more about Claire. And then, that call with Mother!

I turned the south corner of the *piazza* heading for the health food store. I'm picky about wine. Well, I'm picky about most everything. It took me a year of browsing, online and in person, and about four trips to different furniture outlets and showrooms before I decided which sofa to buy. Same thing with the colors to paint the walls, two months of trials and errors with small patches changing shade every few days.

That lamp looks pretty, I thought while passing the antique store. I was interested, until I read the price tag. The cold wind snuck between the folds of my shawl, biting at my throat. I zipped my parka all the way and lifted the hood to cover my head and ears. The health food store was still a good three hundred feet away and the wind blew against me, making me feel weary. *Why am I feeling so tired?* I was glad I made the appointment for a physical.

People on foot on the sidewalks were all bundled up, walking fast, rushing to beat the stores closing or carrying grocery bags home, keeping the lapels of their coats together with one hand. I hurried up, mentally adding some vitamin C to my shopping list. Just in case the exhaustion was, indeed, a leftover symptom from my flu.

Chapter 5
CLAIRE

Somewhere in the sky above Las Vegas, 5:05 p.m.

From above the thin layer of clouds, I peered out at the last reddish streaks of a brilliant sunset. But how was I supposed to appreciate it? Inside the cabin, it was all neon lights, engine roar, flight attendants clanking carts in the aisle. I sank in my seat, my sister's letter from Bangalore in my hands. My eyes were moist.

I exhaled loudly and turned in the cramped economy seat, unable to get comfortable. I closed my eyes and let the letter slide out of my hands.

A vision of a stingray swimming toward the light followed by a memory that felt like a movie, the action unfurling in front of your eyes but you aren't sure if you're part of it. In that scene, I heard before I could see. The clippety-clop of small running feet moving closer. More than one person running on a pebbled path in a great big garden. Two girls, running and laughing. The oldest led the other by her hand. They looked almost identical but the bigger girl had dark brown curls while the younger was light-haired. They were dressed in matching striped t-shirts, shorts and sandals. The older girl made her sister stop behind a big persimmon tree.

"They're coming for us, Chiara. They'll take our treasure away. Let's hide it."

The little girl opened her small hand and looked at a tiny, ruby-red, heart-shaped pebble that she'd just picked up.

"Here!" She pushed the pebble up her right nostril with her tiny index finger, a triumphant smile brightening her face. "They won't find it here."

"Mamma mia!" shouted the dark-haired girl, bringing her hands up into her hair. "What if it doesn't come out?"

The captain's voice rustled from the speaker and shook me up. "We are expecting turbulence and it might last for the next forty-five minutes. For your own safety, please buckle up. Access to the restrooms is temporarily denied."

I wished to still inhabit my memory, uninterrupted. But it was just another wish I'd not get granted. I'd never treasured memories before. I was confounded to feel that way.

I looked around for other means to distract myself, to avoid thinking about Ondina on an operating table thousands of miles away, a scalpel digging into her open skull. But the lights were still up in the cabin and I saved movies for the darkest hours when everybody would be asleep and I wouldn't dare to turn the lamp above my seat to read. I leaned over to find my computer case under the seat in front and shuffled through the few books I brought with me. My new book launch was a week away and even if it sounded now as remote a possibility as a meteorite striking us down, I couldn't leave Nails unattended. I grabbed my ear-marked, heavily under-lined copy of *Dark Desert Nights* and opened it at the chapter I selected to read from. I dove in like my life depended on it. Maybe it did.

(passage from *Dark Desert Nights*):

"Nails is in the squad car, listening to the soundtrack of *The Last Samurai* on the surround stereo system. *A Way of Life.* She's in Twentynine Palms, parked on Lear Street, a block south of the address on Two-Mile Road.

"She's near a compound with a ratty trailer house and two rusty sheds, dotted by an east view of Copper Mountain. She's following on a snitch's tip, hoping to snag the criminal she's been after for months.

"She's excited, sensing the opportunity to catch the freak in the noose of the trap that she has been fashioning. *Stay in control* is the name of the game, so she takes a few deep breaths to slow down her heart rate."

Stay in control. I should aim for that, too. Don't let any dark thoughts creep into my mind.

I took a few deep breaths to curb my anxiety and plunged back into Nails' world. A dangerous milieu wrapped in dark shadows and inhabited by criminals that I preferred to my new, unbearable unknown.

Chapter 6
CLAIRE

Bergamo, one day after the accident

I arrived at the hospital late in the evening, jet-lagged and worn out from the long flight. I'd been unable to eat anything on the plane, and the cab ride from Milan to Bergamo cost me the same as a night in a five-star resort. But I couldn't care less. I wanted to see my sister. I'd been in this hospital years before, when Ondina had to pick up her test results from a routine check-up. A happier occasion.

Ospedali Riuniti looked the same, an ancient structure at the turn of the new millennium, obsolete despite its incongruous modern additions. It had a glorious past and a few name changes since its birth in the fifteenth century. The city had approved the construction of its replacement, but for now this was still the main go-to. Cathedral ceilings and stained-glass windows, large stairways with low steps, a central courtyard with the different departments placed around it. If you didn't know it as a hospital, you could think it was some kind of medieval palace, fitting in with the sixteenth century Venetian walls that surround *Città Alta*: the old town with narrow alleys paved in cobblestone, the Basilica of Santa Maria Maggiore and the Cappella Colleoni with their beautiful facades, the upscale boutiques and pastry shops, the century-old cafes and *trattorias* with a one hundred and eighty degree view of the valley below.

But I was far from in the mood for beauty.

I'd always disliked hospitals, avoided them as much as possible after too many stints in them as a child, the result of my endless antics. I couldn't escape this one now. I sucked in the cold air from my nose and exhaled a foggy breath, shrugged the dread off and approached information. Directed to the first floor of the neurological department, I walked up a wide and crowded stairway, making my way between the columns and the streams of people. I found myself walking along a doorless, deserted hallway. Linoleum floor, walls painted in a drab light brown, dusty ceiling lamps and a strong bleach smell. Only at its end, I could spot two huge plate glass doors under a sign: *TERAPIA INTENSIVA*. The Italian I.C.U. The sound of my long strides on the tiled floor echoed. The full-length coat I wore flapped around my legs, sprinkling tiny snowflakes behind my steps.

I rang the bell, knowing I'd arrived past visiting hours but I'd come a long way, she was my sister! A nurse answered the door and directed me to the waiting room, to talk to the doctor. I heard two nurses murmur behind my back. "She's the sister of Twenty-one." "They could be twins," said the other, "I mean... before the surgery. She flew all the way from America."

Luckily, the wait wasn't long. I was ushered into the doctor's empty office. It was small and unwelcoming. A desk and a swivel chair, two metal chairs for the visitors. Bare walls but the usual crucifix and a sad print of overburdened donkeys climbing up an unidentified trail. The heater was blasting.

There wasn't any window and the air was stifling. I removed my coat and sat, drumming my right hand fingers on the edge of the desk.

The doctor entered and offered me his hand to shake before sitting down. He looked about my age, worried. "Nice to meet you, Ms. Strada, despite the circumstances. I'm your sister's neurosurgeon."

"Can I see her?"

"Let's talk first."

I braced myself. I had a hunch that nothing good was going to be said next.

"I want to make sure you understand the gravity of the situation. I operated on your sister. I decided to perform the surgery despite the terrible condition she was in when she arrived here. CAT scans and MRI showed that she had been hemorrhaging for too long. The cause was an arteriovenous malformation or AVM, a condition present since birth that, unfortunately, in most cases doesn't give any symptoms until the bubble bursts, and when that happens it's already too late."

Too late. Two words that sliced into the heap of questions fast-crowding my mind. So Ondina had this so-called AVM in her brain since she was born. Did she know about it? Hmmm. If she knew, I doubt I'd have not known. But if she knew, could she have done anything to prevent what happened? And *how* and *why* did it happen? But again, *too late!* It was past the time for these questions now.

The doctor went on. "Her brain had been compressed by the huge mass of blood in her skull with a lack of oxygen lasting twelve minutes, the amount of time it took for the ambulance to get there and for the paramedics to intubate her before transportation. Most of my colleagues wouldn't have operated. There was a one in a thousand chance even for survival. But she is still young, with a very healthy body, and

I thought, who could make better use of that one chance, after all?"

The doctor paused as if I should thank him but I remained silent, eyes locked onto his while the churning in my stomach increased, acid burning the back of my palate. I had this habit of looking directly at people that in the States was often considered unacceptable, like, staring. It made Americans uncomfortable but here in Italy it's perceived as the opposite— the will to establish a direct connection. In this case, it was just awkward. I glared at him, hoping to read his face, shocked by his words. He operated on my sister when there was only 'one in a thousand chances even for survival', as if survival was going to be enough. *Survival* how? How was Ondina's life going to be now that she *survived*?

Registering my lack of applause, the doctor proceeded with his medical explanation, answering my unspoken questions. "The subarachnoid hemorrhage started in the left hemisphere but soon invaded both. It shut down the centers for speech and movement. She's tetraplegic, that means entirely paralyzed. She cannot talk or understand either. We have to keep her in a pharmacological coma to give the brain time to recover before allowing her to breathe on her own, without a ventilator. Only when she recovers her vital functions, we'll be able to determine the extent of the damage. Her score on the RTS Scale is so low she's almost clinically dead. You have to understand, Ms. Strada, that her chance of recuperating any of her abilities is extremely slim."

I resisted the impulse to jump the desk and scratch his hollow cheeks bloody. I felt nauseated but I couldn't let it go. "Weren't her chances just as slim when you decided to admit her into your operating room?"

The doctor looked surprised, maybe offended as if nobody ever challenged his choices, his medical authority. "My duty is to save lives. I'm the surgeon. The rest is up to neurologists, physical therapists, and rehab programs."

"Rehabs that my sister probably won't ever be admitted to." I was unable to restrain myself. "Because of the 'terrible state' she was in when she was brought in here. So, you're telling me that if I'm *lucky*, I'll end up with a sister who, at best, might smile or frown, but needs diapers, and a chalkboard to express herself. Am I right?" I didn't wait for his answer. "And you know what my sister made me promise when we were girls? *If something really bad happens to me, don't let me suffer. Shoot me.* But now she's here. In the care of a hospital in a Catholic country that doesn't allow relatives to pull the plug, regardless."

I paused, trying to regain composure. The doctor seemed at a loss for words. No point in carrying on our exchange.

"Can I see my sister now?"

Reluctantly, he directed me back to the nurses' station, walking as far as he could from me like I was holding a grenade ready to go off. He wasn't the only one relieved when he turned away. I wanted to gouge his eyes out, but I doubted they would let me see my sister if I did.

I put on the mask and the blue disposable paper slippers that were handed to me before I could enter through the heavy doors of the I.C.U.

Once inside, I stood and scanned the unit, tried to recognize my sister in one of the twenty bulky metal beds. Ten on each side, facing each other and surrounded by light curtains that could be pulled or drawn for privacy. They were all open. The patients lay still in their beds with frozen expressions. Their limbs contracted in rigid, unnatural poses, their eyes closed. Their bodies trapped in a web of hoses strung up to their veins and orifices. Small boxes with different buttons hung to the metal bed rails seemed to operate the hoses, programmed to pump solutions with salt, morphine, glucose or dopamine and liquid nutrition in, urine and blood out.

I walked lightheaded and disoriented, forced myself not to look too intensely. Until a nurse pointed me toward a bed where one of these bodies lay, covered only by a white sheet despite the snow now falling outside the windows. A body was there. *A person*, I reminded myself, with a bandage wrapping half of an abnormally swollen and shaved head. A note was pinned on the bandage on the left frontal side of the head. "Attention, bone missing." Stuck right in the middle of all that gauze, a drain carrying blood out of the wound. Stuck between the person's teeth, a gray tongue hanging. Her body rigid like a frozen bird. I looked in disbelief. Ondina.

The nurse approached. "We had to pull her tongue out so she won't choke on it."

"Can she hear me?" I whispered, although we were the only two people standing there and talking.

"The doctors stuck a pin under her nail this morning, and she didn't react."

Each of her words felt like a pin in my heart. Too painful to absorb. The nurse moved on to check on the machinery at the next bed, leaving me with the hard shell that had been my sister. I swallowed my tears and dared to get closer. Careful not to trip on any of the hoses, I bent to kiss her cheek, right under the bandage. I then took her hand in mine to stroke it. I was surprised it was warm. I stayed there. With her. In silence.

When I felt ready—well, the maximum 'readiness' I could summon in that moment—I circled around the bed and walked to Ondina's right, assuming that her hearing, provided it still worked, might be better on the less affected side of her head. I put my lips to her right ear, where there was no bandage, the way I whispered her a secret when we were kids. "I'm here,

Sis. I came for you, as soon as I could." I lifted my head to scrutinize her face. No reaction. "I know you're scared. It looks pretty bad now. But we can fix this. You're strong."

I paused. My voice tinged with sorrow when I'd wanted to sound reassuring. I took a couple of deep breaths.

"I know you can hear me. It's alright if you don't know what to do. You might not know if it's worth crossing back, now that you've been down that tunnel. But if you decide to, I'll be here for you. All the way. I won't leave you alone, I promise."

Still no signs of recognition whatsoever. I went on.

"You'll be my absolute priority. There's nothing more important than you. I'm sorry for all the times I didn't show you how much I love you. What I *can* change is the present. We'll do this together, alright? You do your part, the bravest one. Whatever your choice, I'll always help, love, and respect you." I stood up and caressed her yellowish cheek. The nurse caught my attention, gesturing that the time was up. I was the only visitor, the only one not in a nurse's uniform or lying silent in a bed.

My sister's place was only a few blocks away from the hospital but the darkness, ice hidden beneath the snow on the sidewalks, and cold air had made the way treacherous. I retrieved the keys left for me under the doormat. Guilherme had already come and gone, advised to rush to the hospital the night before. He'd jumped on a train immediately but had to go back to Tuscany right after—he couldn't miss his work. We'd talked on the phone and he'd left me the keys that Filippo gave him. Meeting in person had to be postponed.

I opened the door and exhaled in relief, stepped in after

shaking snow from my boots. I caught a glimpse of myself in the mirror. I looked ugly and pale, deep bluish circles under my eyes. I hung my coat and took in the scene. Everything always seemed to fit so well together at Ondina's. Her travel memories with the antique Persian rug in the entrance, Mom's present for her fortieth birthday; the Louis Sixteenth accent table holding the phone and a vase of dried white flowers; the colorful beaded curtain screening the living room with Frida Kahlo's portrait threaded in yellow, blue, red, and black wood spherules.

I brushed my hand on a couple of travel photographs taken in different places of the world, adorning the wall by the entrance. I ran my index finger on my first book cover, framed and hung close to the pictures. *Harder than Nails*, with the same pretty woman that graced all my other book covers. The detective stood on the side of a partially open door, ready to enter the prison of a kidnapped teenage girl tied to a chair and gagged. Left arm bent at the elbow, hand with long polished fingernails firmly gripping her gun. *Wish I was as strong as you, Nails!*

I moved into the kitchen and opened the fridge, my stomach grumbling. I hadn't eaten anything in almost two days. Chia seeds and yoghurt made from grass-fed cows' milk. Kale, artichokes and eggplants that made me salivate thinking of the *parmigiana* I could but would not make. Brussel sprouts and Indian ghee, coconut oil, quinoa and chicory coffee. A feast of organic food, a party banquet for microgreen-worshippers. You couldn't find a hot dog, ketchup, mayo or white bread even if you combed the shelves. A natural over-reaction to our childhood menu of processed food, risotto Knorr and Campbell soups, frozen chicken tenders and everything that you could cook in ten minutes out of a can or a box. Our single, working mother didn't have much time to spare in the kitchen.

Across the city, families gathered at the dinner table in

front of steaming plates of *casoncelli* tossed with burnt butter and sage and sprinkled with parmesan cheese and black pepper, a sort of ravioli specialty of Bergamo that Ondina had insisted I taste. "You need to try it at least once," she'd said, and she was right, despite me pouting and teasing, "Maybe I should order *bucatini alla carbonara* instead, or *rigatoni all'Amatriciana.*"

Memories of our meals together flooded my mind. The two of us sitting, facing each other in restaurants in Milan, ordering tiny plates of exquisite appetizers that left you starving, wishing for a simple, robust portion of *spaghetti olio, aglio e peperoncino*, but the presentation was all the rave. Us again, sitting at the outdoor patios of trattorias with white and red checkered plastic tablecloths covering the long wooden tables that you shared with the other hungry hikers stopping for lunch on a nine-mile trail in Val Taleggio, polenta or *pizzoccheri* the only two options on the menu, but both to die for: literally, both dripping with melted butter and *taleggio* or *bitto* cheese, enough to give toddlers clogged arteries for the rest of their lives. "I don't eat cooked butter," I protested. "Oh, yes you do. Trust me!" And again, she knew better.

I shut the door of the fridge and leaned my back against it with a sigh. I couldn't eat anyhow, my stomach in an angry knot. I let myself slide down and landed on the floor. I raised my knees and crossed my arms on them, dropped my head in between. Ondina's cat, Belinda, came out from hiding under the couch, timidly making her way to my feet. She wrapped her tail around my right calf, purring. "You must be starving, huh? Everybody forgot about you." I got on my feet, picked up a tuna can inside the pantry to feed the cat. "It's all yours, sweetie." Belinda had been alone only a few hours but she must have picked up Guilherme's panic. She was hungry for food and human contact.

I moved to the small table at the entrance and felt the

impulse to switch the answering machine on to hear the outgoing message in my sister's vibrant voice: "Ciao. This is Ondina. I can't come to the phone right now but if you leave me a message with your name and phone number, I promise to return your call. Have a wonderful day!" I felt like crying but they were gratitude tears for that tiny strip left of my sister, of when she was still whole, lively and healthy. I played it three more times before checking the incoming messages. There were nine. The last one was from our mother: "Ondina... Are you there? Why didn't you call me today? I haven't heard from you, and I'm worried. Call me, *bambina*."

I tried to blow out the weight that compressed my ribcage but the evil gnome sitting on my chest had no intention of leaving. I opened the bedroom door and noticed that the king size bed was made. Of course! Ondina would never invite anybody over if the house wasn't in perfect order. And Guilherme spent all the hours of his visit at the hospital before taking a train back to Tuscany. The room was freezing. I instinctively moved toward the heater bolted to the wall. Arctic cold! I tried to make it work but it wouldn't. Ondina probably turned it off to avoid wrinkles.

My eyes fell on the nightgown folded on the armchair. I picked it up and held it to my nose to inhale my sister's scent: amber, citrus and woody notes blended with white flowers. I undressed and put it on, then crashed on the bed. The cat jumped on too, curling up to my back. I slid under the comforter and pulled it on top of my head, shivering. What was that song Xavier made me listen to, on the demo of a new hip hop/rock band? The one that listed all possible numbing prescriptions from Valium to Nyquil? That's what I needed to defeat the monsters, but I had no hope of finding any in my sister's medicine cabinet, probably filled with just herbal concoctions.

I tossed and turned for the most part of the next hour, the

song still playing in my head, until I could no longer stand it. *Let's change music at least.* I got up and moved to the CD player in the entrance. An ejected disc rested in the exposed tray. I pushed it in and *Bougainvillea Sister's* notes filled the room. I hadn't heard it in such a long time! Ondina's dreamy voice, exploring different tonalities at every riff. I turned on the hot water in the bathtub, decided to put in a load of laundry while waiting for the tub to fill. The washer was in the bathroom, as it usually is in Italian homes. I grabbed the bag the nurses gave me at the hospital, then started picking random items and dropping them in. Clothes that Ondina wore when she fell, a long soft skirt, a multicolored shawl, a down coat and an odd light purple garment. I spread it out—a mutilated, shapeless piece of cashmere. Ondina's blouse, cut by the paramedics when they found her lying on the pavement.

I closed my eyes and ran the scenario in my mind. *How do you think it went, Chiara?* The usual question at the end of each morning dedicated to composition in fourth grade, when Miss Corolli, my teacher, asked the class to turn a topic into a collective story, weaving each twist into the previous kid's section. How much I loved it then! That isolated spark of inspiration in the whole boredom of school. The glimpse of a future forged by imagination instead of algebraic expressions and capitals of countries I couldn't imagine I'd ever visit. *Like this, Miss Corolli. Most likely:*

The ambulance arrived, the siren blaring. Paramedics tried to revive her, spoke loudly, asked what happened to the neighbors and friends gathered around the woman lying on the concrete. A friend tried to explain: "She said she'd go down to the store and get some wine for the party. She wasn't back after half an hour. This neighbor called us on the house phone."

"I found her on the entrance floor," started the neighbor, *"close to the elevator. She must have fallen and hit her head*

trying to open its door. Her key was still inside."

Then her other friend, Filippo, the one who'd called Kata-rina and then my brother: "We carried her outside after calling the ambulance and not seeing anybody arrive for more than... Ten minutes? We thought to put her in my car and rush to the hospital, but we were afraid of hurting her. But now you guys are here, and it will be alright... Right?"

Then the gurney slammed on the pavement close to her body with a loud metallic bang. The paramedics crouched. One lifted her lids to look at dilated pupils that did not reflect the flashlight, irises black as a raven's wing. The two paramedics talking medical jargon. "Pulse and vitals, weak. Difficulty breathing." They took Ondina's coat off, cut her sweater front with scissors, moving very fast and nervous. "Hurry up. We need to intubate before moving her."

The scene dissolved like a dream that disappears as soon as you open your eyes. I felt the impulse to throw up and kneeled at the toilet. I barfed the content of my empty stomach. Bile. Uncertainty. Despair.

No fear! Nails' life motto, right? *Where are you Nails? I need you.*

I remembered the book I'd just seen on my sister's shelf, the first of the Nails' series that I hadn't read in years. I dragged myself to my feet and went to pick it up, hoping to escape once again inside Nails' world. I'd rather spend the night in the company of cops and bad guys than among critical patients and nurses in the neuro I.C.U. where my sister lay, rigid and absent, in an induced coma.

Chapter 7
CLAIRE

Bergamo, the night after the accident

I picked up *Harder Than Nails* and brought it to the bed with me. I didn't have any hope for sleep, so losing myself in a fictional world was the best option. I opened the book at its index and chose a chapter from the first part. I read the first paragraph aloud to the cat, snuggled close to my hip on the plump down comforter:

"Nails and her partner, Carlos Mendez, are parked in front of Stan's hardware store on Twentynine Palms Highway in Yucca Valley. They are in an unmarked police car, dressed in plainclothes. To avoid raising any suspicion, Carlos has gone inside to buy sodas and snacks at the vending machines. Nails isn't new to the valley. People have seen her around before. She hikes in the nearby Joshua Tree National Park and sometimes sleeps at the Super 8 motel a few blocks away. Pretty basic, but better than camping in one hundred and fifteen degrees. She enjoys the outdoor pool at the end of the day, the air conditioning and that the customers are mainly families of the marines stationed at the Twentynine Palms Military Base twenty miles away. This time, though, she's here on duty, surveying the Twentynine Palms Highway about a hundred feet from before a turn to a dirt road."

Belinda had started purring. I burrowed myself more inside the covers feeling the temperature in the room dropping even more, the night going into the wee hours. I went on reading in silence. Nails' magic had already worked and I found myself transported into the Mohave desert in California where she stalked her suspect:

"The country road winds toward the hills for three miles to end up in front of an isolated house with a backyard full of junk. According to Nails' source, it could be the hideaway of the newly nicknamed Desert Rat—the prowler who's recently upgraded to murderer terrorizing the communities along the San Bernardino highway, all the way from East Los Angeles to Palm Springs. In early 1995, he'd made a name for himself sneaking undetected into houses in Echo Park, Eagle Rock, Pomona, Riverside, Indio and Cabazon late at night.

People inside were asleep and he was light footed enough to rob them and get away with his bounty, no further damage. Until April 10, when a householder in Riverside woke up sensing the stranger's presence in his bedroom. He immediately reached for the nightstand drawer where he stored his weapon, but didn't grab it in time. The prowler panicked, opened fire on him, his wife, the two young children in bed with them, and the baby in her cradle. As he was fleeing the scene, the killer stumbled upon two older girls aroused by the commotion, running toward their parents' bedroom screaming in terror. He killed them, too. Seven dead bodies left behind. Colleagues had described the crime scene as a blood bath.

A neighbor who'd spotted the killer on his frantic way out was able to provide a useful description. The hood of the suspect's sweater had slipped off in the frenzy when he'd climbed the fence separating the two backyards, revealing his bald crown and ratty hair in a loose ponytail. He'd run away before the cops arrived. The Riverside Police Department released a sketch showing a man in his 30s, unmasked. He was slim, white, and small in stature. Calls rained in, claiming possible sightings around town, but none of them helped trace his movements. Vanished.

Two months later, a woman was assaulted in her sleep at her home in Cathedral City. Her aggressor had slipped in through the bedroom window facing the backyard. He'd silently cut the screen and lifted the unlocked single-hung window left slightly open to let the night breeze in. He killed the woman in her bed, and also her elderly bedridden mother sleeping in the other bedroom. The woman was found partially naked, her nightgown pulled up and bunched around her neck, suggesting sexual assault, but the rape kit came back negative. The autopsy determined the cause of death was the same for the woman and her mother, asphyxiation. They'd been strangled with a metal wire. None of these findings would have prompted a connection with the shooting in Riverside if an insomniac neighbor hadn't seen the guy slipping out the same window he'd used to get inside. A full, bright moon lit the night sky and the neighbor hadn't switched any light on inside his house, on his way to the bathroom. He gave a pretty reliable description of the intruder to the officers alerted on the scene. Their man was the same who'd committed the homicides in Riverside. Criminal psychologists recommended not to divulge this conclusion since the change in the homicide style suggested a new profile. He appeared to have become a hard core killer who targeted women, possibly to obtain sexual arousal before or from strangling them. The profile was distributed to the desert police divisions but not made public. Raising panic wouldn't help to catch the perpetrator."

I recalled the endless hours spent researching serial killers' crimes and psychology at the Los Angeles Central Library, the many interviews with the profilers from the FBI Behavioral Science Unit. I'd felt like an explorer in a still unknown territory, the excitement of each discovery refueling my dedication to go further in my quest as a mindhunter. Making every character believable, the setting realistic. It seemed all so far away now, but I clutched at the memory like I was drowning, clawing at the oar of a lifeboat. I turned another page:

"At the end of July, an item from his first robbery in Echo Park, a gold chain with an ivory angel pendant, showed up at a pawn shop in Palm Desert. Selling hot merchandise was risky, but he might not have other means to support himself after his mug had been broadcasted by all the TV networks back in June. If he was working before, he'd surely resigned and disappeared. What could he do then? Apply for a job at Home Depot? Nails, who'd worked the crime scene at Echo Park with Carlos, confided this news to Hugo, her local friend, asking him to keep his eyes open. Hugo loved to browse pawn shops and thrift stores. He might have come across some useful information. And, guess what? On September 12, Hugo spotted the Desert Rat exiting the convenience store at a gas station in Joshua Tree.

He'd cleaned up his look and sported antique-looking spectacles. His wispy hair cut short, goatee shaved away. But the triangular shape of his face and the slouch in his shoulders were unmistakable. So, Hugo followed his white Ford Econovan along Twentynine Palms Highway, keeping a good distance, until the Desert Rat turned onto a dirt road in Yucca Valley. He didn't dare to follow him further, but made a mental note of the location of the road. When he went back the following day, Hugo waited to see the white van leave the dirt road and disappear on the highway before driving in. He followed the road to its end in front of a small house. Run down, little more than a shack, its sides stacked with old shovels, racks, wheelbarrows and tools for a nonexistent garden, a couple of rusty cars no longer working, piles of used tires, posts and planks from a previous fence. Military blankets hung as curtains from the windows and Hugo didn't want to push it getting too close on foot, despite the fact that there wasn't anybody in sight.

Nails was there right after receiving Hugo's tip, and carefully checked the suspect's movements with binoculars from a distance. She needed more before asking a judge for a warrant to search the property. She couldn't confirm identification yet, visual wasn't clear enough. On top of that, it wasn't her turf. She'd need special permission from her boss to team up with the local enforcement, to get in on the investigation."

I closed the book, my fingers almost frozen, my mind unable to focus on the story, and turned on my left side. A gray dawn light infiltrated the joints in the heavy *tapparella* rolls at a diagonal angle, slanting lines of dashes on the comforter duvet. I fought the heaviness taking hold of my eyelids, fearing to enter a world of nightmares populated by hungry-fanged monsters like I was still a five-year-old, asking my sister to hold my hand until I fell asleep. My sister wasn't there to comfort me now. She was all alone in a cold hospital unit, fighting even worse predators aimed to rip her to pieces, separated from me and the whole world by an unbreakable glass bell.

I sighed, feeling powerless for the first time in my life.

Chapter 8
CLAIRE

Bergamo, two days after the accident, 6:45 a.m.

I woke up to the unpleasant rasp of Belinda's tongue on the dry skin of my cheek. I felt groggy and my mouth was sticky and bitter, my throat ablaze. Minutes later, while cursing at the cat who'd jarred me from much needed sleep, I heard the distinctive tone of my cell phone ringing from the living room couch. I scrambled to get there, wiping my mouth and eyes on a small towel abandoned on the nightstand that also smelled of my sister.

Susan, my publicist, calling from New York, evidently unaware of the time difference. "Hello, Claire. How is it going over there? How's your sister?"

I gathered myself. "It's pretty dire. She's in a deep coma. They have to pump drugs into her and keep her hooked to a ventilator just so she stays breathing."

"Did the doctors give you a roadmap?"

"Doctors don't know shit. All they repeat is: only God knows. We are in his hands."

"So, you can't know when you'll be able to come back?" I could hear the disappointment in her tone. "I hate to remind you, but we had to cancel the book-signing and it's time to reschedule. Maybe you could leave and then eventually go back after the event? I mean, if your sister still wasn't well?"

Seriously? Was she asking me to go back to the U.S., leaving my sister?

"I can't leave my sister now and I don't know when it'll be possible. Certainly, I won't come back there while she's here in a coma! I won't, with her sleepwalking on the edge between life and death, and my mom still in the dark about it."

"I understand you." Honey in her words. "Believe me, I do. But you know publishers. It's so hard to keep up at the top, particularly nowadays, when fewer and fewer are buying books. It's not enough to write them. Authors have to market them. You know that. Claire, listen to me. You can't forget yourself and your career."

I pictured Susan as a snake in Prada ankle boots, holding her leather briefcase made of the hide of a relative. I sketched a snake on a paper napkin that I found on the hardwood floor close to the couch, flown there from the table still set for the dinner party. I've always had this curse. Images materialize in my mind like dream fragments when things happen, giving life and colors to the stories that people tell me. An unpleasant ability, sometimes. Just as my very fine nose can smell rotten flesh, body odors and carbon emissions three times faster than the average person. I even *smelled* the snake, trying to hypnotize me like Kaa in *The Jungle Book*. But no.

"I don't care about my career at the moment. I don't give a damn. So do me a favor. Tell anybody who'd push me in this moment to go fuck themselves. I don't even feel bad for letting them down."

How on earth could I care about promoting my book when I had to bring my sister back? How could Susan be so heartless?

As I dropped the call, I noticed the laptop that Ondina kept on the antique desk in the living room. I wanted to Google 'brain hemorrhage' and research some more, but my attention shifted to a notepad with a red cover. The first ten pages were filled with Ondina's elegant handwriting. A long journal entry from a week before her accident:

15 January 2008

On the train, returning from Florence.

There was this magnificent full moon yesterday. Finally, Guilherme and I went out on our own. Neither kids, nor a hundred of friends around. It has been very intense since I came back from India and decided to spend the rest of my vacation at his place. Maybe I'm just not used to that. Maybe I need to feel like the center of his attention more often.

Last night was great. We talked and listened to lots of music, one of the many things we have in common. We both feel emotional when music fills the air. Guilherme plays the saxophone and likes jazz and R&B. I'm open to variety. Some-times I wonder how it would have been meeting him when I was a young singer/song-writer, and... playing together? When we both were free spirits with no strings attached, able to build a life together in a simpler way? Maybe bearing his children? Sometimes I wish my life had gone another route.

Oh, well. Anyhow, it was interesting trying my best to fit into his very structured life. I tried to ignore the mess in his house. The piles of dirty dishes accumulating in the sink, that veil of old dust covering every surface, the stains on the tiles. Restrained myself from the need to play housekeeper.

The worst, though, was to deal with his ex-wife's presence everywhere. I asked Guilherme to put away some of Beatriz's clothes still in his closet, since he had told her that he made his choice and she cannot come back. Beatriz had gone home to Brazil at the end of summer, trying to handle the alcoholism that destroyed their marriage. She entered a rehab clinic and was released in early December with a clean bill of health. Wrote to Guilherme and said she was ready to try again, that they owed it to the children. Fate plays tricks, though, and Guilherme and I had just met in October. It was clear since the beginning that this wasn't just another of his affairs.

We fell in love. And as it is with love, it was nobody's fault. Love just happens, like a sudden thunderstorm conjured out of clouds. Love doesn't consider what is best and when, neither accepts age nor class restriction. It refuses to play by the rules, dances naked on the public square in broad daylight. Love doesn't give a damn about balance and appearances and chooses to ignore the basics of politeness. Love is ruthless, likes to surprise and embarrass, swallows you whole and spits out the bones with a loud burp. What would we live for, without this kind of love?

Guilherme made his choice, and he chose _me_. After five years of flakey guys unable to decide, going back and forth like rubber bands stretching between the new (me!) and old loves in their lives, finally a man who had the guts to choose! And be honest about it. He took the kids to visit her and told Beatriz that there is another woman now in his life. I should feel happy. Instead, it's bittersweet. I can't help being sad for Beatriz. For the two of them and their love story gone bad. Am I an idiot for feeling that?

Guilherme went all the way to make me love his life in these few days. He took me around his beloved Tuscany, visiting friends on the coast and then skiing in the mountains. He's one of those immigrants who's really pushed hard to fit in. Speaks perfect Italian, surrounds himself with Italian friends, eats, cooks (well!), and appreciates Italian food. He doesn't exile in a closed community with passes allowed only to other expatriates.

Skiing came in the end. It was supposed to be a two-day deal, but our plan got spoiled by a weird accident. We were all slaloming downhill. Guilherme tall and elegant. Then me, right after him. And then the kids, still a little clumsy, following at short distance. I didn't see it coming. An out of control snowboarder swiped me off my feet. He managed to run me over and then hit Guilherme too.

I got a sprained knee ligament out of it, Guilherme a broken rib.

It almost made me think of a macumba placed on us both. South American women 'tienen sangre caliente.' Who knows what a jealous woman might be capable of? I told Guilherme my thoughts, but he laughed. Beatriz could never hurt a fly, he said. Only herself.

I'll need an MRI when I'm back home. Maybe I should also throw in some other tests, and a physical to find out why I feel so tired all the time. Thought it was still jet lag from the difference with Indian time, but now it's been too long. I hope it's nothing serious. 2008, in my opinion, should be a fun year. A barrel of monkeys. I'll be forty-seven in April. I'm still young and I'm in love. I look in the mirror and see a beautiful woman. I'm healthy and financially independent. Nothing should prevent me from enjoying life.

A sadness spread on me, thick like molasses gone bad. *A fun year, just like a barrel of monkeys.* I shrugged the thought off and checked the time on my phone: ten past seven. If I hurried up, I could get to the train station earlier than I'd planned.

I made it to catch the 8:05 train heading to Milan. It was full of commuters. Gray, foggy landscape ran out the windows. I sat with five other people in a crowded, dingy compartment. Lucky, since others had to stand in the aisle. I wrote a letter to Ondina on my notepad. Since she couldn't read, my crooked handwriting didn't matter. I'd be the one to read it to her. Forty-eight hours since I landed and I already felt like Italy was swallowing me back. I was on the same commuter train Ondina embarked on every day to go work at the advertising agency in Milan.

I turned on the padded bench, uncomfortable on the window side, crammed against it. I tried to make myself smaller while a hefty old guy kept falling asleep, leaning his head toward my shoulder. On the facing seat, a young woman applied fingernail polish, formaldehyde fumes filling the stuffy air. The schoolboy on her right chewed gum and made bubbles. A woman snored loudly.

I had an imaginary conversation with Ondina, except I knew she couldn't talk back. "Mother always knew what was going on with us. Remember? Lying to her was useless. It might be Parkinson's disease. It might be that she doesn't want to know. She might be scared as you are. But so far, what she knows or wants to know is just that you fell and hit your head. And she's waiting for me to go tell her that her 'other baby' is going to be alright."

I watched out the crusted window. Gray fog wrapping the bridge on the Adda River we were crossing. I closed my eyes and saw Ondina and me, maybe nine and six, run into the river in our white underwear, splashing and laughing. Those Sunday afternoons when Father would take us fishing with him. Him, standing still in the shallow water in his waders and tall green rubber boots, calling after us: 'Don't go far. And you, Ondina, be careful. Keep an eye on your sister.'

"You always had to take care of me. How unfair, having to be the one always responsible, particularly with a daredevil of a sister like me. But anyhow: Mom. I think I'll lie some more to her. Fed up enough with all the lies our parents told us, I convinced myself that truth is always better. This time, I doubt it. Not this time. Not for an elderly ailing mother who relied on you to take care of her through all these years that I spent away. How can I tell her what really happened when we don't know what will ensue?

"I'm so grateful to you for helping her, so sorry that life took me so far away from you both. I will take care of her from now on. Don't worry. I'm prepared to go back and forth from California just like you commuted from Bergamo to Milan. I'm not afraid of distances. You know that. I'll come and go for as long as you need me. But first, I'll wait for you to come back. You've got too much to come back for."

The train whistled and the speaker announced "Milanoooo, Stazione Lambrate." The familiar approach to the station, run-down stone foundries and the narrow paved streets of my childhood.

"I know all we said and promised when we were little. But the truth is, we don't know how it'll be. There's a chance that you can make it. That's why you can't leave, not yet. That, and the fact that I can't conceive of a life without you in it."

It felt weird to write it as a pronouncement. Didn't I tell her I'd support her whatever would be her choice? And how could I have her believe that she could make it while I wasn't so convinced myself? To make it *how*? What the hell happened to my resolve? My emotions were a jumbled tangle of hope, despair and an irrational willingness to believe that 'everything was going to be alright,' just as Xavier had told me, making me go ballistic.

Chapter 9
CLAIRE

Milan, two days after the accident

Going from the railway station to my mom's house was another quick trip by subway. I like cities that provide good public transportation, particularly those that have an underground fast train system with multiple lines. Under the surface is where life pulses, an intricate nervous system that gives pace and purpose to the city. That's one thing I miss in Los Angeles.

Mom lived northeast of Piazza Loreto where, at the end of World War II the body of the fascist dictator Benito Mussolini, known as *Il Duce*, was executed by a partisan firing squad and hung upside down at a service station. The gesture was criticized by some as excessive and welcomed by others as a symbolic conclusion, intended to publicly confirm his demise so that the oppressed Italians could celebrate the end of his regime of terror. Mom had been a young partisan, fighting for change. She told us horror stories of what fascists did to contain the people.

She didn't like the neighborhood where she lived now. In Milan, they called it the Kasbah. Immigrants from Arab countries and North Africa moved there in the second half of the eighties and now counted for almost half of the inhabitants. She had nothing against immigrants. I was incredibly proud of her for not giving into the anti-immigrant sentiment that most old timers shared since Milan had become more cosmopolitan, quite different from the almost all-white city of our childhood. What she found offensive was being forced to move from the apartment where she started her family and raised her daughters. She didn't appreciate change and never got used to the new geography of her life. She could never understand how I could move from one place to the other in a heartbeat and find it exciting. I had moved at least twenty times since I'd left here at sixteen.

Wilma greeted me at the apartment door and let me in. I took off my coat at the entrance, hearing my mother's voice from the family room. She spoke with a thin, wiry voice, almost a whisper. "Who is it?" She was sitting as I imagined her, in her electric lift chair in front of the TV, all wrapped in a plaid blanket. "Chiara! What happened? Something bad happened to your sister?"

Had Wilma spilled the beans? I had not told her much. But I also knew my mom—despite her illness, her mind was still razor sharp. She was intuitive, knew how to sum up facts and extract a conclusion. I dragged a chair from the dining table, taking hold of her hand on the blanket. Her hands were still graceful, still smooth. So different from my rough, boxy ones that had worked with tools, made repairs, gardened and painted. Hers were thin and elegant, with long tapered fingers and perfect smooth nail beds shaped like hazelnuts. Her nails were painted with a pearly pink polish. The same color I used to apply on them when she let me, when I was little and in awe of those princess hands. I believed they were magic, that Mom could just move them in the air to clear away anything ugly. I wanted to believe it again, right now.

"We don't know yet how bad it is, Mom."

"Can she talk?"

"No."

"Can she walk?"

"No."

"But she recognized you?"

I looped my fingers through the beads on the leather string with the medicine bag I wore around my neck. "I hope she did. But I can't say for sure. She's still in a kind of coma."

Mom's eyes went wide at my last word, her irises lost in the double white. "But who did it? Who pushed her and made her fall?"

"We don't know that either, Mom. Nobody saw anything. But remember, it was icy outdoors. She might have slipped on her own with wet soles and hit the marble."

"But she'll recover, right? Did the doctors say that she will?"

I felt my heart jumping in my throat, choking. I took her hand to my lips and kissed it. The TV kept buzzing. The talk show host screamed "That's right!" I wanted to repeat him. A sound like the jackpot of a slot machine followed. The Italian version of *The Price Is Right*.

"They're not sure yet. It was a bad fall. The hemorrhage was just as bad. Her recovery depends on lots of factors that may or may not happen in the next few days."

Mother turned her head away from me, looked out the window, the slightest tremble in her lower lip. "How do they feed her?"

"Through a G.I. tube. An opening in her belly and another one in her trachea to help her eat and breathe while she's unconscious."

Mother burst into tears. "*Che tragedia!* Everything happens to us. Look at me, already crippled in a wheelchair. And now, Ondina. I hate God!"

I rose to hug her, feeling guilty for her crying "Hush, Mamma, hush. Don't be pessimistic. It could have been worse."

"Worse! How? She doesn't talk, eat, or walk. She can't even breathe on her own. How could it have been *worse*?"

I felt myself shrinking inside my pretend-adult clothes. "She could have died," I mumbled. "The surgeon might have decided not to operate and let her go."

"I wish that surgeon had let her go in peace! It'd have been a blessing for her. You don't know what it's like to live as a disabled person. I'd rather die than be in this chair all day. Alone with that one!" She gestured with her head beyond the partially closed door. "Breathing on my neck like a vulture!"

"Come on, Mom. You're lucky to have Wilma," I whispered, grateful for once that Mom was bringing the focus on herself, as she often did. "She's affectionate and capable."

"If you say so," she added, pouting. "But shouldn't you go back to California now, take care of your business?"

"Business is just business. California can wait. You and Ondina are my family. You two come first, this time. Don't worry. I won't leave you now."

"Always the optimist! Just like when you were little. When you broke your leg, you were there on the floor in terrible pain, trying to hold it together with your small hands. I almost fainted when I saw you that way, but you said: 'Don't worry, Mom. It could have been worse.'" She chuckled, then went on. "You brought home all the strays from the street, no matter how ugly and wounded they were, thinking that you could fix them all."

"Well, it turned out that I *did* fix most of them. Didn't I?"

I was trying to lighten up our conversation but Mom got all serious and sad again.

"What if this is not one of those times? What if you can't fix Ondina?"

"I... We... We'll fix her, Mom. We'll fix her, and she'll come back to you, almost as good as new. Please, Mom, believe it. I need you to try and believe it, alright?"

I had to believe it but Mom didn't need to know that. She nodded, a doubtful look on her face. "Go now. Go to her. I'm tired. I need to rest."

Dismissed. She was still taking charge and calling the shots. Relief washed over me like a lunar tide. She didn't ask any other question that would have forced me to go deeper into details. Some things are better left unsaid. I started to see the reason behind holding back certain truths.

I made it back to the hospital for visiting time. The hallway leading to the I.C.U. was alive with many people. I looked around and had a vague sense of recognition. Some faces I knew. Others, I recognized from pictures at Ondina's house. I straighten my shoulders and marched towards the group that was huddling together.

"Am I wrong, or are you my sister's friends?"

"You are Claire, right?" asked a young woman offering me her hand to shake. "Paola. I'm Ondina's colleague at the advertising agency. How's she doing?"

"I didn't arrive in time to talk to the doctors before visiting time. I visited my mother in Milan."

"We did. I'm Nicola, by the way," said a tall man with a kind smile. "Nobody was here, so Filippo and I went in. The doctors know us since we accompanied Ondina the night of the accident and stayed through the surgery." I followed the direction of his eyes to find Filippo, dark haired, brown eyed, slim and about my size.

"Doctors are very pessimistic," he informed us all. "Ondina

isn't responding to any neurological stimulation and her clinical situation is critical. Basically, they don't know if she can pull it off." Straight forward, no beating around the bush. I liked that, though not everybody else did. A woman in the group burst into tears and turned her face away to hide her embarrassment.

"Doctors know nothing," I said calmly, hoping to placate her. "I wouldn't trust them to put stitches on a cut on my arm. Certainly, they know nothing about the brain. There was no brain science until twenty years ago. It's such a young field that most of their diagnostics and therapies are still in the experimental phase. I know this because I spent time reading a lot of stuff on the web about alternative therapies that were attempted with people in the same situation as my sister, and I'll definitely pursue them... I mean," I added after a couple of seconds to avoid sounding too assertive, "if Ondina wants me to."

"But how can you know what she wants?" another friend, Maddalena, asked.

I smiled, trying to stay upbeat. It was too warm in there to keep on a coat so I unbuttoned it while searching for the right words. "The doctors are keeping her in a coma, giving her drugs since the pain must be too much to handle. As soon as they stop the painkillers, we'll wake her up. That's the most immediate goal. Finding clues to catch her attention. Memories of good times that can make her want to come back and be with us all." I tried hard to throw Ondina's friends a rope.

"I can help," Maddalena said, grabbing on it to pull out of the swamp of worry and despair. "We spent last summer holidays together traveling throughout Mauritania. Ondina loved every minute of that vacation."

"So maybe you should come in with me when they call. I know they allow only two at a time. I'm sorry that no others can see her tonight, but I think, in this case, the doctors are right. It must be too much for a person in her state to deal with too many. Maybe we can find a way to coordinate and you can come in one at a time?"

The door of the I.C.U. opened and a nurse called.

"I.C.U. visitors can come in now. Two for each patient. No exceptions."

Chapter 10
CLAIRE

Bergamo, two weeks after the accident

The chilly morning air hurt my lungs at every breath but the view was inspiring. I gazed at the landscape underneath the *mura*, those huge walls surrounding Bergamo Alta, erected in ancient times to protect the town from invaders. Fields and houses were still sprinkled in fluffy white flakes from the last snowfall. I ran with an iPod and headset, secretly wishing to be somewhere else, on a warm beach. Far away from hospitals, doctors, metallic beds, beeping monitors, prescription drugs, patients' charts and visiting times: my new normal.

I stopped to catch my breath. My phone vibrated in the pocket of my track suit. I checked my messages. A new one started with *"Drago says."* I clicked, and a picture of Drago in the yard filled the small screen and made me curl my lips in a smile. A handwritten sign hung to his collar, "Come Back Soon. We miss you!" Below, a message from Xavier.

Dear Claire, I tried to talk Drago out of it, explaining that you cannot return now, that you have things to take care of in Italy. But he's an old stubborn dog and an attention monger. He didn't go on hunger strike like last summer, when you went to New York to discuss the contract with your agent and publisher. On the contrary, he convinced me that he needed a T-bone steak for dinner to make up for your absence.

The wildflowers are blooming in the canyons. We already spotted yellow mustards and brittlebrush on the crest of Elyria Canyon where the castor plants seem ready to start sprouting their red blossoms. We'll send you pics with our next email. Take your time and let us have some news when you can. Your roommate/ gardener/dog-sitter/whatever

I closed my eyes and smelled the mix of mustard, creosote, chaparral and sage. That scent you smell in the canyons surrounding my house in early spring. I missed it. And I also missed Xavier, but I was glad he wasn't in Italy with me, exposed to my moods and crises. I had trouble myself to be with *me,* this unrecognizable, insecure and doubtful person who held sway over Claire in these last couple of weeks.

Nothing had changed in Ondina's situation. *Only nothingness,* I thought, immediately visualizing the Japanese character *mu* painted in black brush strokes. I'd visited her every day but couldn't detect any improvement, so I'd asked the neurosurgeon to show me the test results and prepare a report that explained everything that'd been carried out for my sister's care. I trusted him even less than I usually trusted Americans in that profession. It seemed to me like he did nothing more than just kept her breathing and feeding her that sour-smelly, milky concoction through her G.I. tube. I had an appointment with him in less than an hour and I badly needed to shower after my run.

The CAT scans were already hung on the wallboard when I entered the windowless doctor's studio. It was a place so barren and plain that you immediately wished to get out. I always wondered how doctors might feel, spending so many years studying and hundreds of thousands of dollars for an education that brings them to spend most of their lives in ugly places like these.

"You wanted to see them, Ms. Strada, and it's your right," Dr. Bardone said, pointing at the board. "But you must realize that even though we're doing everything we can, your sister's situation is... tragic. Such a shame! Such a beautiful woman with a healthy body, younger than her age."

"She's not dead yet, Doctor. Maybe it would help to think about her as somebody who can still have a future?"

The doctor glared at me. He proceeded. According to the script, or had he revised it to silence my concerns?

"See this?" He took out a pen from his pocket and pointed it to a black area of the brain scan displayed on the illuminated board. "This is the extension of the subdural hematoma that I had to remove. I could not avoid extracting a huge number of neurons. And surgery has most likely affected this other area toward the back..." He moved the pen a bit on the right, to the nape area of the skull. "Where the pineal gland is. That means that your sister's ability to understand and interact could be irremediably compromised. If she ever wakes up, she might just remain in a vegetative state."

I stared into his eyes, in disbelief. Was he fucking crazy? How could a sound-minded doctor decide to perform such a surgery! But the milk had been spilt. What I was left with was a clean-up job that looked almost impossible. Yet, I wasn't ready to give up on my sister. And I had my own script this time, to counteract his. I made an effort to look unimpressed, not discouraged.

"I guess there is only one way to know, Doc. Take her off the drugs."

His cheeks became as white as his coat.

"No offense, Ms. Strada, but this is such an important decision, it would comprise a personal risk for me. I know it's your sister, but I think that you should be authorized by the court, first. Officially, I mean, to make such a decision."

"I didn't ask you to pull the plug off the ventilator. I just asked you to stop keeping her unconscious so I can try to communicate with her." I was fuming. "But you're probably right. All these years abroad made me forget how horribly slow and complicated Italian bureaucracy can be. I'm Ondina's only sister and our mother's an invalid. I'm the next-of-kin, the only one who can authorize such decisions for her. I don't need to get 'approved' by some court!"

"I'm afraid you do. And the fact that you live abroad might be an issue. The court will grant you a tutor status only if you are willing to stay and be part of her recovery."

I felt a swell of rage mounting, hot acid boiling in my chest and creeping up my throat. I stood up abruptly. "Tutor! My sister doesn't need any tutor. But if it's necessary to get her off your drugs and out of here, I'll be her tutor. I'll come back tomorrow with signed papers."

I strode out of his office slamming the door, charged down the hallway and then ran down the stairway until I was outside and in fresh air. I slowed down my breathing, exhaling with a double count compared to my inhales.

I sat in the courtyard on the rim of a flower planter with a few dry rose branches. February, but there weren't any fragrant buds that would sprout by June. This wasn't California.

Chapter 11
CLAIRE

Bergamo, fifteen days after the accident

I'd been able to act quick as soon as I went home, the night before, and I'd summoned everybody I needed for the first available hearing. It was another cold, damp day that remained gloomy even at noon. I reached the courthouse and climbed the stairs to the first floor in a hurry.

I entered a hallway with several closed doors, small groups in front of each one. I approached a bench outside of "Room 27, Judge Molinari." Three people I recognized sat on the bench. A younger guy that bore a stark resemblance to Ondina, my half-brother, Fabio. A pretty older lady, his mother and my stepmother, Katarina. Ondina's ex-husband, Giovanni. Nicola and Filippo stood in front of them. Nicola with his lanky frame, leaning more on his good leg, the other one shortened by poliomyelitis contracted when he was a young child. Filippo with his baby face framed by black curls, deep set brown eyes and straight nose, fair skin with red cheeks that made me think of a ripe apple. Everybody had their coats draped on their arms. Hot inside, snowing out. Another icy February day.

I bent toward the youngest in the group and kissed him on both cheeks, the Italian way. He was handsome, looking like my father when he was his age. "Hey, little brother. Thank you for coming. Thanks to you too, Katarina. Giovanni, so nice of you to be here to testify. As I told you on the phone, I need to be supported in my petition to become Ondina's tutor because I'm no longer an Italian resident. Apparently, I don't have the right to legally represent my sister unless you guys testify to my intention to switch back my residence."

"Are you really going to do that?" Giovanni asked.

"I don't think so. But I'll stay here as long as it takes to get Ondina out of the hospital. Into rehab. You know, a place where they have the best therapies and devices for brain damage. The first step to achieve that is becoming her tutor."

"Shouldn't the doctors take care of it all?" asked Nicola.

"They should, if the system worked. But they made it very clear that, due to the system's limited resources, only patients who're already at a good stage of recovery and have the best chances of fast results get transferred to these rehab clinics. That way the clinics—which are funded on the basis of their results—can keep their cash flow."

"What happens to the others?" Giovanni intervened, swiping the index finger of his left hand in the hook of the other hand like he meant to clean it from some invisible dirt. He never got over Ondina leaving him and I knew he cared about what happened to her.

"They get transferred to long-term care. Nursing homes for the elderly where they're lucky to receive physical therapy once a week, a neurologist visit once a month. But since the waiting list is as long as a giraffe's neck, they usually get sent home. To families who are absolutely unprepared to care for them."

"What will you do with Ondina?" inquired Filippo.

"I want to get her accepted at this private clinic in Switzerland. Very expensive, but I don't care. I'll raise the money one way or the other. But they won't take her in if she's still in a coma or, like Bardone put it, in a 'vegetative state.'"

The sudden swing of the door interrupted us. Two people exited. A loud, high-pitched voice from inside announced: "Next!"

Chapter 12
CLAIRE

Bergamo, eighteen days after the accident

Long ago, in a life that now felt as distant as the Borgias of early Rome, I'd enrolled in a massage therapy school in Santa Monica, the Tao Healing Center. I studied shiatsu, an ancient Japanese style based on traditional Chinese medicine and acupressure applied in specific points, charted accordingly on the meridians that guide the flow of energy, or *chi*, through our bodies, the same principle of acupuncture. Instead of needles, though, the therapist uses her fingers, elbows, knees, or sometimes feet to apply pressure and stimulate those points to release blockages.

I love the approach of Eastern medicine that considers the body not just as a bundle of organs and glands, but holistically. According to this vision, symptoms are messages to listen to, not nuisances to medicate or repress, and most illnesses are mainly a *disturbance* in the flow of energy. I didn't intend to take up massage as a career, but following those principles, I cured myself. I haven't used prescription drugs since I was old enough to make my own decisions. Proper nutrition and lots of exercise gave me a platform for a healthy life. Herbs and supplements integrate what's missing in produce from impoverished soil and polluted air. It works until a brutal turn of fate befalls you. And when it happens, the fact that you lived a healthy life counts like a Two of Spades. You are plunged into the same nightmare as somebody who drank himself to cirrhosis, ate fast food twice a day for thirty years and considered lifting a six-pack of Budweiser an acceptable workout daily routine. Like in Ondina's case.

I kneaded Ondina's legs under the white sheet while Maddalena stood on Ondina's other side. She held one of my sister's limp hands and murmured in her right ear. I hummed chants I'd learned in meditation, did Reiki on her. But Ondina remained still. Eyes closed. I'd brought in my computer and the screen was open to the page I read last night, which I'd spent surfing the web, researching. Sleepless, like almost every night since January 21.

"People in a coma cannot see, and we don't know if they can hear. But neurological tests have shown there can be neuronal response to music and other sensorial stimulation at times. Touching is very important and can provide some comfort to people confined in a hospital bed..."

I've never been religious. Unfit to follow any doctrine. Quite incompatible with commandments and the unappealing idea that we need to be punished for wishing for anything good. Like sex, unless it is "excused" by the sacrament of marriage. Such patriarchal bullshit. But I was surprised to find myself praying to every god on Olympus and every Christian saint for my sister's healing. I would have gladly traveled to Lourdes or Mecca, climbing up the trail with a backpack full of stones, if any of it might have helped her.

I wore Ondina's clothes. Not only for practical reasons—I'd left Los Angeles with just what I had on my back and little else.

I'd not dismissed the suggestion read in Ondina's journal that a *macumba* must have been placed on her. Irrational, but just in case, I hoped that wearing my sister's clothes might divert the *brujo's* attention away from her already devastated body. To me. *And now even yoga!* I taunted myself. *So that I might add Shiva and the Green Tara to my personal menagerie of gods.*

I'd committed to go to the yoga teachers' meeting right after the hospital. I was curious to know more of my sister's life, to discover missing pieces of the puzzle. Some forgotten *tessera* of the mosaic that could help me see the whole picture, gain some insight, break the mystery that obsessed me. Why did this happen to her?

Yoga had been a great help in her life, giving her tools to deal with her anxiety. It also gave her a slim and fit body, muscular without any bulk, flexible as a twenty-year-old. I never cared to dwell on the past. I prefer to live in the present as it inches me into the future. But I'd learned to seek clues during my excursions into dreamland, to discover what my rational mind couldn't conjure in a waking state. I sensed that scraps of my sister's recent existence could help me and I was determined not to leave any stone unturned. Plus, Filippo had invited me, and what's the nastiest some yoga could do? Worst case scenario, I would just stretch and move.

When I entered the yoga studio, Filippo, dressed in loose white cotton pants and t-shirt, sat cross-legged on the floor. He was in the lotus position, speaking quietly to a group who squatted down in 'easy pose' on the linoleum. I left my shoes in the rack by the entrance door and grabbed a yoga mat. I recognized Nicola in the middle, nodded to him discreetly and crept silently toward the back of the room. It didn't work.

"Welcome!" Filippo smiled and waved at me, then turned to face the class again. "You all know that Claire is Ondina's sister. I invited her to join us in a little meditation to help our friend recover. We'll start by closing our eyes, focusing on the energy coiled in our first chakra at the base of the spine."

I closed my eyes, intending to follow the guided meditation. I found myself drifting into daydreaming instead. At first, it was only quick colorful bits of images running through me. Dream fragments pushing each other and bouncing in different directions like several balls pocketed at once by an expert strike on a pool table. Then the images organized and aligned themselves. Behind my closed eyelids emerged a starry night. Not the kind of black sky mapped by a million shining dots that I used to see while camping in Montana or New Mexico, far away from the city. But a vivid night sky that held a promise. And in it, the thirteen-year-old version of myself, blonde tresses long to my waist, my slender body dangling out of the second-story window of the apartment building where we grew up in Milan. Thirteen-year-old Chiara hung on a rope made of bedsheets, holding it with her thighs, feet, and hands. She was now descending in a spiral movement, like a firefighter on the old station pole. She lifted her head to look up to where she'd twirled from. Another figure framed in the window, hands on the sill, head projected out.

"Hurry up!" young Chiara hissed. "Come on, Ondina."

But Ondina seemed to hesitate. "I don't know, Chiara. It's so high!"

Chiara had let go of the rope to cover the remaining few feet to the ground, then jumped as high as a basketball player to grab the rope again and held it straight for her sister.

"You shouldn't have to do this. You're sixteen! You should just tell Mom you're going. Come on!"

Ondina hesitated, afraid but excited. "Damn you! You are

out of your mind. We'll both end up busted or in hospital."

The young Chiara contained her laugh. "Last call!"

Ondina relented, turned around and hoisted herself out the window, starting her descent. Music swept in from some remote fold of my mind, a choral applause for Ondina as she winched herself down three inches at a time. Radiohead's "Exit Music." A song about escaping from the house before the father wakes up. But we had no father in our house. Our mother played all the roles.

Ondina, gripping the rope with such tenacity her knuckles looked white, made her way down until she reached Chiara. "Know that I hate you," she said.

"Not as much as you love me."

The image dissolved and became something different. I was inside a huge black and dark red coil spinning like a tornado. It was violent and fast. I needed to get away from it so I opened my eyes and stood up. I rolled up the mat and mouthed to Filippo a silent "I need to go."

I slid out of the studio, careful not to make any noise, leaving the group in their meditation.

I couldn't find Belinda when I got home after yoga. I looked under the bed and the sofa, inside the washer and the dishwasher, on top of the kitchen cabinets and in the laundry basket. I finally opened every drawer in the house and the terrified cat jumped into my arms from the middle of the bedroom chest of drawers, meowing frantically out of Ondina's folded socks. I didn't blame her. I'd have been scared too, locked inside a dark place. I couldn't help thinking about the darkness where my sister was trapped. The idea that I might have lost her precious pet had crept along my nerves like circling seaweed. I was relieved, but still uneasy until I realized Belinda must have been hiding in the back of the drawer when Olivia, the cleaning lady, accidentally closed it. Olivia came once a week, she had keys to get in when my sister was at work. She was silent and efficient, communicated only through notes left on the kitchen counter. Italian wasn't her first language. She had come from Romania only four years earlier, but had managed to learn the language pretty well.

After finding Belinda, I still couldn't sleep. I tossed and turned all night and finally got up, more exhausted than when I went to bed. I put on my track suit and sneakers, and went for a run. It was very early morning and the path along the Mura was empty, aside from the occasional early-risers walking their dogs. I needed to sweat off the toxins of another sleepless night. Warriors conquer their fears. Worriers get consumed without achieving anything. I'd used this conviction to free myself from anxiety in my teenage years. I wished I could summon that warrior willpower now.

The cobblestone streets gently curved and converged into a square that I remembered filled with tables and chairs in summer. I spotted the coffeehouse in the little plaza on top of the walls. 'Marianna,' named after the owner. People would sit there sipping their morning coffee or enjoying their cocktails in the evening. I'd enjoyed both there with Ondina. Aperitif is an honored ritual in Italy. Coffee is almost a sacrament, though most people swallow their espresso or cappuccino standing at the counter, a habit I rarely witnessed outside Europe.

Attracted by the rich bakery smell that invaded the crisp morning air, I resolved to sit down, having run already three miles. I ordered a cappuccino and brioche, the sweet pastry breakfast preferred by most Italians. They looked delicious for a second when the waiter put them in front of me, but then my stomach turned, shooting acid reflux up my esophagus. I couldn't eat hardly anything, those grim days after the accident. My sister was always on my mind. I was hungry for answers, for her to open her eyes, not for food to fill my stomach. A young African vendor asked me to buy a little booklet with recipes of Ethiopian cuisine. I bought the book and told him that I had ordered a breakfast I could no longer eat. He happily dug his teeth in the flakey pastry and thanked me with a guileless smile. Despite the burn of my muscles, I felt the urge to leave the coffeehouse and run on, all the way down to Bergamo Bassa and toward the hospital. I didn't care that I was sweating or that it wasn't visiting time.

When I reached the hospital, there wasn't anybody in the I.C.U. hallway. I rang the bell and eventually one of the nurses opened the door. She was the one I'd interacted with the most. Her name was Cinzia and she was young. She tried her best to convince me to visit later. "If I did this for everybody else," she said, "I would be fired on the spot." Then, perhaps moved by the dark circles under my eyes, or the fact that I wore my workout clothes and not much else, she resolved. "Okay. I'll give you a few minutes with your sister. Just because her blood pressure keeps rising and falling today." She tightened the blood pressure strap around Ondina's arm and gave her a light caress on her cheek. "God knows she needs a miracle. Why's he's not answering?" She shrugged and added: "If the systolic pressure goes under eighty-eight, the alarm should beep. Keep your eye on it. Sometimes this old equipment can be tricky. If it goes under, push this button, and I'll come."

As Cinzia left, I approached the raised bed. It was so elevated that it looked like a scaffold. I had difficulty finding a decent position to get close enough to my sister. Her face wore a painful expression, but at least there was expression. I took her hand in mine under the sheet. "Hey, Sis. Bad night, huh?" No answer. I kept going. "This morning I got up at six. It was still dark. I knew they wouldn't allow me to come here, so I went running up the walls of Città Alta. It was chilly. But beautiful. This city you decided to make your home."

Ondina's teeth started biting her lips and tongue or maybe she was just mouthing.

"How many times you invited me to spend time here with you, and I always had some great excuse not to. Wish I'd made time. Gone on that trip to Nepal. But it's not too late, right?" Ondina remained still and rigid, breathing hard. The only thing moving was her jaw, jerking forward and back. "I went to your yoga class. You have lovely friends. I'm sorry I never met them when I visited before. I know that was my fault, rushing off to check up on Mom and fly home." I had so many regrets about the things we didn't do together, the things I left her to handle all alone. And just like with memories, I was so *not* used to regrets that it was hard for me to sail through them without becoming an emotional wreck.

I felt a slight pressure on my palm. My eyes turned to Ondina's hand in mine under the sheet. "Did I feel it right? Did you try to squeeze my hand?"

She still looked the same, rigid in that elevated metal bed. Her eyes shut. Her jaw chewing some invisible bite or maybe trying to free her tongue. But I felt the first tiny hope in almost three weeks. "Ondina, if you can hear and understand what I'm saying, can you squeeze my hand again?" And there it came, that almost imperceptible pressure on my palm. I looked down at our laced hands, amazed. "Oh, babe! I knew it.

I knew you were trying to cross back. You should, you know. There are so many of us praying. You're so loved, Sister. If you come back, we're all here ready to help you. Don't listen to the doctors. You are not 'average,' you're extraordinary. Who said you can't wake up?"

The blood pressure monitor beeped louder and the nurse arrived running. She took Ondina's left arm with the IV needle already stuck in and secured it to a tube coming out of a bottle hung on a support. A clear solution, saline water to hydrate and reintegrate mineral salts, or medication to alleviate the pain brought by the myriad symptoms my sister experienced in her condition.

"Not again! I have twenty patients, and my colleague is sick with the flu!" Watching the nurse moving quickly around my sister, I tried to share my discovery.

"She squeezed my hand when I asked her if she could understand me."

"Oh, OK," said Cinzia, not showing much excitement for what seemed extraordinary to me. She kept her eyes on the IV. "I'll tell the doctor later. Now I have more important things to take care of, like stabilizing your sister so she doesn't die. You better go. Come back tomorrow during visiting hours."

But she squeezed my hand! I kept telling myself as I walked away, repeating it to make it real, to reassure myself it happened. *She squeezed my hand!* And for the first time in three weeks, I smiled while exiting the hospital.

Chapter 13
ONDINA

Bergamo, twenty-two days after the accident

Bzzzzzz. Beep beep beep. Clang. CLANG.
   So loud. All these sounds.
   Steps, running. Where?
   Fog. Dark. I can't see. Eyes don't work. Only shadows.
   A song I used to sing:

> *Scarred my eyes looking straight at the sun*
> *I drank his bloody boiling fire*
> *Like an alien vampire*
> *Scarred my eyes looking straight at the sun*
> *And I'll never regret it*
> *Since it was helluvafun*

It isn't fun now. Where am I?

> *I never felt so warm and one*
> *Like that moment*
> *Blink and blind*

When I jumped with my van
And we crashed into the ocean
Blunt and kind

I don't remember a crash. Where is here? Why this song?

Now I'm lying on a rock
With my mermaid blue skin
Bruises and wounds on my tail
Broken bones and no fin

Broken. Yes. A bunch of broken bones and not functioning
parts.

But I got fire in my eyes
A red lizard on my irises penciled in
By the sizzling ink of dreams
That's what I got in my veins
What pulled me back by my ties
Fire, that's what I got in my eyes

I don't feel fire. I'm cold. Hurt. Everything hurts.

I dared beyond where very few have been
I faced things that very few have seen
I scratched my soul spinning
into the vortex of fire
I hit the "off" button on my parachute
And let myself just slide
Down in the ring of fire

But I don't want to jump. Don't want to slide in the fire.

I never felt so clear and one in life
like the moment I went blind
Jumping in that ring of fire

STOP. Useless song. I want out. Out of this darkness.
I can't move. Not arms. Or legs. Nothing bends.
I am NOT the Fire Woman.
I just want my life back.

Chapter 14
CLAIRE

Lake Como, twenty-seven days after the accident

The bar lifted to allow us access to the parking lot. We'd driven there in Filippo's silver Golf Sport. Me in the back, my brother in the passenger seat, Filippo at the wheel. We all got out at the same time and marched across the parking lot toward the entrance.

"Did Cristiana say that her friend who suffered from an aneurysm got better in this place?" asked Fabio.

"Yes!" I replied enthusiastically. "She got me a meeting after the Swiss clinic refused to accept Ondina. Cristiana said the new-patient intake doctor is a character. His colleagues call him Dr. House, like the doc on that TV show who doesn't follow the rules."

The clinic was managed by the Nuns of the Sacred Heart. Ondina would have killed me if she knew I'd tried to place her in the care of a *Madre Superiora*. But I didn't care. I'd given up church at nine, when I discovered that my mom couldn't receive the communion because she was separated from my father. Maybe I wasn't a churchgoer, but if Ondina could be cured in this clinic, I didn't care if it was run by Catholic nuns, Hare Krishna or Muslims.

"How about God?" Filippo'd asked me days before. "Do you believe in God?"

I believed in a pantheistic higher power. I perceived a divine energy in ceremonies held at a Native American reservation, where Xavier's uncle led them. That old medicine man reconciled me with my spirituality, but I was still not buying into any structured religion. Yet, I prayed for my sister.

I stepped into the clinic and took in the bright light and the huge picture windows. No religious icons, so far. Modern. Spacious. "Wow!" I exclaimed. "This, compared to the hospital in Bergamo, looks like a dream."

The receptionist called me close to her window. She scribbled our names on the log. "Take a seat. The doctor will see you in a few minutes."

Fabio, Filippo and I sat on one of the two long benches placed on opposite sides of the lobby. Soon a door opened and a doctor walked through hurriedly. Forty-five, give or take. Longish blonde hair and spirited blue eyes. He wore his white coat open on denim jeans and an aqua cashmere sweater. No tie. Hospital clogs on his feet. "Ms. Strada? I'm Dr. Moltacci." He extended his hand to shake mine and I introduced my brother and Filippo as my sister's friend. "Let's go to my office," the doctor invited us in, keeping the hallway door open.

We followed his quick strides past a hallway with wheel-chairs parked in a row, inhabited by patients with heads lolled on one or the other side, waiting for their turn inside the gym. Others stood and tried to walk, helped by two physical therapists.

"We strive to give them as much therapy as we can since movement and touch are what can awaken the neurons. What kind of physical therapy are they giving your sister so far, Ms. Strada?"

I was unable to hide my frustration as we arrived at an office behind a double plate-glass door. "None. The neurosurgeon in charge of my sister said that a public hospital doesn't have the resources to give physical therapy to patients still in a coma."

The doctor opened the door and gestured toward the chairs in front of a desk. "And how do they expect her to improve without any stimulation?"

I liked him already.

"We are a public facility, too," he continued. "We, too, have budget limitations. We have a double system for funding our research based both on government grants and donations by private foundations. That's why I have to be firm in recruiting patients who are promising, in terms of results. But if I do recruit them, then it's my duty to provide them with the best available therapies." He pointed toward the portfolio in my hands. "I see you brought me the data and test results. Let's take a look at your sister's situation."

I handed him the files with trepidation. He examined Ondina's CAT scans and paperwork. The corners of his mouth turned south.

"It looks worse than I expected. The damage to her brain is so extensive that..." He raised his eyebrows. "I must be honest. It makes a full recovery unlikely."

I interrupted, determined not to let this last opportunity slip away. "My sister is an incredible person, Doctor Moltacci. She can do unlikely things. And she was in great shape, with a strong body and perfect health before this horrible incident. She ate only healthy, organic food. Never smoked or drank alcohol."

The doctor kept his eyes on me. I could see he was intrigued. "Interesting. A brain that wasn't contaminated by drugs, smoking, or alcohol has more chances, speaking in neuronal terms. And nutrition is very important. We have a great dietitian here who personalizes the patient's diet according to needs."

I felt encouraged but I knew I had to keep the momentum, pry that small window open. "Ondina also meditated, went to the gym, ran, swam, practiced yoga consistently, for years. She's in great shape and doesn't look her age."

The doctor looked at me with a sympathetic smile. "You're trying to convince me, and I wish I could be convinced since I also care deeply about relatives. We want the family to be involved in the recovery process. We want to be assured that once the patient is released, the family will welcome her and will care for her at home. Can you assure me of that? I see here your sister is divorced."

"But she has us!" Fabio chimed in. "Her brother and sister, and lots of friends."

"How about her apartment?" asked Moltacci. "Is the house disability friendly? Does the building have an elevator where her wheelchair will fit in?"

Fabio seemed worried. "How long will she have to use a wheelchair?"

"I can't promise anything," the Doctor admitted. "I'm not God. God is the only one who can also determine if your sister will wake up from her coma. Every patient is different. They make their own progress. But I can't keep everyone here until a full recovery. I can only give them the starting push. Then I send them home. I don't abandon them. They can come back for periodic visits or also stays, if they make any significant progress."

"She will!" I almost shouted, shameless. "And we will be with her all along."

"I know you live in America, Ms. Strada," Moltacci continued. "If I take your sister in, and I said only *if*, who will be here with her?'

My brother lived in another city and worked like a maniac to keep his company floating and support his mom, as he'd done since my father's passing. He could provide some emergency support but couldn't guarantee a constant presence. Neither could Guilherme, living hours away with two children to raise on his own. And my mom was an invalid who needed caregiving herself. Not many options left. "I can stay as long as I need to, Doctor."

The doctor lifted a hand up to signal a time out. "Your enthusiasm is contagious, and I admire your determination. Should I take your sister in, you'd better take advantage of us, knowing that she's in good hands. Go back, settle your affairs and be back at your sister's side. Because, I've got to tell you: even if God gives us a hand, it will still be a long road. It could take years. Are you prepared for that?"

"I am," I exhaled. "It's just that talking to you, I'm feeling the first bit of relief in a month. So far, I've only been told that this is a tragedy and that I'd better give up hope."

"This *is* a tragedy," Doctor Moltacci confirmed. "But there's always room for hope. As long as there is breath, there's life. Nonetheless, I'll have to see your sister in person before making an ultimate decision. And she'll have to wake up from her coma, first. My requirements are that patients who enter my clinic need to do so with open eyes and at least a vague cognitive state. I rarely take patients in a vegetative state. I could make an exception, as long as she has recognizable periods of sleep and wake. I expect you to get back to me as soon as your sister wakes up. We can set an appointment for me to visit her then. Meanwhile, let me show you our therapy rooms."

The doctor stood up and we followed him on a little tour. Fabio, Filippo and I exchanged glances, observing patients doing exercises with machines in the physical therapy rooms, on computers in other rooms. Could Ondina be soon one of them?

Chapter 15
CLAIRE

Milan, twenty-eight days after the accident

Half stoned by my lack of sleep and the lizardly movement of the train to Milan, I recalled fragments of my childhood summers spent at my grandparents' house on Lago Maggiore. Grandma's hands were all knotted by the arthritis she'd suffered for decades, their fragile bluish skin freckled with dark spots. "Liver," she explained, following my gaze while turning another card. She placed it face up, adding it to the deck of her solitaire game spread out on the coffee table.

Afternoons, she would sit alone in the living room of her apartment on the ground floor of the matriarchal vacation house, one room for each child and their family on the first floor, yearlong caretakers on the upper floor, curtains pulled together to keep the rooms cool in the summer heat. She either played cards or crocheted intricate doilies.

"Three of clubs." I could barely make out the card in that darkness. I squinted to detect the expression on my grandma's face. Poker face. She was a bridge multi-champion. Her mug could remain stone-still through any game. It wasn't the card she was hoping for, though, so here came the scold. "It's your fault. Stop watching me like a hawk!"

She was tough on me, resented my presence, maybe the same fact of my birth given the circumstances of it. But I was fascinated by her power. In my mind, she was a shaman more than a witch. A dreamer, a gambler, a sorcerer and the best cook in the whole world. I attributed her bad temper to the colostomy bag she wore. The colon cancer surgery had removed two feet of intestines, leaving her weakened and psychologically wounded. She'd been a gorgeous young woman; she turned heads.

Grandpa told us the story of how he got to marry her on a bet. *Nonno* Nico was a captain in World War I, as a young man. Toward its end, he lost his left eye to a flying grenade and was sent to the military hospital, wounded also in the other eye. Grandma was a voluntary nurse. She was the talk of the soldiers. They all daydreamed about taking her home once the war was over. Grandpa couldn't even spot her through his bandage but he trusted his best friend's judgment: "She's a goddess," he'd assured him. So, the two men bet. The first one of them to propose would marry her. Grandpa won. He took home a gorgeous but temperamental woman, who became both his muse and his tyrant. In some odd way, though, they lived together in perpetual, compatible conflict.

Each summer, we were seconded to their *Villa Serenella*, that huge country home on the lakeshore of *Lago Maggiore*, and left there for three full months. Our busy parents came to visit on weekends. Not only Mom but also our uncles and aunties, parents of our cousins Manuela and Stefano, who were Ondina's age, born just a few weeks apart from each other.

I was the little one, and they made a point to keep me out of their business. That didn't leave me with options since our grandma forbade me from accepting invitations to go play with kids outside the villa. Not only that. She adored Ondina but couldn't stand me, a walking earthquake in her eyes. A nuisance, since I could never be quiet. I got into trouble a lot. I climbed tall trees and rocks, hung upside down like a bat from the iron wrought poles of the gazebo. I ate wild berries or mushrooms that I gathered in the woods, getting sick. I hammered my fingers while building my refuge from her authority: a platform so high in the big persimmon tree that she couldn't spot me from the ground.

Her revenge was to blame me for whatever the other kids did, and scare me to death with her stories of spirits inhabiting the house. She realized that fear was the only thing that might keep me still. She threatened to tell the spirits to come get me, or transform me into one of the big toads I heard at night, hidden in the garden. I believed she could. She was powerful and I was her prisoner. I prayed for Friday night to come so that Mom would arrive and shield me from her evil powers.

She terrified me, but also fascinated me because she was an adult who still knew how to play. Not just card games, cheating on herself since she couldn't bear to lose. She could play with her imagination. She could see behind the appearance of things and transform reality. Imagination was our common ground. And that allowed me, over time, to become her confidant.

"Watch carefully," she'd tell me when some distant lady relatives came to visit. "They want you to think they're good women, but one is a vulture and the other's a spider. They're after my money." I didn't understand the last part, but I did observe the two women closely during their visit, from my privileged spot hidden in the tree branches. And I saw their real nature, the marauding spider and the flesh-hungry vulture.

She'd tell me what she dreamed and ask me to interpret it

from a gambling perspective. "Win or lose?" My answer determined her mood for the following days, until Saturday came when she was freed from childcare. *Nonna* and *Nonno* crossed the border to the casino in Switzerland to play roulette. She'd still go and play if I said 'lose.' Then, once they lost, she made us kids pay for my prediction by dragging us to church on Sunday to confess our sins. My rebellion against Catholicism came straight from Grandma's notion of sin. "I committed many sins out of love," she once revealed when I asked her why she'd suffered so much, getting ill with rare diseases. *Love sins? Love could make you sick?* I rejected that possibility even then.

But she was the one who taught me to believe in the power of visualization, and that made up for the rest. She adored only Ondina. Her first grandchild and a mirrored mini version of my dad.

So where are you now, grandma? Can't you come and wake up your favorite? It's been almost a month, and she's still sleeping.

When I left Los Angeles, I didn't know whether I was going to bury my sister or she'd wake up again. I still didn't. I was focused on helping Ondina escape her pain, in case her injuries proved too extensive for a full recovery. Her words were emblazoned in me: 'Don't let me live a miserable life, sister. Don't let me end up complaining every day and cursing my fate.' How many times we'd told this to each other? So, what made me believe that no matter how horrible the doctors' reports, I could still hope for a full recovery? But it was actually more than hope. I held this strong conviction that Ondina would stick out her tongue at all of them, and make it all the way back.

I dreamt of her talking. Eating at the table with her friends. Walking the trails all the way up to Ca' San Marco, the mountain where she loved to ski. I cherished those dreams, relied on them to endure the harsh reality of our daily hospital visits, the time when I was forced to go home leaving her in that hideous hospital.

I understood what mothers with premature babies must feel when they had to leave their newborns in incubators. Mothers of sick children who are taken out of their arms and attached to machines and tubes. Babies who have to sleep in rooms with bare walls and beeping instruments instead of pastel colors, plush toys and lullabies.

My sister wasn't a baby, though. She was a grown woman with her own strong will. And she was suffering an incredible amount of pain. Did I have the right to make her live because of my hope, my dreams? Or should I accept the doctor's grim evaluation and be true to what I'd promised her long ago? How can you know what's right for another, even a sister you love? What if Ondina wanted to take the risk to come back to full consciousness and fight? What if she didn't?

I wished I didn't have to face this truly unsolvable mystery. A 'career' in solving them felt useless now. I had to get myself together and woman up. I needed to channel Nails.

I arrived at my mother's, slouched on the armchair uphol-stered in worn blue velvet set near her chairlift. The television, buzzing as always like a giant bee, with some talk show. They talked about Eluana, a thirty-seven-year-old woman who'd been in a vegetative state since she was twenty. Her father wanted the clinic to stop feeding her. The Vatican stepped in to forbid it. Everybody in Italy participated in the heated debate. You couldn't step into a bar in the morning to get your espresso without hearing about it. Catholic country, lots of believers. Controversial topic.

I tried to drag her attention away from the screen. "Doctor Moltacci's clinic will do wonders for Ondina."

"If he takes her. She's still in a coma. I don't know how you can be so optimistic. She'll end up like this poor girl on TV. All bad things happen to us." She broke into tears. Ashamed, she covered her face with the blanket. I gently stroked her hand.

"Mom, don't cry. Trust me. She'll make it. I just know. She's strong."

"I was, too," she interrupted. "Look at me now. I can't stand by myself. My hands shake, and I pee in my underwear because, most of the times, I don't make it from my wheelchair to the toilet in time. I can't read anymore, because of the eye disease, macula degeneration, whatever that is. Oh Chiara! And now this with your sister. I just want to die."

"Don't you dare to leave me alone now!" I tried to lighten up her mood, make her feel still useful, important. "I need your help, Mom. Ondina needs you. We need you to believe she can make it."

"I just wish that damn surgeon had let her go in peace."

I interrupted her negativity flow before it engulfed also me. "Okay, Mother, enough! I'll come back in a few days to check on you. I'm going back to Bergamo. I'll call you." As I got up and put on my coat, she called after me.

"Put on your hat, too. Stay warm. You getting the flu, it's all we need!"

It was almost dark when I made it back to Bergamo. Visiting hours had already started. I hurried along Via Papa Giovanni XXIII, walking fast from the railway station to catch the bus to the hospital.

Cinzia wasn't on her shift. Ondina was practically naked,

with the white sheet down to her waist. I glared at the closest nurse, then marched toward her. "Why is my sister exposed like that during visiting time, strangers staring at her?"

"She had a fever," explained the young nurse. "The doctor ordered that she be uncovered."

"With her bronchitis? And, regardless, do you think it's appropriate?"

"We do what we can. It's only me and my colleague here, with all these patients."

I went to Ondina's bedside, pulled the sheet up and felt her forehead. It was cool underneath my fingers, but not as cold as her chest.

"Wake up, Sis. We need to get you out of here. I found a great clinic in Lake Como. It's more like a big gym than a hospital."

I hoped for some kind of reaction. There was none. Ondina remained absent, unresponsive.

"You can do a lot of therapy there and learn everything again. It's nice and bright, and they use the most advanced therapies. I think you'd like it. We'll stay only the time necessary to make you better, then go back home. Don't you miss home? Belinda misses you. She always asks about you. I miss you, too. Can't wait to hear your voice again, see those beautiful brown eyes of yours looking into mine."

Ondina remained still as a statue, her eyes closed.

"But you need to help me. The doctor there says he'll take you in, as long as you are awake. Would you try, Sis? It's been twenty-eight days."

No reaction.

"You know what I found on the stereo the first day, when I arrived at your house from the airport? The CD with the song you wrote for me when I was sixteen, "Bougainvillea Sister." Now you've become my beautiful bougainvillea sister, like those bright flowery shrubs in Grandma's yard. Silent and still, but vibrating with life inside. I know you have it in you, Sis. Nobody else believes it. Nobody else can see it, but I believe in you. I know you."

I bent over and started humming softly into her right ear, singing the lyrics of the song.

> *I was nothing like her! My bougainvillea sister*
> *Climbing womanhood*
> *Clinging hair to rosewood*
>
> *Oh Sis, let me hold you tight*
> *Let's go fly our kite*
> *How can I let go of*
> *Diving into your purple eyes?*

Ondina slowly opened her right eye. In the following seconds, it became clear that she couldn't focus. But she could see some. She was scanning the strange environment of the I.C.U. Her eyes finally found my face. I was still singing with tears streaming down my cheeks. Ondina squeezed my hand and pulled hard on it to lift her face up close to mine. Her left eye remained closed. I made a huge effort to remain calm and reassure her. "Don't rush, Sis. One thing at a time. You're so brave! I'm so proud of your courage. But let's take it slowly."

I quietly sang the healing song used by the Lakota Sundancers.

> *"Tunkashila, hoye wainkte.*
> *Namahon Yelo! Maka sitomniyan*
> *Hoye wainkte.*
> *Mitakuye obwaniktelo*
> *Epelo."*
> *I am sending a voice.*
> *Listen to me.*
> *I am sending a voice through the universe.*

I will live together with all my relationships.
This is what I am saying.

I paused to explain. "I sing this healing song of my Native American friends to give you strength to heal yourself, just like you're doing. Xavier's uncle, Bitten by The Snake, said it would help you when you're ready. I think you're ready."

I rang the bell to call the nurse and showed her what Ondina could do. The nurse had to admit that Ondina was now awake. "See? My sister answers to me, not your doctors." I turned back to Ondina. "You love to be stroked, don't you, Sis?"

I showed the nurse that when asked to relax her left hand, then the left foot, right foot and right hand, one by one, Ondina did, letting me bend each one of her fingers and toes. There was still rigidity and contraction in her body but when I asked her to open her mouth and let me refresh it, lightly brushing her teeth, she complied.

"She never let us do that. This is so great! I'll tell the doctor as soon as he arrives."

"Let's show her a little trust." I pressed. "Let's reward her. Detach the tube from the ventilator."

"That's up to the doctor."

"I beg you. If only for a few minutes. I assume all responsibility. I'll be glued to the monitor. I'll call you immediately if it starts beeping."

The nurse looked conflicted. She knew she could be in serious trouble but she was moved by my begging. "Only a few minutes, like you said. But I must stay here."

She detached the ventilator and we both stared at Ondina as she drew her first breath on her own. And I was the one to hold my breath then, afraid to break the spell. After a couple of minutes, Ondina closed her right eye, relaxed, and quietly slipped back into the dream world. The nurse reattached the ventilator.

Another song popped into my mind while I looked at my sister sailing into her slumber. "White Apple Tree," by Snowflakes. I hummed it while gently letting go of my sister's hand. She'd utterly just come back from the remote distance of a profound sleep.

Love, hope and snowflakes rained from the evening sky through the darkness of the window. "Rest well," I told my sleeping sister as I got ready to leave. "So good to see you looking at me again! We still have a lot of work to do but you'll wake up from your beauty sleep soon. You'll be looking a lot younger, energetic and ready. Screw the doctors who doubted you. Now rest."

That night, I slept in Ondina's bed, in her nightie with her cat, Belinda, curled up in my arms. And I dreamed that I was with my sister. Ondina and I, at nine and six, were following our grandfather up a mountain path. I was last in line, panting, following in my sister's footsteps.

"I can't go on," I whined. "My feet hurt."

"I'd carry you, but I'm having trouble myself," said Ondina. "We're not far. You know, when we get to the top, Grandpa will let us rest and drink some juice. Come on, little one. Just a little more effort."

I reluctantly took hold of her hand and followed her.

The dream vanished, but my lips remained curled in a smile. And for the first time in weeks, I slept through the night.

Chapter 16
CLAIRE

(a post from Claire's new blog, *Road to Recovery*)

Five weeks after the accident

Dear Friends:
Thank you all for standing by us. I'm sorry for not having enough time to answer each of your emails, texts or phone calls, but you can read about my sister's journey here. I started this blog today to chart Ondina's progress. And progress we've made, as you already know.
It's been one week since she woke up and we are fighting to find the best way for her to return fully to this world. It's a bumpy path, a great exercise of alternating determination and kindness, which are not opposite but complementary. It's very much like skiing or surfing, or any kind of sport that requires you to climb up and slide down. Elegantly. Softly. Impeccably.
I'm trying to teach Ondina to surf the waves of her return to earth. I explained that it's okay for her not to speak yet. She's always been very talkative, but now she'll be better off investing her energy in recovering other abilities first. I'm also trying

to get Ondina to use her heart more than her brain. I use very few words to share feelings with her. I use my emotions and energy instead.

I got her used to waking up when I put my right hand on her heart. Very lightly at first, almost not touching her skin, then laying it on her chest and letting my body warmth be the wake-up call. Ondina wakes up without being alarmed that way. We should all have this possibility every morning instead of jumping when our alarms ring. We should all use our hearts more in our daily life instead of letting them just exercise their muscular pumping function.

This whole adventure is showing me how much heart people still have, buried under fear and daily worries. So many friends all around the world have warmly expressed their feelings and encouragement. This is the most refreshing energy I've ever experienced, and I'm convinced it's also what brought Ondina back. This is a path that needs heart. Ondina has an incredibly big one but it has been partially frozen for a while, as happens with most of us.

The mind takes over, and we don't notice since the mind is usually very skilled at playing commander in chief. But the heart is the true way of the warrior. Ondina was already learning to be a warrior, not a soldier. She is now. A great warrior on a peaceful mountain path. She'll keep climbing with the steady pace of people who know how to walk up and down hills.

That is what we were taught by our grandfather, Nico, when we were just toddlers. She has longer legs now. It will be easier. She'll just need to keep a child's heart to show her the way, and I'm convinced the path will be revealed.

Chapter 17
CLAIRE

Bergamo hospital, seven weeks after the accident

Early morning, the wintry, dark sky was still. I'd already been upstairs to check on my sister.

She looked scared. Who'd blame her? I'd have felt scared, too, in her condition, unable to fully understand why they woke me up and washed and dressed me—a first in almost two months! She couldn't grasp that they were getting her ready to leave the I.C.U., no matter how many times I told her. She just kept glancing around, alarm in her big brown eyes. Alert, yet not fully aware. I was reluctant to admit it but I had to. Some moments Ondina seemed to fully understand, but her awareness didn't last long before slipping away again.

I paced the courtyard until Filippo's Silver Golf entered the hospital parking lot. I gestured for him to park behind the ambulance that had its back doors already open in the loading zone.

Filippo got out of the car. "Thank you for letting me come."

"Thank you for giving me a lift," I answered. I'd made

arrangements to rent a car but it wasn't ready yet for me to pick it up. "I can't believe that they wouldn't let me ride with her in the ambulance." About to say more, I followed Filippo's gaze toward the hospital doors.

"Here she comes!"

We both rushed to the gurney to reassure Ondina as they wheeled her toward the van. "Everything's going to be okay, Sis. We'll be right behind you. See you at the clinic, in a little bit."

The drive to Lake Como behind the ambulance was slow, winding through narrow streets and frequent roundabouts. The ambulance didn't turn on sirens. It wasn't an emergency, just transportation duty. My thoughts raced fast while I caught glimpses of houses and stores following each other in my window view. *Was this the right choice? The right place? How would she react? Would she be up to the Doctor's expectations?* I couldn't stop the internal dialogue, useless as dust. There I was, after all these years and healing paths, buzzing with anxiety and hating myself for it.

Filippo didn't try to start a conversation. The silence didn't make him uncomfortable. I liked that. I shifted my attention to the hillsides covered with some early velvety green: a hint of spring, of possibility. The earth was coming back to life. I hoped my sister was too.

Finally, we arrived and the paramedic carried Ondina inside. She looked listless, as if what was happening had nothing to do with her. Had the EMs given her a tranquillizer on the way?

They parked the stretcher right in front of the admission desk as I asked the clerk to call Dr. Moltacci. He promptly appeared, directed the carriers to an examination room. I wanted to follow him in but there were two other doctors and a nurse who stopped me, shutting the door on my face. Fifteen minutes later, the three doctors returned. "So far, she's not responding to any of the neurological tests we performed," Doctor Moltacci informed me with a severe expression.

I had to fight the instinct to fold in on myself. I didn't want him to see the effect his words had on me.

"You can go inside now," he added. His cerulean eyes scanned my crow's feet, my complexion that had lost any trace of the California sun, the Cupid's bow of my upper lip, usually pointing up to the tip of my nose and now clamped with my lower lip. "Come back in the afternoon and you'll see her sitting in her *seggiolina*," he informed me, with pride, like I should consider it big progress..

He'd called the pachyderm monstrosity I'd seen in the hallway *little chair,* the way Italians have this habit of sweetening nouns with diminutives, sounding like people talking in baby blabber: *passeggio* is stroll, but for stroller the Italian language uses the term *passeggino*. *Pochettino* equals just a little when *poco* isn't already small enough. *Patatine* for potato chips. *Cavolini* for Brussels sprouts, since they're not big enough to be considered *cavoli,* cabbage.

"Claire," Filippo's voice interrupted the chain of words that could have continued to infinity, "let's go." He put a hand on my shoulder to direct me to the door. Filippo did his best to cheer me up. We'd been thrown out of the clinic and told to grab a bite before the afternoon visiting time.

We chose a *trattoria* that had a patio overlooking the lake, with a pleasant flowery scent. Luscious camellias sported a few buds already, but we had to keep our coats on. You could feel that winter was not yet finished with us.

Lunch was a pitiful affair. The tongue in my dry mouth felt like parched paper. I could only nibble at my grilled *persico* fish. I pushed it around the plate with my fork, surgically examining the corpse. I should have asked for a simple salad. That would have been easier to get rid of, under the camellia foliage.

A boat with two young men plied the water and I couldn't understand what they were up to. They didn't face us. They were turned the opposite direction, looking out onto the center of the lake. Were they going to dive in? Try to find the right spot to launch anchor to set their fishing poles? I followed the lines of their backs until they became just a vague impression, a pale watercolor brushed in light strokes.

"We can go now." Filippo's voice called me back to earth. I checked the time on my phone. He was right.

We arrived at Ondina's room while two nurses were putting her in a net hung to a mechanical metallic arm powered by an electric machine. They were absorbed in the complex operation of lifting her up from the bed to transfer her to the wheelchair. She wore the pink and gray sweatpants and the lilac t-shirt that I'd given to the nurses for her. I'd packed her a suitcase for her stay with other gym outfits, nighties, toiletries and socks that I'd chosen carefully. My sister would have never forgiven me if I forgot her sense of style and color coordination.

The two nurses, a man and a woman, lowered her into the wheelchair. Then the female nurse turned to grab a jar of moisturizer from the shelf, letting go of Ondina's head. It was still bandaged, missing a part of her skull on the left side. Her head fell heavily on her chin, unable to fight gravity, like a puppet whose strings had been let go.

I was in shock.

"Ooops! Forgive me, Ondina," the distracted male nurse vaguely apologized. "I thought dry skin would bother you." He secured a strap from the headrest to Ondina's forehead to keep her head up. "She has no control of her neck," he explained.

"Make sure to keep the strap on all the time. She's scheduled for physical therapy at 3:30 p.m. Get her to the gym by then."

I fought back tears and swallowed the lump of my pain. I wanted to focus only on the positive. "You mean, we can go outside in the yard?"

"Sister Ilaria said so. But cover her up. It's windy out."

The two nurses left and I squatted in front of Ondina in her chair, looked her in the face. She was awake but absent. I grabbed both her hands. "Did you hear that, Sis? Sun and fresh air after seven weeks indoors! Can you believe it?"

Ondina remained indifferent to my words while Filippo smiled. He knew her love of the outdoors, a passion they shared, daylong hikes in the Maresana or in Val Taleggio. I'd only heard of their adventures. I didn't know much about the valleys surrounding Bergamo. And my Italian memories revolved around another lake, not Como.

I was used to brown hillsides covered in sagebrush and fat, oily chaparral where I'd sit on top of barren land burnt by the merciless Californian sun. I belonged more to that harsh scenery than to this sweet landscape. And yet, here I was, pushing a wheelchair through the corridor, determined.

Chapter 18
CLAIRE

Lake Como, two months after the accident

The sun was now warm enough for us to linger in the garden during the afternoon visits, despite the snow still capping the mountains a few miles away. First day of spring, after all. Ondina sat in her wheelchair, a couple of friends standing at her side. Nicola sat over on a bench by himself, a good hundred feet from Ondina and the others, checking his phone. I watched them, out of sight, leaning on the trunk of a beech tree, talking to Filippo in private.

"The doctors said that she wasn't given enough physical therapy while in Bergamo, so she has a very high level of spasticity. She can't move any of her limbs at will, or control her head movements. Her legs and arms are so contracted that the muscles and ligaments are at risk of becoming shorter. He advised me to enroll her for an experimental surgery to install in her abdomen a baclofen pump, which releases medicine in a constant flow. The baclofen should help to relax her muscles."

I exhaled, lowering my head. I couldn't understand how my sister had regressed to that level of contraction while only a few weeks earlier she was able to respond to my commands, opening her hands. A procession of red ants circled the tree root beside my left foot. A few feet above, Paolo and Maria inscribed their names into a heart scratched on the whitish bark, at wheelchair height. I wondered if Maria ever rose from that wheelchair, able to walk again. Did Paolo stay and love her anyway, no matter how much progress she made? Or did he run with Maria's healthy best friend, away from all the dread and pain he could no longer bear?

I turned my attention to Filippo, who'd kept silent. "It's risky," I added. "But Moltacci said that there's not much else that can be done. The physical therapists fight with Ondina's automatic reactions to contract her limbs. Physical therapy happens only an hour a day anyhow. The remaining twenty-three hours, she's mostly left in her 'vegetative state,' as they call it, preventing her from participating in the other activities and neurological stimulations I'd hoped for. Without that stimulation and the baclofen, she'll just get more rigidity."

"Did he explain the risks?" Filippo questioned, sifting inside a bag of stale potato chips bought at the vending machine that neither of us would eat.

"If I agree to the surgery, I'll meet with the scientists in charge of this experiment. I'll need to sign all kinds of releases. In her condition, she could die in the operating room."

Why did this have to be me? My sister? The question I'd always despised—Nails would never ask that. *Why anybody else?* I'd answer my whining friends when they believed they were the only victims of tragedies. Now, I was one of them.

But how can I know what's best for my sister? How would she decide for herself? How can somebody ever make that kind of decision for a smart adult, and know they're not fucking up?

I felt like screaming my tormenting doubts out into the

afternoon breeze. I wanted to curse at all the gods and karma, climb up into the tree and hide out in the leaves, bawl my tired eyes out. But I knew it wouldn't help. I'd already bawled enough.

Chapter 19
ONDINA

Lake Como, nine weeks after the accident

Better.

She said this place was better.

It's not.

I still sleep with a neon lamp on top of my head and people come and go at night, flashing lights in my eyes, turning me on one side or the other.

Then they disappear for hours, letting me stir in my wet diaper without even checking.

I fear them.

I fear the white coats when they burst into my room early in the morning and shout stupid orders one after the other like machine guns. They're done before I can even grasp the meaning of the first, try to respond. They scribble on my chart and vanish, leaving me there alone.

I hate them.

I hate the nurses who fake cheerful smiles while they wash and dress me to be trapped in that horrible fishnet like I was an octopus. They lift me up all wrong, crooked and unbalanced, then lower me to my wheelchair.

They wheel me up to the hallway, where the cleaning ladies keep the doors open at both ends, to leave me there together with other miserable-looking patients abandoned in the cross-winds, their heads bowed, goosebumps on the skin of their bare arms. Some of them so wet with their own saliva that the spit spread from their bibs on their chests. So much for keeping us from catching bronchitis and pneumonia! Of course, this goes on when it's not visiting time, when indiscreet eyes aren't around.

Later, somebody else arrives and pushes me to the gym, where madmen pull hard on my arms and legs like they want to rip them apart. But I don't let them, ha! I fight back.

They think I'm too far gone, I heard them say it.

They don't know that I intend to travel far from here on purpose.

It's my only defense. My 'resistance.' My 'absence.'

Then my sister arrives, still believing in elves and fairies, and she promises great things that will not happen. I'd hate her, too, if I didn't see the pain in her eyes, her need to believe that I can still make it.

At least, she takes me out in the garden.

I live for that hour of air. For 'recreation' in the yard, like any inmate. And sometimes friends come to visit me there. They carry shreds of my past life.

Sometimes I enjoy hearing their stories. Others, I close my eyes and turn my head away, ashamed of what I've become. I wish they'd never come, never saw me this way. That's what I did when Guilherme came, erupting good intentions and reassurances like a mocha machine.

Claire doesn't want to see it. She dismisses my protests like they're involuntary fitful reactions. Can't she see that I don't want to be here? That here isn't any better than there, where I was before? That I have nothing to offer to those who still insist on loving me?

My body's entwined in a long garland of thorns. I'm bound tight in pain, physical as much as emotional. Strapped to a damn wheelchair, my head unable even to stay erect on her own. Is this my life?

What life? This isn't life.

I will not give in to believe that it can be.

Screw them. And screw me, too. This 'me' that I am not.

Chapter 20
CLAIRE

Milan, ten weeks after the accident

Once I'd forced myself to make my decision, I had to go to Milan and tell my mother, face-to-face.

We sat in her family room, in our usual set up. Me on her blue velvet armchair, pulled close to her electric lift placed in front of the TV which was on, as usual, buzzing like a swarm of bees. No matter if it was the news or some talk show, Mom needed the company of background noise even when she had a visitor. A habit that deeply disturbed Ondina as much as me, but I wasn't going to press her on turning it off. Not today.

"I don't agree," she said, her authoritarian tone resurfacing for a second in her feeble voice like a diver coming up for air. Parkinson's had taken away her bossiness, together with her old bravery and confidence. "We don't have the money for this surgery and it will be useless. You'll see."

Italy provided public healthcare but for specialized urgent care without the endless waiting lists, you often had to take the expensive private route.

"Mom," I explained, "it's the only chance we have for her to recover. What would you have me do? Leave her there all twisted-up, unable to walk, speak, or scratch her own nose? I'll sell my house if I have to."

Mother turned her head toward the window and covered her face with her left hand, the one that didn't shake so bad. She yelled for all her faint voice permitted.

"Don't tell me these things! I don't want to hear them. I don't want to think about my daughter that way. I wish she were dead! You're torturing her. And you don't even know if it can work."

Wilma rushed into the room. She tried to calm Mom down. I stood, about to leave. "Well, thanks for the encouragement, Mom. It's nice to know you love her too."

I understood why my sister had such a difficult relationship with our mother since Parkinson's had made her a prisoner in her powerless, beaten old body. I wanted to find compassion for her but I'd spent it all on Ondina.

Chapter 21
CLAIRE

Lake Como, three months after the accident

Doctor Moltacci was in Ondina's room with three nurses when I arrived. His secretary had requested me to come over immediately. The baclofen pump had been installed the day before in the *Ospedale Valduce di Como,* as rehab clinics are not equipped for surgeries. And I'd been there waiting since 6 a.m. Before, during and after the surgery. I hadn't slept the night before the surgery, and spent the day on a metal chair close to my sister's hospital bed. The ambulance had brought Ondina back to the clinic at 3 p.m., and then I'd returned to Bergamo. The call from the clinic woke me up at about 8:45 p.m., after a three-hour crash on the couch. My hands trembled from the lack of sleep. I had to use all my willpower to concentrate on driving, not letting the mounting worry distract me from the road. Filippo would have come if I'd asked him, but I preferred to go alone. She was my sister. My load.

When I got a glimpse of Ondina in her bed, surrounded by all those white uniforms, her mouth was twitching, her body shivering. I knew she was in unbearable pain. The alarm on the blood pressure machine beeped every few moments.

"Can't we pump in the plasma faster?" Moltacci asked the nurse who was applying an IV into Ondina's ankle. The veins in her arms had been poked for so long they needed a new territory.

"I warn you, Doctor. Her vein is so small that it could break," the nurse answered.

"If it breaks, it breaks. If we don't, she'll go."

I followed the conversation, moving my eyes from one to the other, then to the devastated body of my sister. An expression of sheer terror ravaged her face. Her body spasmed and twisted. It all seemed so surreal and at the same time, horribly real.

Moltacci turned to address me, acknowledging my presence in the room for the first time. "Signora Strada. Thank you for coming. Everything was going well after the surgery, as you saw yourself before you left the hospital this afternoon. Then, all of a sudden, her blood pressure dropped. And it seems she caught bronchitis again, as if we were missing some other ailment!"

He moved aside to let me get closer to Ondina. I wanted to recoil inside my shell like a snail when I heard that last piece of news. But it was a luxury I couldn't allow myself. Not with Ondina in that state. I took her cold left hand in mine and whispered in her ear. "I'm here. Everything is going to be alright. Don't worry." But I was more than worried while voicing that idiotic mantra.

The nurses left the room and Moltacci explained. "I'm trying all I can. But I need you to help me. I wouldn't do this with any other person but you have a special relationship with your sister. I've witnessed your dedication and commitment to her care. Not many other patients have their relatives visiting every single day but you've been consistent. I've seen enough to know I can trust you. Here"—he showed me to the end of the bed—"you need to monitor her blood pressure every fifteen minutes and write it on her chart. It should be a nurse doing that, but I don't have enough personnel. I'll be doing my rounds and come back at the end. If something happens, page me."

He left the room, and I tried not to cry. I couldn't breathe. I felt like I was riding on the Twisted Colossus at Magic Mountain, plunging downhill at impossible speed. Ondina alternated between squeezing my hand so hard it hurt and letting it go.

"I'm so sorry, babe. I should have never put you through this." Tears flowed down my cheeks and I couldn't stop them. "Don't leave me, Sis. Please! Don't go away without me. Don't leave me all alone."

All my years practicing detachment, and I'd turned into a fickle, selfish woman just the same. Pleading with my half dead sister to remain for *me,* clawing at the bedsheets covering her body like they could help me hold her down.

Chapter 22
CLAIRE

Lake Como, three and half months after the accident

I'd been summoned to Dr. Moltacci's office. I'd expected just a routine talk about the next steps in Ondina's treatment. The after surgery scare was over. The baclofen distributed by the pump had relieved Ondina's spasticity. Her arms and legs could be bent and I was able to lace my fingers through hers. She was no longer in pain and I was hopeful that increased physical therapy would also bring more awareness.

"I kept your sister longer than I normally would have," Dr. Moltacci started, "but I can no longer convince my boss. Ms. Strada is not making the progress we expected and we have a waiting list that's long like the California Coast."

I was totally unprepared for the news Moltacci just delivered. My mood was already gloomy. The Italians had voted in an authoritarian premier. Silvio Berlusconi, the media tycoon and real estate mogul who'd first assumed premiership of the Italian government in 1994—resigning just after a few months because of accusations of corruption—and then again in 2001.

His bombastic style had appealed to the silent majority, despite the scandals.

I felt ambushed and couldn't hide my outrage. I had a strong suspicion about the real reason behind the doctor's change of heart. "And your investors will open their wallets only if they see good results."

Moltacci didn't comment, so I kept going. "But Ondina has been busy these past weeks trying not to die from your experimental surgery. What progress was she supposed to make?"

"It has been unfortunate, I know. But she's been here for almost two months already. There is nothing more I can do for her."

"What about the foot surgery you said she'll need to stand and walk again?"

Moltacci had explained that the tendons in Ondina's feet, forced in a spastic position by the lack of physical therapy during her first hospital stay, had become shorter and a 'simple cut' could release them and make it possible for her to be put on a vertical stand.

"She might be able to come back for that at a later time. For the moment, I have no other choice than to release her."

I stared into his icy eyes, seeking a trace of understanding. There was none. *I never trusted blue eyes,* Nails whispered into my ear.

The distance between me and Moltacci grew much wider than the few feet between our seats on each side of his desk. Out of the window behind him, I could see umbrellas of milky blooms gracing the cherry trees on the hills. The soft view contrasting with the sharpness of his words. I lowered my glance to the floor. My feet had turned sideways, for the door, instinctively trying to step away from this discussion. But I couldn't follow their lead.

"Release her? Where?"

"That's up to you. It isn't something we can help the

families with. You'll have to find a long-term care facility. A nursing home where your sister—"

I slammed into the backrest of the metal chair. "Long-term care? Nursing home? You mean, you want me to put my young, energetic sister in a sort of hospice, to die?"

"Signora! Not all long-term cares are the same. But I urge you to think about yourself too. You cannot become your sister's full-time caregiver. It isn't fair, and I'm sure Ondina wouldn't want that."

How dare he? What did he know about what my sister wanted when I had no idea myself?

"I urge you to visit some of these institutions," he added, moving the brass paperweight to pick up his prescription pad. "I will write you a recommendation to Don Orione, one of the best, which is in Bergamo, close to Ondina's friends. Listen to me. Go there to visit. Take a look around. Try to find peace knowing that you've done everything you could and more for your sister. And so did I."

"Did you?" I hissed as I stood.

I left his office with the wind knocked from me. I had to hold myself up by the railing in the hall.

Chapter 23
CLAIRE

Bergamo, almost four months after the accident

It took me two days after that meeting to set an appointment at Istituto Don Orione. My mom had stayed there for a month the past summer, when Wilma went on vacation back to Krakow. Mom was housed in a different wing than long-term-care patients and she received physical therapy five days a week. She'd hated it anyhow. But Mom hated everything.

It was a clear afternoon when I arrived. I'd asked Filippo to accompany me. Of all Ondina's friends, Filippo was the one most consistent in visiting, not giving up on her. Most of the others had progressively slowed down, losing hope. Nicola would come almost every weekend and I really appreciated his efforts since he had physical limitations of his own. Guilherme and Cristiana were also supportive, but they both lived in Tuscany and had commitments there they couldn't disregard.

We walked toward the receptionist who directed us to the long-term-care department. I slowed my natural athletic gait to glimpse around.

"We have an appointment with Doctor Giarsi. Doctor Moltacci sent us. The name is Strada," Filippo said to the clerk.

I wandered off, leaving him there to deal with the bureaucracy. Everybody was ancient, just as I expected. Mostly sitting in wheelchairs parked in the corridor, unattended. They looked sad and absent, drooling on their chests. One lady had her head unnaturally bent forward on the right side, saliva all over herself, as nobody cared to help. Her neighbor was trying to lift a hand to the window but the hand fell back in his lap when it reached halfway. Over and over, reminding me of the shock I experienced as a little girl when I saw my grandaunt Giuseppina doing the same, as an aftereffect of her car accident.

I felt rickety. The effort to hold myself together made me queasy. I swallowed the mounting acid and sadness together.

I cannot do this to Ondina. She'd think that I abandoned her.

I hurried back to the registration and grabbed Filippo by his coat.

"Let's go. I can't do this to her. Let's run!"

I hastily dragged him out of the unit, then out of the entrance doors toward the parking lot, like we had a horde of blood-hungry zombies rushing behind us.

Chapter 24
CLAIRE

Lake Como, four months after the accident

A week later, I had another meeting with Dr. Moltacci. This time, I'd requested it. A few days earlier, Ospedali Riuniti called to schedule the surgery to reattach the missing part of the bone to Ondina's skull, now that she was in more stable condition, and this had given Moltacci pause. He'd agreed to transport her to Bergamo and then back to his clinic for the convalescence. The surgery went well. Ondina seemed now much more alert and responsive.

"Many things could change now," he said when I sat down in his office, which I'd left in a huff just a few days ago. "Let's pray it is the case."

I begged him to give me another month, explained that I was determined to take my sister home but 'home' still needed to be found. Ondina's apartment on the fourth floor in the center of Bergamo wasn't an option. The elevator was too small to accommodate her special-needs wheelchair and I didn't want to confine her to a prison indoors. I had other plans—I'd hire a live-in caregiver, find a disabled-friendly van to accompany Ondina to medical visits. But first, after finding a new home for her, I needed to get back to L.A. to tie up my old life.

Moltacci was impressed. This time, he was understanding, cooperative. He confided that he'd never convinced many families to do anything similar and had stopped trying after witnessing the devastating effects on those who agreed. A few months down the road, they all gave up, unable to cope with the sadness, pain, emotional stress and fatigue.

He asked if I not only could but *wanted* to do it. Both of us knew it was a rhetorical question. He told me he wouldn't abandon me nor Ondina, and would put in a request for the right equipment to be sent home, free of charge. It must have won him a big medal to pin on his white lapel, a patient going home to a family member committed to her care. Donations to his state-of-the-art clinic would roll in. Or maybe he wasn't so heinous after all.

My 'doer' mood had clicked right after that short and dreadful visit to Istituto Don Orione. Cristiana volunteered to take my place, to stay at my sister's Bergamo apartment and visit her every day here at the clinic while I went back to L.A. She knew she risked losing her job in Tuscany, but she still wouldn't back down. And Ondina trusted her as much as I did, I knew that as a fact. There weren't many like her. Friends show their true colors in moments of need.

Filippo offered to gather information about possible housing nearby Bergamo. My only requirement was a place with a view and a big elevator or on the ground floor. In a week, I'd accomplished a lot. And the fact that Ondina re-gained her whole skull in place, despite a very visible long scar on her shaved head, meant a great leap forward.

To celebrate, I bought her a pair of golden hoops earrings the size of an orange that made her look a bit like Sinead

O'Connor when the singer sported a shaved head. *Nothing compares to you.* The lyrics of the song kept looping through my mind. It felt great, swinging into action after months of hanging on threads and circumventing roadblocks.

I knew I'd have to play a game that was anything but easy but I was unflinching in my resolution. Sitting on the bleachers was no longer an option.

"It ain't over now 'cuz when the going gets tough, the tough get going." Didn't John Belushi say so, in that '80s comedy that became a cult movie for my then coming-of-age generation? *It will be my new mantra,* I told myself while exiting the rehab clinic where Ondina had been warranted an extension, *and the Blues Brothers my gurus.*

Chapter 25
ONDINA

Lake Como, June 2, 6:30 a.m.

I fight off the light that filters through my closed eyelids, conspiring to wake me up. My head turns from center to left but I can't reach the itchy line of stitches that runs vertically on my shaved head. I glimpsed it yesterday in a mirror in the corridor. Scarier than my bloody and swollen upper lip. And it hurts!

My jaw muscles contract in spasms. Every few minutes, the pain is so deep it makes my legs clasp together, automatically shifting them both to the left side of the bed.

Inhale... Exhale. Inhale... Ex-haaaale. Inhale... Now exhale. Will it ever go away?

I ride my breath like a magic carpet. Flying... Out and away from this noisy place with people in white uniforms and latex gloves touching me, always touching me.

They lift me up in that sort of ridiculous hammock, then lower me in the humongous, squeaking wheelchair. They don't notice when they deposit me in the wrong position, one hip stuck on the armrest, they don't seem to care that I'll hurt for hours afterward.

It feels like a tank ran me over. A big ball of pain that I cannot localize. I can't touch my body! I've lost awareness of what is arm or leg. The only place that constantly burns as a sizzling pan is the left side of my skull. It must be devils' gathering time again, their secret dancing ground in a burrow inside my head.

I cannot talk, I cannot protest. I am the perfect patient.

The nurses wash me as if I were a corpse already. They turn me on one side first, then the other. They give me a sponge bath in bed and gossip above my head, trading dirty jokes they think I don't understand. Sometimes it's true—I float so far away from this place not to hear their discouraging comments. ("Number eight? Nah, she won't make it out of vegetative, she doesn't have a chance.")

I resent their cold touch on my skin.

How did I end up here? What happened to me that caused this? This me reflected in the mirror? That's what I'd like to know, but nobody cares to tell me.

When my sister is here, she squats in front of my chair to be at eye level, keeps repeating my name and tells me how beautiful I am, that everything is going to be okay and that I will return to be who I once was. Based on what?

I roll my eyes sideways, turn my head on the left side and shut down.

She lies to me out of love, I know. But she should know me better than that.

Sometimes, I wish she would give up her faith in my recovery, stop trying so hard. Can't she see that it's too difficult to break this damn glass ball that separates us? Can't she feel how exhausting this is? I get tired even with a minimal effort like turning my head to the right when she whispers my name.

Her determination scares me. Anytime she comes into my

room, I wonder what she's got in mind. What new medicine, surgery or therapy she's been researching. She's so darn resourceful, spending her nights on the web to find new possible cures.

There are times I pity her. It breaks my heart to see her so hopeful and I wish she'd remain in California.

Maybe I'd have died without her, knowing that nobody was going to pull me back. It would have been better for both of us.

Where is she now, by the way? Where the hell did Chiara go? She didn't come today, neither yesterday nor... I don't know how many days. No, wait, last time she came—but when was that? She brought a candle, eucalyptus-scented, and a soft mohair sweater. She said it was a lovely lavender, but I can't distinguish colors. Same with scents. My sense of smell isn't the same it used to be.

I have no calendar in my room. My hours follow the rhythm of the hospital schedule. Six a.m., wake up. Seven a.m., washing. Eight a.m., doctors' rounds... I understand how convicts might feel. Your life is ruled by others to the smallest detail, and pretty soon you are institutionalized, thinking as they'd like.

I'd kill myself—and I wish I could—before feeling 'normal' in a place like this.

I'm in their hands. I'm their hostage, now even without my sister giving them a hard time for their negligence and lack of care.

Where is Chiara? What am I doing here?

Why was I left alone in the hands of my jailers?

Chapter 26
CLAIRE

Los Angeles, June 2, 5 p.m.

Landing at Los Angeles Airport always put me in a good mood. This time, it didn't work. My mind was packed with still frames of my sister alone in her electric bed at the clinic, her shaved head halved by a long red welt zipped by black stitches like a bad hem on a garment. *Will she remember why I had to leave? That I'll be back soon to her side?*

The slim towers along Sepulveda Boulevard lit up in quickly changing colors, neon palettes versus the black silhouettes of palm trees emerging from the marine-layered sky. The vastness of the city was wrapped in that wooly gray blanket that Angelenos dread, the June gloom. The Delta plane completed its descent after an almost fourteen-hour flight, which included a layover at JFK, unavoidable since Alitalia had suspended direct flights to LAX from Milan, Malpensa. Our unofficial city anthem, the wry, tongue-in-cheek, "I love L.A." by Randy Newman boomed from the speakers. I took a long exhale when the aircraft wheels hit the tarmac and taxied with its tires burning.

Home, anyway. Finally.

I'd never been gone so long from Los Angeles. Four months and counting. Some of the darker nights during my stay in Italy, I'd feared I might never get back. An unbearable thought. No matter how polluted, shallow, unsafe, car-centric, vapid, pricey or whatever other unattractive labels outsiders used to describe it, L.A. was my city.

Outside the terminal, people dressed in light summer clothes and sandals crowded the sidewalks. I walked among them, dragging my carry-on filled with my sister's medical reports. I headed to the yellow taxi booth and fell in line. In less than ten minutes, I sat in a cab, silently enjoying the familiar route along the 105 East toward the 110 North.

How many miles had I flown in and out of this airport? A hundred thousand? I was still absorbed in the calculation when the cab drove past the lights of the billboards of L.A. LIVE and the Staples Center, flaunting our patron saint Kobe Bryant with a foot-wide smile. Playoff season. The Lakers were in the finals versus the Boston Celtics, departing for Massachusetts in a few days. Lucky tonight wasn't game night. Traffic would have been murder.

I felt beat up, jet-lagged, dried out as an imported grape-fruit, yet the view of the downtown skyscrapers staggered against the San Gabriel Mountains never failed to revive me. Some epic quality in how they soar above the fumes rising from the freeways. The sheer contrast of steel and glass with the earthy colors of the landscape in their background, here not so overcast like on the coast, was striking. The familiar feeling of awe chased away the deprivations of the past months.

I never felt home anywhere. Lived thirty years in Milan and didn't have a single regret when I decided to move abroad. Italy was too small. Too predictable and orderly while I needed... *chaos*? I longed for something larger than life, as I learned to say in America. Wildlife in the middle of the city. New relationships. Territories to explore. It could have been Cairo or Sidney. A place with sunny skies and bright colors, plenty of trees and a warm climate. Untamed animals sharing the grounds with humans. Movie theaters, good restaurants and a lot of internet cafes at a stone's throw. A beach nearby. Diversity, with an immigrant population coming from different ethnic backgrounds. An international airport and a lively urban vibe. Those were the requirements.

But 'home?' Home at the time wasn't a requirement. Home, in my view, was a locker room to safely store my belongings in between my shuttle trips, my explorations. Roots are meant for trees. But, still, I needed a place to raise my son and it happened to be Los Angeles. This city of dreamers living on shaky ground, earthquake faults roping the desert beneath a sketchy urban structure riddled with too many architectural styles. Neighborhoods sprung like snakes from a Medusa mane. Buildings popped out of the cracks in the soil like prickly peyote cactuses.

L.A. fit me like a glove. I loved each one of the nine million residents of the county who said hello asking what's up, granting random acts of kindness. In Milan, people always ignored each other despite living in the same apartment building for years. They 'politely' avoided making casual conversation and didn't greet anybody they didn't know. Europeans are convinced that Americans are superficial, their 'nicety' only skin deep. I'd choose nicety and kindness in a second.

The cab passed the Hollywood Freeway interchange and exited the 110 toward downtown onto Broadway. Guys wearing suits and women wearing heels and pantyhose with black leather briefcases under their arms hurried out of the rolling glass doors that gave access to tall glass buildings housing insurance companies, bank headquarters and law firms. Six o'clock in the afternoon, and the intersection of Broadway and First Street transmuted into the corner of Fifty-sixth Street and Fifth Avenue in Manhattan.

A couple of blocks farther, in Chinatown, Asian-American women carried umbrellas to protect themselves from the heat, not the rain. I lowered the cab window to let in the aroma of the city. I took a deep inhale. A mix of dirt and rubber, car fumes, soy sauce, fried food and smoke.

In Los Angeles, shacks huddle beside Tudor mansions with white picket fences, often in neighborhoods not yet completely gentrified but already infused by Korean, Armenian, or Indian money that pushed out the less wealthy Latino residents who once 'owned' the Eastside after skipping the West beach towns curling up from Santa Monica to Beverly Hills. The new money targeted the more approachable East L.A., Echo Park, China-town and downtown, the true guts of Los Angeles.

My son and I lived in Venice when we first arrived from Italy. I was a beach girl, an ocean worshipper. I spent hours watching the waves, letting my thoughts dance at their roaring pace. "The sea once it casts its spell, holds one in his net of worth forever," according to Jacques Cousteau. I've been under its spell since the first time I met the Pacific. Pretty soon, though, I realized that Los Angeles didn't breathe there. Neither in Malibu nor in Marina del Rey. And Long Beach was a world unto its own.

You could smell Los Angeles and get intoxicated by its scent only in Chinatown, Little Tokyo or the Garment District, where the fashion industry was once thriving and now almost vanished. It's the core of the city, wrapped around the dry concrete riverbanks and wound around the labyrinth of freeway overpasses, that spices up its abundant bouquet. The ocean lived far away from the Mexican vendors of Olvera Street, flashing the gaudy colors of the Oaxacan hammocks or

Cuernavaca ponchos in the camera lenses of the tourists who just got off the Greyhound buses with Minnesota and Ohio plates. Far from the homeless picking their lunch out of trash cans at the four corners of Pershing Square.

"Stop here, please," I told the taxi driver who kept a picture of his five kids left behind in El Salvador on the dashboard of his old Dodge van. He braked abruptly and hot sauce from his taco lunch spilled from the Styrofoam container onto the tan-colored fabric of the empty passenger seat in front.

I apologized, though it wasn't exactly my fault.

"I meant on the corner of Second. I'm sorry."

I gave him a big tip to silence my guilt and got out of the car. I hurried across San Pedro, wheeling my carry-on through the narrow streets of Little Tokyo, too tired to haul it up by its handle. Fatigue forged its way through my body. I should have let Xavier pick me up at the airport but I needed time alone with the city before going back to my house in the hills, to a wagging dog and a welcoming roommate, to my giant oak, the bluejays and the hummingbirds. I wasn't ready to melt down.

I walked through a smelly stretch of back alleys. My nostrils burned with the stink of piss mixed with the vapors of hot dogs and burgers charring on the greasy griddles of the food trucks parked on First. I focused on the cool sweetness of the azuki bean flavor served by the ice cream parlors in Little Tokyo, instead. But I still breathed in all of it, savoring like it was crispy mountain air. 'No attachment' had been my religion. Lately, though, I'd let Los Angeles get under my skin.

I started whistling the Red Hot Chili Peppers' song, "Under the Bridge." It ringed so true. Maybe my only companion *was* this city, populated by lost angels who'd washed up here, just like me. Lone wolves don't feel lonely in L.A. I walked past storefronts adorned with pastel-colored paper lanterns, sushi counters where customers crammed in the raw, fishy smell that would rest in their hair. Teens in baggy jeans and fleece hoodies swarmed out of graffiti-painted sneaker stores, lined behind the Manga toy booths.

I turned into a hidden courtyard between a novelty shop and a soba restaurant where three huge trash bins, each one sealed with a big lock, were being investigated by a litter of stray kittens. I took the remains of the stale roasted veggie sandwich that I bought on the plane out of its paper bag and gave it to the kittens, who crowded around the open wrapper. They even ate the red peppers.

When I pushed it open, the heavy gate of the ramshackle building shrieked. It led into another narrow alley with stained and slippery pavement marked by mounds of rubble. I skirted around, jolting when a rat crossed too close to my boots. No other way to reach the Tattoo Heaven's blue door. Pacific blue ink is what I wanted, and to see my old friend Nakamura.

Chapter 27
CLAIRE

(remembering her first meeting with Nakamura)

I'd met Nakamura at a downtown bar, the 7 Grand, several years ago.

He was drunk, sitting on the next stool at the bar counter. He could barely bring his shot glass to his lips and mumbled nonsense, laughing. At some point, he stripped down to his waist to show some guy he was hitting on the intricate tattoo that covered his back, shoulder blades to buttocks. A tiger pacing the jungle. Dragon snakes with mean eyes hung from the trees, threatening the tiger with their forked tongues. Water lilies laid his path through the supple greenery. This tiger was fierce but also graceful.

Are you the tiger? I'd wanted to ask him. Instead, I'd looked for a silent answer in the intricate design on his skin and in his eyes. I longed to be part of the secret connection between him and his tiger. Eyes show more than a mouth can tell. In my childhood, I learned to detect lies in the adults' eyes while they tried to make me buy their explanations of reality.

Mom? Not her. I didn't need to see her eyes to know when

she was making things better or worse than they were. Mother loved embroidering on the truth. Any tragedy or happy event, win or loss, was never enough for her. Her version of reality had to be augmented. But her 'biggerness' involved inevitable elaborate lies. So, growing up, I regarded truth as so fundamental that I tried to fish it out of people's eyes.

Nakamura didn't like it.

"You staring at me, lady?"

"I know Americans don't like eye contact with strangers," I muttered as a half-hearted apology. "I have no idea about the Japanese. But you just showed me and all these strangers your butt."

The background laughter and smacking of glass on glass came to a sudden stop. "Too many eyes staring now," I added, not breaking eye contact.

"You're edgy, lady. Real edgy." He sounded suddenly intrigued.

"And you're drunk, sir. Real drunk."

That made him laugh, and everyone went back to their chattering, cutting the tension.

I wasn't as tough as I pretended to be, not as tough as Nails. My alter ego lived right there, working the hills and neighborhoods of the seediest and sauciest part of town, the Angeles I loved the most. Despite my fronting, I was much softer than Nails. I shot my Glock 19 only at the range, aiming at still targets. Nails could hammer a bullet in a running armed suspect from fifty feet away. Without blinking. We were both tomboys but Nails was one of the boys, while I was just a wannabe. When my sister and cousins didn't want to have me around, I got used to isolation, inhabiting other worlds. Since then, my genie escaped the lamp only when I was alone. Teamwork didn't work for me. I had trouble thinking straight in a room with other people.

At the 7 Grand, Nakamura insisted on buying me a drink.

I'd not been drinking for years. I winked at the barman who knew what I meant—7 Grand was one of my favorite hangouts after moving to the northeast part of town. I dropped there at the wee hours of the night, when walking under the bridges would call for crime scene yellow tape. I drank a bubbly cocktail of cranberry juice and tonic water that could pass for Vodka, my usual trick when somebody insisted on offering me one. Nakamura and I sealed our new friendship with that pretense.

A few days later, I had the opportunity to appreciate Nakamura in his sober state, when the artist scraped through layers of my subconscious with his penknife.

Chapter 28
CLAIRE

Little Tokyo, June 2, 6:30 p.m.

I pushed the squeaking door of the tattoo parlor. I walked downstairs with thoughts about my first time here, when I'd come to visit determined to learn more about Nakamura's tiger. Hours later, I emerged back to street level with the symbol of the Tao permanently scarred on my forearm. A black tear, a drop of Yin, in the white Yang field. A tear of white Yang in the black half of the circle that represented Yin. The wheel of life. *When something is too full, it will become empty. When there's emptiness, fullness will follow.* The Great Book of Changes, the *I-Ching* oracle.

Nakamura, like so many Japanese, wasn't so passionate about the Chinese culture. And although he'd never use his ink on somebody he didn't like, he remained open to the ideas of those he favored. He never tried to impose. He wasn't that kind of man. He made suggestions and showed sketches of the client's ideas, usually beautifying them.

I recalled looking at the still raw tattoo on my forearm

when the inking was done and Nakamura was discarding his pen knives, which he preferred over the noisy machine-whirring version. He was an old-school artisan.

"You're a beautician at heart," I'd teased him. "I never had to sit so still."

"I wouldn't mind tattooing the dead."

According to his vision, all tattoos should be ceremonial. Ink as an opening to rites of passage, like Samoan men tattooing their thighs to mark different life stages. Death is just a door, a transition to another stage.

I used to think I'd die young and reckless, and had no problem with the plan. We come into this world to die, and my Barbarian heritage—the Lombards, Norsemen descended from Germany to Italy—made me fear only death in bed. Dying is not the end since we're on route to the next attraction. What's unjust, intolerable, unacceptable is to be trapped like a rat in the wall. Not having the right to a dignified death. That thought brought the blues back.

I arrived late for my appointment. You never know with international flights. Custom and rush hour traffic just piled on. Nakamura was busy with another client but got up from his work stool to greet me. What remained of his almost shaved hair had been dyed a reddish brown. A warm cinnamon shade. And he'd shed a few pounds. He looked sharp.

I hugged him as tight as I could, his physical substance reassuring.

"You're shivering, Claire," he said. "And you look like shit."

"Always the gentleman."

"I got your O'Doul's in the fridge. I'll pour you a drink."

It would take more than a non-alcoholic beer with lime to heave me from my sulks, but by now the man knew I didn't drink.

"Ma' girl looks like somebody ran her over. Roadkill for the hobo stew."

Nakamura had been in the States how long? Eleven years? Still, he learned his English from rap songs. Self-taught to become a 'brother' before boarding the plane with his immigrant baggage. The rest of his linguistic abilities were acquired in local gay bars.

"I know what ma' girl needs."

He stepped behind the desk that doubled as a sort-of cash register. He took the money and gave the client his 'receipt,' a piece of paper scribbled on the desk where he kept his collection of CDs and the player, always on during business hours. He'd never upgraded to an iPod.

A few other people were in the shop, his two assistants and two prospective clients who'd come to scroll through his designs.

"Here, princess. To your return! Have some of this." *This* was Tupac's "California Love," blasting from the speakers above the tattoo stations. He started dancing toward me. More than a dance, it was a groovy walk, keeping his knees bent and bouncing, pushing forward his chin and one shoulder at a time.

Advancing until he got close enough to take both of my hands, he gently pulled me up and had me tapping my feet to his beat. We clicked butts, and he whirled me around, dragging me to squat low to the midnight blue concrete floor, then pulling me upward for another spin.

I couldn't resist him when he got flamboyant. Nobody could, apparently. The others were all smiles, thumping the floor with one foot and clapping their hands. Party time!

"Cool, sistah. Cool that you can still dance. I worried you let all the monkeys run out of your barrel."

A few minutes later, I dropped on the purple velvet sofa, the focal point of the parlor's funky décor. My head spun like a tornado over the prairie, but it felt good to be Claire again. Too many in Italy still called me Chiara. It got worse when I dealt with banks, courtroom orders, hospital releases, bills and other bureaucracy. Then I was Signora Strada. I never cared for my first given and last name. Some people stick to their names like chewing gum to a shoe sole, for life. Branded by their parents before birth. I liked better the idea of sampling different names in different places, different stages of life, like choosing clothes from a wardrobe.

There are some worthy names. Take Ondina, which my father gave her to celebrate his love for the ocean. He hoped that his firstborn would inherit it together with his olive skin and dark curls, and he got his wish. But mine? Mine didn't have that musical quality, that Italian lilt and roll. So, I chose to be Claire Waters when I started my career as an 'all American' writer. Claire sounded better and Waters kept me linked to my sister but included all running waters: rivers and falls and lilyponds. And it sounded American, an advantage when I first stepped into publishing. For a while and thanks to a 'creative' biography on the back cover of my first book, my U.S. readers didn't suspect that I wasn't born here, which was fun.

Change is the beauty of going out to sea. You leave behind your old self and reinvent your identity from scratch. It's always been an opportunity dear to outlaws who'd head to a different state, get a new driver's license, sever ties with the past. There were still places in the American West where you could get lost, just like Nails' desert rats.

"Knock, knock, sleeping beauty. Your seat has become free."

Nakamura's touch on my arm was gentle. Less so when he pulled my sleeve up to check the state of his first artwork on my skin.

"Ouchiiiiii. Look at this!!!" he screeched. "It's all faded the wrong way!"

"Because you did a lousy job."

"Because you burnt your skin in hot showers and ruined it."

I didn't confess that every day I'd been in Italy, I took a shower in the morning and lay in the bathtub every night, hoping hot water would soothe my aches and sorrows. It never worked for my soul but did wonders for my muscles, strained by standing endless hours next to the elevated hospital bed. Ondina's hand in my hand, tears pushed back into the bottom of my lungs. I knew the hot water treatment could blur my tattoo. But I had more on my mind than those fading colors.

"You'll touch it up, and it will look like new, *Maestro*."

Nakamura had a soft spot for Fellini's movies. He knew Fellini was called Maestro as a sign of respect. I kissed ass to be forgiven. The tattoo on my arm needed a touch-up as badly as the gray roots of the hair on the guy who'd just left his chair to me. It was a mystery why those guys needed tattoos, the ones with slicked-back, gelled hair like they were still in the eighties, or Chicago mobsters from the thirties. Tattoos that will be hidden under dark blue suits. But what did I know? I wasn't sure why I got my first. Curiosity? Temptation? Desire to belong? Like the homeboys of the Gang of the Avenues who got their affiliation tattooed in lettering on the nape of their shaved necks?

What I did know was that I wanted *The Great Wave off Kanagawa* to be printed on my back. Nakamura had tried to warn me in his emails, discussing it while my desire was taking shape. But just talking about it, imagining and sketching the design, gave me strength. The wave would be my private act of rebellion against what had befallen my sister. An act of hope, trusting that she might find her way to the surface of the abyss that had closed over her head. "It needs to be big, unlike your little Tao," Nakamura wrote. "Not a lil' tramp stamp. I can't do a good job unless it's big, almost as big as the original."

He referred to the woodblock print by the Japanese artist Hokusai, an example of ukiyo-e art. It was the first in Hokusai's series of *Fugaku Sanjurokkei* or *Thirty-six Views of Mount Fuji*. It depicted a huge wave threatening three boats. But I wanted the boats gone and also the mountain—I had no use for Fuji. "Mount Fuji doesn't speak to me," I'd written to Nakamura. "The wave alone screams."

The trouble restarted when I insisted that instead of Fuji, I wanted a bougainvillea flower to be part of the design.

"Bougainvillea? Nasty, thorny vine! We got better than that in Japan," he replied. "We got lovely lotus flowers. You should get a lotus."

I explained about the song that Ondina wrote when she was young and how the bougainvillea flowers enveloped the walls of our grandma's house. "They were magic! They climbed the walls of our fortress like the sweet pea climbed the walls of the tower where the fairytale Princess was imprisoned."

Purple was our symbol of freedom. When Ondina got on stage to sing "Bougainvillea Sister" for the first time, she wore silk purple flowers braided into her hair.

"I have to have those flowers on my back," I'd written. "Close to the stormy blue ocean."

"I never do purple," he replied. "I wear purple but that's not my ink."

It was true, he painted only in primary colors. But I couldn't let go.

"You're like your pitbull, Claire. When you get hold of an ankle, you bite until the foot comes off. You're like that dog of yours."

"Drago is only half pitbull. And only half mine." I felt compelled to defend Drago's character but also to clear any misconceptions. Technically, Drago was Xavier's dog. But "the traitor likes you better than me now," as an annoyed Xavier put it when he was mad at his dog for showing a soft spot for me. "It must be all those biscuits you sneak him under the table when I'm not looking."

At the end of our serrated email exchange, Nakamura had surrendered to my purple rain explanations and pulled out a pretty sketch. More cherry blossoms than bougainvillea, red more than purple, styled like the flowers on a surfer's shirt. Beautiful, though. Quicksilver would have paid Nakamura big bucks to get their hands on something so cool, but he didn't play that game.

"Remember, Claire. It's big, and it will be there forever."

"I know what a tattoo is."

"Yeah. But not all people have a problem with forever like you."

I didn't like forever. I never married, because I couldn't commit my tomorrow. How could you know that you'd still love somebody tomorrow with the same intensity you loved them now? I didn't buy the bullshit about love evolving through time. I liked change only if it meant more passion. Less, and I'd be gone. I needed a Jedi knight to be with, who accepted that I might not be with him forever and I didn't need protection. I liked to be gone often, all by myself. I enjoyed the inebriating freedom of walking alone at night. I'd never give up the adrenaline rush that went through my veins when I'd finished writing and there I went, finally free, out into the sleepy city. Cruising, keeping my lights down low to avoid attracting attention. Or walking up and down dark canyons, sharing the night with the king coyote and the night owls. "Coyote Heart," like the title of the song Ondina had written after she broke up with her bassist bandmate.

She sang it the last time I saw her on stage with her band, before everybody went their separate ways. What a sight she was in her red dress, dark curly hair long and loose. Switching from the lowest notes to high pitches, kicking her shoes off and dancing barefoot, shaking like she wanted to get rid of her heart, her coyote heart:

> *Veins blockage, clots of fear in my heart*
> *Nobody said it was easy*
> *I wish I knew it was busy*
> *My wandering heart*
> *That can't stop*
> *Can't stop*
> *Ever wandering*
>
> *Coyote heart*
> *Cruel twist of fate*
> *I didn't want any part*
> *In putting it in a cage*
> *My wandering heart*
> *That can't stop*
> *Can't stop ever wandering*
>
> *I fell in love with a shadow*
> *Followed his scent*
> *To a green meadow*
> *I was flying then I bent*
> *Saw a piece of my heart*
> *Ripped off, laying in the grass*
>
> *My wandering heart*
> *That can't stop*
> *Couldn't stop*
> *Needed...*
> *Wandering*
>
> *Coyote heart*
> *I was cruel*
> *I put myself in a duel*
> *I wish I knew you were not*
> *As strong as I thought*

Coyote heart
Torn in pieces
Nobody said it was easy
To give away million kisses
Without ever stopping
The wandering

Nobody said it was easy
I wish I knew you were busy
I shouldn't have had any part
In putting you in a cage

My wandering heart
I didn't know you can't stop
Can't stop
Ever wandering

It was also the last song she had sung before she stopped performing. Coyote heart, that was what beat in my chest when I wandered out after dark. The animals of the night sensed it and left me alone.

I got in position to get my tattoo done. Jeans unzipped and lowered to expose more of my skin, leaned forward on a stool that I rode saloon style, hugging the backrest. Nakamura held a makeup pencil to sketch on my lower back.

"Stay still."

I barely breathed, concentrated on getting out of my body before the needle started buzzing. He'd trace the contour with the electric needle first, then fill in the colors with the pen knife, all according to his traditional technique.

Let it sting and prick. I'll be floating out above this parlor, in the darkness. I'll breathe the early summer scent in the air. I'll be a low cloud exploring the thrill of the night sky. I'll be with you, Ondina.

Still, when the needle hit a spot where the skin was thin

and the nerves were close, burning electric waves invaded my brain. It's like sex the first time. You know it's going to hurt. Your vagina doesn't seem to fit what's coming for it. And yet it's what you want. Cross the line and become who you're supposed to be next. Grab a glimpse of your future. No matter how much blood you've got to spill, you'll show the world that you're mature enough.

Nakamura had worried about working on me after a fourteen-hour plane ride. But I was already aching, my body numb as my spirit. The pain was sort of a relief.

It had been hard to leave Ondina defenseless in the hands of doctors, nurses and a system that I didn't trust. As hard as leaving L.A. months earlier, completely unprepared. That caused quite a bit of damage. It'll always be sculpted in my memory, that sequence of odd events as they unfolded one after the other. The telephone call from Italy that changed my life in a heartbeat. The speedy run to the airport with a day's change of clothing thrown in the carry-on. I had no idea if I'd be gone just a few days or longer. No idea if I was going to see my sister dead or alive. Instinctively, more than anything else, I feared what I couldn't fathom, the reality I'd have to face soon. An infinite series of days walking the edge between hope and distress, left alone with a motionless body that showed only clinical vital signs. Not knowing what to pray for.

"Don't shake, ma' girl. I'm all done for now. Just a couple minutes more and you can march out of here. Big boy coming to pick you up?"

Yeah, Xavier would be on his way as soon as I called him. It was a quick run from the house to Little Tokyo. I should have felt happy. But my happiness had been stolen by a phone call from Italy, months ago. And I was afraid that I'd never be able to call it back.

Chapter 29
CLAIRE

Little Tokyo, June 2, 9:30 p.m.

Xavier's pickup arrived at the curb. Brakes screeching. Xavier and Drago burst out, both from the driver's door, both excited. Drago wagging his tail at high speed like a maniac and moaning around my legs, while Xavier lifted me up and spun me around in his arms.

"I almost can't believe it. You've been gone for so long!" He put me down on the pavement.

I bent down to pet Drago and let him kiss my face. "Good dog! What? You thought I won't come back for you? Of course, I would. Hey. Hey!"

Drago had jumped on me, licking any spot of skin he could find, my face, my neck, my arms. Good thing the fresh tattoo was on my back, protected by layers of clothes and clear foil.

Xavier threw my luggage in the back of the pickup and we got into the truck. The pickup left with a loud tire squeal, exhaled carbon exhaust to add its polluted breath to the city bouquet.

Xavier knew when I didn't feel like talking. Silence slowly wrapped its soft familiar around us. A waning crescent moon peeked through the truck rear mirror. Jacarandas bloomed purple along the boulevards.

Hours later, the moon had risen high in the night sky, bathing it in its milky ivory light. The uncanny brightness battled the petulant voices in my mind as I lay naked on my bed, alongside Xavier, my head on his shoulder. Drago snoozed on his dog bed on the wooden floor. He had his own bed in each of our bedrooms, free to choose where he wanted to be when Xavier and I didn't spend the night in the same bed.

"I'm sorry. Can't do it tonight."

"It's okay, Claire. You've been through so much. Hopefully, Uncle Bitten by The Snake's medicine will help you."

I pinched his arm playfully. "What? You mean, he'll put up a sweat lodge to help me fuck?" I tickled Xavier, who laughed but was swift to catch my hand on his stomach, stopping it.

"Oh, babe! That would be pretty good. But I guess you have some more specific healing in mind." He relaxed on his back again.

"I got a sister to rescue from hell." I adjusted my head on his shoulder. My gaze wandered through the reflections of the moonlight that spread through the shutters, across the mottled ceiling.

"How long will Moltacci keep Ondina in his clinic?"

"Long enough for me to sort things here. I promised that as soon as I rented out this house, I'd go back. I'm going to take Ondina away from that place, with me. I can't leave it up to doctors and hospitals. They're not going to help her. I'll enlist the best physical therapists. Reflexologists and nutritionists, too."

"But how will you take care of Ondina at home? By yourself?"

Xavier's questions didn't bother me. He was just asking out of concern. Not trying to change my mind. "I found a lady, a former nurse from Ukraine whom I hired as a caregiver. She's going to the clinic every day with my friend Cristiana, while I'm here. And just before I left, I saw a ground level apartment with a nice patio in the outskirts of Bergamo. A town called Sorisole, just a few miles from Ondina's place. Her apartment isn't accessible for her in a wheelchair."

I wanted to sound convincing. I looked at Xavier. His straight nose gave a certain severity to his profile. But it was just above his sensual lips, the bottom one always slightly open as an innocent child. *Would he miss me?* "I need money for all of this. I'm so sorry but you won't be able to stay here. I have no choice but renting the house out."

"Are you kidding? Ondina's your sister. And I was thinking of going back to the rez for a while anyhow. Uncle is old, he can use some help. And I can use the time to regroup. It'd be good for me. I got some trauma from my time in the force I'd like to confront with Uncle's guidance. Driving back and forth once every two weeks to record my show here in L.A. isn't a big deal. Man, I'm young enough to endure it! I'm not your problem. I admire you for all you're doing for your sister. I'm proud of you for doing what you're doing. She's lucky to have you."

I lifted my head on my elbow to look into his eyes. "*Lucky* isn't a word I would choose for my sister."

He kissed me tenderly on the lips. "Sleep. You need a good night's sleep after all those bad nights. We'll have to leave early tomorrow to drive to Uncle's place. New Mexico is thirteen hours away. It's good that he's back on the Laguna reservation, or we'd have to go to South Dakota."

"Why's that?" I meant, why he'd left New Mexico.

"When his wife passed away, he felt lost. He had to go back where he was from, find his strength in the land where he grew up. It was hard for a Lakota to give up the Paha Sapa and the green prairies to settle down in our red rocks and dusty canyons. But love makes you endure the craziest things. He stayed in South Dakota for a couple of months and now is back in New Mexico, with his wife's people who got used to relying on him."

"I was so sorry to hear about Martha's passing, I wrote him a card, letting him know that I was thinking of him and his loss, but I sent it to his P.O. Box in Laguna."

Drago whined, looking up to me with his head bent on one side.

"He knows you're not here to stay. He's saying 'don't abandon me again.' You better take him with you to Italy, babe. I'll miss him, but he misses you more."

"That sounds like a cowboy giving up his horse! How could you survive without him?"

"I survived without you, didn't I? And Drago is not even as good in the sack."

I threw a pillow at him. "Get out of my face!"

I got up, put on my lounge pants and the top I wore before plunging into bed with Xavier, and moved toward the bathroom door. Good thing Nakamura let me take a shower at his place before our session because washing up with a tattoo still fresh on my back looked complicated. Making love too. So maybe abstinence wasn't such a bad thing, after all. But I couldn't recall a day in my adult life when sex had not been on my mind someway, so it felt odd.

I guessed I felt guilty doing things that my sister could no longer do. That also explained my lack of enthusiasm for food. Ondina and I shared our father's passion for great food and cooking, turning on the stove with joy for a *fritto di pesce* or *brodetto di cozze* even if we were home alone. Now it was takeout pizza swallowed without even sitting, and disgusting tuna salad sandwiches wrapped in plastic bought at the vending machines in the hospital hall. No wonder my ribs were sticking out. I'd already gone from a 34C bra size to a B cup. Even my boobs looked starved. Ondina's friends tried to take me out to dinner, but the rare times I accepted their invites resolved in agonizing experiences for everyone. No matter how fancy the entrees, a couple of morsels was all I could take before giving up.

Part of the problem was the hospital smell, that mix of human waste, disinfectants and germs. I felt it in all my orifices, including every skin pore. I could never wash the odor off, out of my nostrils. I scrubbed and sponged as soon as I got home, but still!

"Oh, stop it! What do you think, that doctors and nurses are all anorexic and sex deprived? Get over it!" Ondina was in my head, in the mirror. "Man, Chiara! You lost your spunk," she buzzed, disappointment in her voice.

The jetlag and tattoo had me dizzy. "But..." I tried to counter. The only rebuttal I could come up with was humming the lyrics of "Nothing Compares to You" by Sinead O'Connor. I really felt like a bird without a song, so lonely without my sister.

"Oh, *piantala*, Chiara!" Ondina said in my mind. "Fuck it. That's right. Or even better, fuck him."

But what if I broke down, once I let go? I didn't want to break down. I couldn't. I had to keep strong, no weakness allowed.

Should I go Nails' style, then? Pick up a dude at a bar? No emotional involvement?

Like I was really going to enjoy that! I marched back to the bedroom.

Chapter 30
CLAIRE

Mount Washington, June 2, 11 p.m.

Xavier was still naked on top of the bedspread, the recording of his last night show playing from the iPod on his nightstand. The familiar sound of his voice gradually rose into song. Yellow Wolf anticipating my return at the beat of Dirty Heads. "Dance All Night" blasting its notes.

Should I dance all night, get through my jetlag and sadness? This man who never asks me for anything, who accepts me without flinching, might he make me right?

I stopped at the footboard of the bed and watched him. Handsome as ever, even with his eyes closed, right knee up and foot tapping the tune. I ran my eyes over the leathery tan of his skin, his long eyelashes and lovely lips, his tight stomach and long muscles. He was so at ease with his nudity! At home in the temple of his body.

The knee wasn't the only body part of Xavier up, and I was pleased by his hard-on. With one nimble jump, I was up on the bed, turned on my back. I stretched from my toes to my shoulders, relaxing my neck. Then, I rolled over and landed, kneeling on top of Xavier, straddling his waistline.

"Hey," he said, widening his eyes, "weren't you?..."

His question remained suspended in the air like a party balloon. I pasted my index finger to his lips, smiling cryptically like somebody with a secret, guarding it like a four-aces hand. I leaned to his chest, keeping pace with the music, my hips rolling like waves. I slid up and down, from his waist to his upper chest, letting him feel the push of my breasts through the silk of the camisole. Gaining pace. Adding a peck on his lips when up, brushing my lips on his abs going down.

He tried to lift his head and arms to answer my kiss when I rose up again to his face. I took hold of his hands, bending his arms and pinning him down, spreading his elbows open on each side. He liked it when I took control. He just surrendered, let me play my solo show. I heard him saying to his radio listeners, "... and this is still my favorite makeup song."

"Sexual Healing," coming up right on cue, erupted with the beautiful voice of Ben Harper. I felt a sudden wetness on my navel area, looked down and saw Xavier's cock head glistening. In Italian, the head of the penis is called "*cappella,*" chapel, the same place of worship where one gets married or sings hymns to the Lord. But I sang my tunes to the Lord of Sex, humming them into Xavier. My kind of sacrament. Thank you, Marvin Gaye.

I pictured Pan sitting on a VIP courtside seat, watching the game. An ancient Greek god disguised as a goat, cheering for my free throws against all odds. Almost summer, after all. Let's enjoy renewal and fertility! Let's be wild! And wild we were. Exquisitely wild.

Xavier couldn't hold it. It was getting stronger and stronger, just like the lyrics say. He placed both hands on my waist, firmly gripping but careful not to touch the wrapping of the fresh tattoo on my back. He lifted me in midair and I arched my back like a gymnast. Holding me there with one hand, he tried to pull down my lounge pants. I helped him, bending on one side to free one leg, then the other, like a bamboo shoot rustling in the morning haze. He caressed my bare butt, searched inside my bush. He slipped two fingers inside me, glided his thumb on my swollen clit, drawing tiny circles.

"I want you now," I heard myself saying as he lowered me, guiding me down as I spread my knees wide. We were both so wet that I effortlessly swallowed him easily. He pulsed inside me while I pressed my knees on his hips. I posted on him like I was riding a horse, rose and stopped halfway, using my thighs and pelvic muscles to sit there for a while. Still like a thief caught by a flashlight. Feeling it, sucking it all up.

It was meditation for the genitals, but I doubted anybody could teach it at tantra classes. Clocks stopped running, the world came to a halt within the bedroom. And I felt happy and empowered like a natural born vestal, cultivating the sacred fire in the depths of my musky vessel. I savored that long minute of suspended stillness, a lizard soaking up the warmth from the sun, then plopped down and picked up the pace. Up and down, up and down, swelling and flowing like the tides.

Xavier arched his back when I sat down, pushed his pelvis up when I rose, to give me more. We made love the way snakes do, twisting in a tight grip. Our limbs and souls entangled. What a pace we were able to keep, what a dance! Moaning and wriggling on top of the notes of *Jam with the Yellow Wolf*. Humming and dancing, utterly intentioned to dance all night.

Who remembered that it felt so good?

I traveled at light speed into a galaxy with constellations resembling illustrations of the Kāma Sūtra. I felt like a daredevil fired from a cannon into a net fifty yards away, an astronaut on speed going to the moon and back in twenty seconds.

Somewhere below me, on that distant planet that everybody called Earth, Xavier thrusted deeper one last time, and a whirlwind spun inside my head, a tornado of bubbles in a glass of champagne. I felt him recoiling, spent, and saw my body double deflating on Xavier's chest. His arms wrapped around my upper back tightly, holding me there. My head on his shoulder, covering most of his face. Beads of sweat graced his closed right eyelid and forehead, the only part of Xavier that was in sight, apart from his legs.

The scent of our lovemaking lingered in the room, thick and fragrant as incense.

Chapter 31
CLAIRE

Laguna, New Mexico, June 5

The new moon, bright crescent the color of an egg yolk, hung over the Laguna Pueblo reservation, gilding the dome of a sweat lodge built with willow branches and covered with military blankets. Gemini Moon, double-edged like a traitor's kiss. In a couple of weeks, it would ripen to a full Strawberry Moon. Rose Moon, according to Europeans. Full moons have several names.

The air was perfumed sweet by the sage burning in an abalone shell. A buffalo skull rested on a dirt mound in front of the lodge entrance door, a flap cut in a blanket that opened to the east. I stood behind Xavier in a line of people waiting their turn to enter. I wore a ribbon skirt long to my ankles, a shawl around my shoulders. Modest, out of respect for the traditional ways. "The ways of our ancestors," Bitten by The Snake had explained to the newcomers. He despised the New Age-y sweat lodges where a bunch of 'disrespectful wannabe youngsters' were half naked. This was a sacred ritual, not a sauna. "They show up with the girls in shorts, bare legs distracting the men, and the men down to their underwear. It's disgraceful."

Come my turn, I stepped in front of the altar and smudged myself with the sage smoke. Then I raised my arms and prayed to each of the four directions. *"Mitakuye Oyasin! To all my relationships!"* I completed my circle, turning a quarter at a time, and faced the lodge entrance again. I got down on all fours, and passed under the raised flap.

The cool, damp darkness inside awakened in me the forgotten feeling of finding myself in the right place, at the right time. Once everyone was seated, the first heated stones were brought in and placed in the pit dug in the center. They were each blessed with cedar and water that made them sizzle. Every round, it would get hotter. More stones were carried in and the songs grew louder, the prayers stronger.

At the end of the fourth round, after an hour and half, the flap was opened. One by one, we got out of the lodge, letting the night breeze lap our skin. We sipped water, careful not to guzzle it down all at once. A young woman discreetly removed her drenched clothes and changed into clean ones. I wrapped myself tight in a dry Pendleton blanket.

Everybody sat around the fire for the communal feast that always follows a sweat lodge. I kept a little apart, perching myself on a big rock, a plate of food in my lap. I shared my baked potato with Drago, who'd patently waited outside the lodge but now looked disappointed. "I'm sorry, bud. You might get luckier with your master. More meat on his plate."

Xavier and Bitten by The Snake stood together a little further away, talking. Then, Bitten by The Snake walked toward me. "I know you want to go back to your sister. *Waste cante!*" he said when he stopped. He beat his heart with his right fist to reinforce the Lakota words for good heart. "But remember, you are not a *wasicu*. Your place is here, on this land. Tunkashila will want you back here." *Wasicu* is the name used by Lakotas to despise unfriendly whites.

I stopped eating my half potato. "As long as Tunkashila brings my sister here too."

"He might. You help her get back her strength, fly her to America with you then. I can do more if she comes." He paused, winked at me. "Also, we have better doctors here."

I wasn't sure if he meant native healers or Beverly Hills specialists, or both. "I wish I could, *leksi*. I talked to a doctor in Tijuana who cures brain stroke patients by injecting stem cells. He would take the stem cells from my bone marrow and inject them in Ondina."

Bitten by The Snake sat down close to me, rested a hand on top of mine. He stared into the fire with such intensity, like he was reading my future with my sister in the dazzling flames. "You will need more than Western medicine to heal your sister, *tun'jan*. But remember, what she needs most is love. Your love. Make her feel how much you love her." The old man paused, keeping his gaze on the fire. "At the end of the day, love is all that matters."

He got back on his feet and slowly walked away. He looked more his age now than when he was inside the lodge, drumming and singing to convey a rainbow bridge to the other world. I felt a tickle on the back of my left hand. He'd placed an eagle feather there. A precious gift.

Chapter 32
CLAIRE

Mount Washington, June 9

Morning light. I walked in the yard, followed by Drago. I enjoyed the fresh scent of the gardenias, honeysuckle and jasmine in full bloom. They were fated not to last when summer temperatures would rise past ninety degrees, but I'd learned to enjoy their bounty for the short time it was there. White flowers always felt more fragile, maybe that was the reason I favored them. I couldn't help comparing them to my sister, so delicate now while she used to be so strong. I yearned for those days, when Ondina was my harbor after every storm, my confidant and refuge, my playmate. Now, she was my disappearing half.

I breathed in the mist, detecting also a trace of jacaranda. When it is jacaranda season in L.A., the thick purple carpet of fallen petals transforms the city streets into a fairytale. Blooms also covered the parked cars, sap sticky on their windshields. Angelenos have a love-hate affair with not just jacarandas, but also tall eucalyptuses that perfume the air and shed their bark to reveal their mottled white nakedness, that fuel the wild-fires. L.A. is a city spreading out across a desert, but a desert adorned with live oaks; weeping pepper trees; protected black walnuts; sweetgums with changing color foliage; cedars and aspen trees; acacias with their gray-green fernlike leaves and feathery yellow flowers in spring; Italian cypresses, so out of place standing close to the tallest and thinnest California fan palms; crepe myrtles that compete with the jacarandas in spring, turning streets deep pink; native and fragrant iron-woods. Trees in Los Angeles seem to have sprouted by the seeds brought in by the winds blowing from different directions, just like the people from different countries who pepper the maze of streets.

I recalled the emotion of the first view of the city tinted in purple jacaranda blooms, a May of many years ago with my son still a teenager. He was now head researcher in the archeological site of Delos, a Greek island in the Aegean Sea's Cyclades archipelago near Mykonos, directing the restoration of the ruins—Doric temples, markets, an amphitheater, incredible houses with mosaics still partially intact and the iconic Terrace of the Lions statues.

My phone rang in my pocket. I picked up the call, walking toward the house.

"Susan! What's up?" I listened to her, silently petting Drago, who was rolling on the grass that already looked parched, not at all like the lush green spreading through the Italian meadows in springtime. "I don't know, Susan. I can't commit to any date. Listen, I understand it's hard for you to be my publicist and 'care for my interests despite me.' And I appreciate you. But Ondina is my sister. She depends on me. She doesn't have anybody else, so I have to get back there soon. I have a schedule already full for the next few days."

"Be reasonable, Claire. The book already sold more than I'd ever expect without any promotion on your part. It made the New York Times bestseller list, again. And it's been nominated for The Edgar Award. You can't insult the publisher by avoiding at least a small celebration in your hometown now that you're here. We can have a reading, the signing we never had."

"I'd have loved that under other circumstances, but my priorities have changed. I need to fly back to Italy as planned. I'm sorry, Suz. Tell the publisher whatever you want. And if it's really going to be the end of my career, as you're saying, then so be it. This time, my family comes first."

I was resolute. Susan's pushing irritated me, but I didn't want to spoil my day. I recalled Ondina talking me into the need for compartments: "It's like clothes out of season. You pack and store them on the top shelves in your closet. Out of sight, out of mind, until it's the right time to deal with them again." In Los Angeles, though, seasons were quite different from Northern Italy, days borrowing from one another so that summer might suddenly break into winter with eighty degrees at Christmas time. Accordingly, my closet was a messy pile of clothes good for every season, a bunch of jeans and t-shirts, a few sweaters and hoodies, a couple of more-or-less formal dresses and jackets, sandals beside boots.

I never learned to compartmentalize, so my mind was sizzling with disturbance.

What's up with all these people who feel it's their right to tell me what to do? Like they know what'd be best for me? It'd be best for me to think about my interests and career? Right. Eating good meals, resting more, sleeping at night, and making time for myself? But what about Ondina? Who's going to do what's best for her?

I wasn't about to give up and be like many of Ondina's friends, who'd stopped coming around because she 'wasn't the same person.' Because she couldn't talk or show any interest in the never-ending tale of their steamy affairs and/or midlife existential crisis? Because she couldn't smile, or follow along on their shopping sprees, give them advice on what looked good with their new red menopausal hair?

I stared at the screen of my laptop, blinking and buzzing. I intended to update the blog before heading out to brunch, but this internal dialogue spoiled it. The blog was a good way to inform Ondina's friends all at once. In fact, they hadn't totally disappeared. They still called and asked for information. They kept inviting me out, like I'd really be up for dinner or cocktails while Ondina, their friend, lay alone in her bed, helpless and starving for human contact. The truth was, most of them probably couldn't bear standing close to her, witnessing her pain and offering the simple comfort of their presence. In a world without words, they were lost. So much for all the yoga and meditation retreats and their ability to be in silence.

I wanted to be understanding. I realized that not everybody could be like Cristiana, who dutifully went to the clinic every day to reassure Ondina and every night sent me detailed reports of what music they listened to, what books she read to her. But I'm not perfect either, so I kept being mad.

"Breathe in, acknowledge the thoughts, let them go when you breathe out. Breathe in, breathe out," Ondina kept repeating the first time she attempted to convert me, making me sit in front of a lit candle.

This time, they didn't want to leave. Thoughts could be stubborn beasts, hanging on a foggy mind like lazy bats in a cool cave. Perfectly comfortable where they were, feeding on confusion, rage and anxiety. Yoga may have worked wonders for Ondina, Filippo and Nicola, but it wasn't my medicine. Walking worked better for me.

Chapter 33
CLAIRE

Mount Washington, June 9

It wasn't time yet for brunch. I decided to go for a hike to clear my mind. I always feel more alive and relaxed when I move my body, but walking is my true medicine. Better than running or surfing, which give me other kinds of benefits. No matter where and how, my automatic mental response to walking is a natural desire to slow down. I like to walk alone so I don't waste time and energy chatting. My brain goes into alpha mode, starts humming only in sets of alpha waves. They rise like a swell from the occipital lobe during all kinds of wakeful meditation with closed eyes. But with experience, you can walk at the pace of alphas even keeping your eyes open, managing not to bust your nose. My eyes notice things like the colors of the greenery, a kid kicking his ball against the wall of a courtyard, the flowers sprouting from rocks or from the cracks of the asphalt. Enhanced awareness.

Walking gets me out of the claustrophobic prison of my mind anytime I need to do so. Walking should be a special class in grade school. Especially in Los Angeles where nobody walks, unlike in Milan or other European cities. Angelenos jog, run or push kids around in those lightweight three-wheelers that allow the new mommy to get back in shape. Or they jump in their cars to go to the grocery store, or to pick up the kids at their school just a couple blocks away. If you walk in Los Angeles, you look suspicious. Cops follow and stop you. How come you're walking around by yourself?

While making my way through Walnut Canyon, I recalled Werner Herzog joking about it at his Rogue Film School, a series of weekend workshops around the world that I attended with my screenwriter friend. The director was sharing his love for traveling on foot and his adamant conviction: two years spent globetrotting is undoubtedly worth more than two years in academia. He also shared he'd be questioned, not just once but regularly, as he'd walk from his house on Laurel Canyon down to Sunset Boulevard for his morning coffee.

I could relate, but never mind. Without walking, I wouldn't be myself. Which brought me right to the beef, the real burning question churning in my mind for a while. *What if Ondina couldn't walk again? What if, despite all the therapies and love, she remained confined to a wheelchair? Just like our mother?* The most dreaded fate, falling under the same spell that took away Mom's wit and sense of humor. Depending on others for every single need. *And who was I to make such decisions for my sister? How could I, knowing that I'd never want to live if I couldn't walk?*

Filippo tried to convince me that Ondina might have reframed her needs and wants, that she might be happy to live despite her disability, enjoying the breeze on the porch tending basil, parsley and tomato plants, watching kids at play. I admired people able to do it. But knowing what Ondina felt was a guess. Deep down in my guts, I sensed that Ondina wouldn't want that kind of life. But admitting it and facing the consequences was a lot to bear. I'd always escaped pain through action, but I couldn't run away from it now. Ondina's life was at stake.

I passed the coyote den in the canyon. I could hear them from the house at nighttime, yapping, their claws and fangs on a possum or neighbor's cat. They wouldn't mess with Drago, but they'd feast on Chihuahuas and Yorkshire Terriers, not to mention the chickens that the clueless guy up on Averhill let wander around, uncaged. They were street smart and able to avoid cars, but they couldn't help looking like dinner. Sadly, they disappeared one by one in less than a week, the last one eaten by a couple of raccoons.

It's a wild world, out in the canyons. Northeast LAPD patrolled this area looking for corpses since the gangs of the Avenues started dumping their kill up here. That's why I always carried a four-inch serrated blade pocket knife. Not as effective as the Glock but safer to take around, besides, it could still do some damage. I also used it to cut sage, the white variety with the fat velvety leaves, so different from the taller silver sage of the Plains with its elongated thin leaves, but still good to smudge. I needed some to burn while praying for answers to solve Ondina's mystery, but there was none. Only tall, dry, wild barley, still uncut despite the Fire Department warnings. Homeowners in the hills of Los Angeles are required to trim their trees away from power lines. Dry branches, brushes and shrubs, or anything else that could catch fire, must be removed. It's mandatory to comply with the ordinance by the end of May, or you get fined. But 'Canyonland' is a bitch. There are big stretches of open land that don't belong to anybody. Unattended areas that are often the culprits of our storied wildfires. Come October and the hot, devil Santa Ana winds blow from the southern desert inland toward the coast, pushing north and west toward Malibu, Hollywood, and downtown. Fires take up thousands of acres of the Angeles Forest, destroy hundreds of houses. You can become homeless at the drop of a dime in L.A. for many reasons: fire, earthquake, mudslide. It's crazy how precarious our lives are here, but nothing in L.A had prepared me for the tsunami of Ondina's accident.

I'd fed a woman who lost her house in a fire three years back. She got used to living on the street. When social workers offered her a space in a women's shelter, she refused. "Thanks, but no thanks." During the day, she stationed her wheelchair in front of the Bank of America on Colorado Boulevard, in Eagle Rock. She thrived on the attention of compassionate bank customers, who'd ask the sweet lady questions after noticing the sign in her lap. They'd spare a couple of bucks toward her next trip for coffee and the restroom at the Starbucks in front of the bank. Some precious human contact that had been starved from her in her lonely house. They dropped enough coins in her collection cup for her to get by on 7-Eleven sandwiches, and she was also entitled to a disability check for $375 arriving every two weeks, plus the occasional gift of homemade food.

No way Ondina would want to live in a wheelchair for the rest of her life, exposed to strangers' pitiful looks. I saw her expression when she was out on the patio and neighbors went by on their way to their own apartments, sneaking curious looks at her. The thought rammed into my mind, chasing away all that had still seemed possible before coming back to L.A. I kicked a stone out of the path, and noticed some foxtails. I made a mental note to check Drago's nose, ears and paws when we got back. Otherwise, their microscopic barbs can get caught in the fur and become embedded. Their sharp ends can penetrate the skin, causing infection. They can make their way into the dog's eardrum or up a leg into a vein. They can be fatal.

Drago knew none of that and wasn't worried. He paid

more mind to the 'ghetto birds' now circling above us. The LAPD helicopters windmilling their rotor blades, flying forward and back, stalling laterally. On the hunt for who knew for whom. The noise grew louder with Drago adding to it with his hyper, excited bark. I decided to put him on the leash and turn back toward the house, still irritated with Susan despite the walk.

Sometimes, no medicines work.

Chapter 34
CLAIRE

Malibu, June 15

Xavier left at dawn to park the pickup on Point Dume Road, not far from the start of the path that wound through the grassy dunes. Surfers walked half a mile with their boards under one arm to avoid paying the ten-dollar parking fee at either one of the beaches, Zuma to the North, Point Dume to the South, toward Santa Monica. Not worth the money when you mean to stay only a couple of hours, just enough to get some waves before going about your day. But you had to get there early to get a spot.

He'd bought a shell for his pickup and packed it to its full capacity, clearing out his stuff from my place. I'd moved my boxes to the garage so the house could be rented as soon as I flew back to Italy. But I gave Xavier my surfboards to move them to the rental my son kept in Santa Monica—the eight foot six, balsa and redwood, Hawaiian looking, that I used to ride the bigger waves, and the light, fiberglass six-footer that allowed me to dance on the lip, turning the board swiftly a few times before checking out of the wave. He tied the big one on the racks, together with his own long Brewer board. He was a tall man. He wouldn't mess with a small gun, a board shorter than his own length.

He'd told me to get mine from the roof rack when I got to Point Dume. No one was going to steal it. All the boys knew it belonged to me. And they'd seen Xavier's pickup around long enough to accept him as a local. Surfers tend to be territorial. To go out paddling to the wrong lineup in a place you're not familiar with can be problematic. Let's say you find yourself in Dana Point, San Clemente, or another beach in Orange County, spoiled rich kids' grounds. That can be risky, especially if you aren't white.

Malibu wasn't that bad. Rich kids mingled with homeboys from inland with gang tattoos plastered on their upper backs, their butt cheeks poking out of cargo shorts worn two sizes bigger. Hippies descended from their cabins and campgrounds in Topanga Canyon, at night they shared their greasy hot dogs and s'mores roasted on bonfires with model-looking blondes. Leggy teenagers who sneaked out and came down to these beaches to escape the boring golfers' parties that their parents threw in their villas built on the bluffs. Up there, it was either six thousand square feet mansions or the gated communities of multimillion-dollar townhouses with white walls and Mediterranean roofs. The local crowd had its advantages, though. Most people were polite and respectful of the unspoken code of wave riders.

There was a leftover three-quarter moon reluctant to leave the overcast morning sky when I arrived. A big swell was expected. Not such a common event in summer along this coastline. Xavier was not going to miss it, no matter the long drive to New Mexico planned for later on. And I couldn't stomach letting him leave without a last ride together. I hoped I could just say *Tókša akhé,* see you later, again. Lakota doesn't have a word for goodbye. But I couldn't shake off the melancholy that shrouded our last days, the sense of loss mixed in our morning coffees, shadowing our smiles.

Surf was our thing, the ocean the place where we both felt freer. Authentic, undressed. I hoped we could still surf together one day. Drago had taken the lead before me, jumping into the grass to hunt ground squirrels and jackrabbits.

"Sets have been coming in twenty minutes apart," a guy informed me while running away from the beach with his black neoprene wetsuit rolled down to his waist, probably in search of a spot to take a leak.

I looked out to the point where the bay met the open ocean. Despite the distance and the bright light bothering my eyes, I could spot a nebulous gray mass that had begun to build. It was just a subtle undulation on the horizon, its crest starting to boil with small whitecaps twirled by the wind. I tried to spot Xavier but couldn't make him out among the surfers straddling their boards and looking out to sea.

I'd taught him to look for intervals, how many waves and how many seconds apart, to calculate the moment they would break and which one was going to be the best to ride out. It worked with the surface waves, the ones prompted by winds and lunar pull. It worked for swells too, waves that start right in the guts of the ocean when it gets heartburn and it roars with gigantic burps, thunderclaps that can travel thousands of miles afar. Waves like that can suck you in and spit you over the falls just to be swallowed in another undertow.

I also taught him to watch for riptides and sharks. "But more than anything else," I pointed out, "you keep yourself in check. No matter how bad it gets, don't panic. First rule on the street, first rule in the ocean, which can be as scary and treacherous as any alley after midnight. Panic is what kills most people in the ocean. They drown because they lose it and can't control their fear."

I didn't have that problem. I felt totally at home in the ocean. Xavier had only experienced the fresh river waters at his reservation, where Native kids learned to swim by throwing each other off big truck tires used as floats, so he was introduced to the big waves by me. If it wasn't for me, his skin would never have met salt water. He'd have kept his feet on the sand, happy to just sit there and watch the game from the bleachers. But I wanted to share the thrill of the waves.

"Man, I could kill for you!" I'd commented, clapping my hands, the first time he was able to pop up after several unsuccessful attempts, a couple of big bruises and a rash. He later told me that my passion did the trick. Made him a surfer for life. Now, he dug surfing even without me. The homeboys called him 'Redskin' or 'Indian Boy.' He didn't seem to take it personally. Every regular got a nickname on the water. Mine was 'Shred.' I earned it for the way I shredded a wave after poising on its lip for a while, gathering energy from the wave itself before climbing up. I rose to the top of its feathering crest and immediately started slaloming down—shredding in surf lingo.

I checked the wind and was pleased to notice that it blew lightly offshore. It helped to hold up the waves once they broke, blowing right into their faces.

"Need some wax for your ride?" It was Jaxxon with his dark, almost black skin and once brown, now sun-bleached dreadlocks. We used to be lovers when I lived by the beach. Six foot, ripped. Ex-Marine, lifeguard in Venice during tourist season. His shift started only at 11 a.m., so mornings started early for him, trying to fit in as many waves he could before slipping out of his wetsuit to change into the red trunks that lifeguards wore on this stretch of the California coast.

"Is Xavier out there?" I asked him, while accepting his wax offer.

"Yeah. But you guys gotta watch out. Today's waves are no joke."

Waves like that could snap a board in half, making it fly into your neighbor's head before the other piece crashed into the rocks. Waves that tangled leashes and ripped their Velcro off ankles, leaving the surfers orphaned of their boards.

"I see," I said, waxing my board. If Xavier was out there, I was going too. "Not many kids around today."

No green surfers in sight, the fast learners, convinced there was never a problem, believing it was all fun and games, until they saw someone more experienced get swept out by a riptide or caught up underwater in a kelp bed that had silently drifted close to shore. Then they got it. And stayed home when the surf report announced a big swell approaching.

It was one of those days, and it was good to have the beach to the seasoned riders. You could smell danger in the salty breeze. The winds of a change coming up strong, unavoidable and thundering like the swell. The waves were announcing themselves, saying "after today, nothing will ever be the same."

Chapter 35
CLAIRE

Sorisole (Bergamo), five months after the accident

I'd landed at Malpensa early in the morning after a sleepless night on the plane. I was jet-lagged but eager to see how the new place in the countryside had come together in my absence. Filippo had offered to set it up while I was still in Los Angeles and I'd welcomed his involvement. He'd already moved the furniture and unpacked all the books from Ondina's apartment in Bergamo. And he'd come to pick me up at the airport. It was a big relief not having to wait for a cab after such a long flight.

We arrived at the old converted farmhouse that had been remodeled into a condo. The town was minimal—a couple of grocery stores, a bar, two restaurants and of course a church—sitting in a valley called Val Brembana. The apartment on the ground floor had a big patio under a roof with exposed beams, overlooking a playground where children were at play. I spotted two swallow nests hidden under the roof with the little ones inside, waiting for their mothers to feed them. The air smelled of freshly mowed grass. Forsythia bushes and cherry trees patched the hills in yellow and pink. The walls of the house were two feet deep. Solid and protective. Not at all like American houses. Wood framing in ancient Europe? Nah! Houses are made of stones and bricks, covered in reinforced concrete.

I walked through the rooms with a sense of wonder, touching the walls and expecting them to talk. I wished they could communicate their secrets. Who'd inhabited these rooms? Were they happy? Did anything bad go down here? I hadn't detected any sick building syndrome the first time I saw the apartment, that sensation of something being off, sad, when all appears in order. I've always been sensitive not only to people but places. Earth energy in natural settings, house energy inside where people lived. Feng Shui teaches you how to correct the energy, how to avoid potential problems, but I felt positive here. These walls seemed not to hold bad memories or vibes.

I stood in the airy, bright three-bedroom on the ground floor. These stones had been here for centuries. Erected before electric lights replaced candles, before the birth of Luigi Galvani and Alessandro Volta, whose genius and research contributed as much as Benjamin Franklin's to develop the path to Thomas Edison's filament lamp.

A couple of centuries ago, without electric power, Ondina could never have come home. Most likely, she wouldn't have survived. It took a huge amount of amperage to work the motorized bed that rose up at the push of a button, to inflate at will the mattress designed to avoid pressure sores that plague immobile patients and also to work the pump slowly dispensing into Ondina's G.I. tube that stinky, chalky nutrition blend that smelled and looked like spoiled milk.

Her diet was one of the many things that were going to change—I was going to teach Raissa, Ondina's caregiver, how to blend fresh organic veggies, fruit and protein powder instead of that disgusting formula. Together with an obvious lack of exercise, it made Ondina gain weight, which wasn't an advantage to put her back on her feet. As crazy as it might seem to take home a person in her condition, according to everyone else's opinion, her coming home meant freedom to make my own decisions for her care.

I swirled from one room to the other. On the plane, all my trapped fears had bubbled up and tangled my stomach in a tight sailor's knot. I was uncomfortable with my insecurity. Before what happened to Ondina, I never second-guessed my decisions. Now? I had to struggle to find my footing and be confident. But now, the long night of shallow breaths in the claustrophobic tightness of the airplane seat was behind me, and I felt hope.

Filippo stood with one shoulder leaning on the doorjamb, outside the kitchen. Ondina's yellow cabinets were already anchored to the wall, appliances hooked up. Drago, who'd flown back with me, leaned against his legs, the way dogs do when they like somebody. He'd liked Filippo from the first moment they met at the airport. Couldn't blame him. He exuded a calm energy that animals could sense. I could picture him enchanting cobras to rise up off the floor. And he'd been so respectful, keeping quiet the whole time to let me take in the new place. I hoped having a dog around could console Ondina about Belinda's absence. Moltacci had explained cat dander was too dangerous for Ondina's lungs, so Belinda was now staying with Giovanni.

"Finally!" I exhaled. "This is it. When are they going to deliver the electric bed? How about the special bathtub stretcher?"

Filippo knew how much Ondina loved water and hadn't tried to talk me out of getting that special bath stretcher that had cost a lot of money, something my mother had promptly done. He smiled, bent slightly to scratch the dog's head, and gave him a command. "*Seduto.*" Drago sat, and Filippo turned his face up to look at me. "See? He's already bilingual!"

"Of course, he is!" I snickered, pointing at the biscuit hidden in his hand behind his back. "Come on. Let's go now. I'm still on California time and my head's spinning. Now that I've seen all that you've done here, I might get some sleep."

The next day was going to be tough at the clinic. I'd have to sign paperwork, get all kinds of instructions from Moltacci. It'd be worth it, though. Just a few days and I'd no longer have to drive that dreaded road each day, leaving Ondina and yet another shred of my heart at the end of visiting time. No more distracted nurses and beeping machines. No more slammed doors and squads of white uniforms entering her room for their 'neurological tests,' saying: "Look here, Ondina. How many fingers are these? Oh, she's not answering." They'd write 'still veg' on her chart and move to the next room.

I hoped she'd keep stable and no incidents delayed her homecoming. My sister-queen. We'd celebrate once she settled in. Right now, I needed a long shower and some sleep.

Chapter 36
CLAIRE

Milan, end of June

Wilma opened the door. Drago ignored her and immediately hurried toward Mom, playful and curious. This time the television was on some kind of *Wheel of Fortune* show. More than half of Italians wanted gypsies to be forcefully removed. Refugees arriving from Libya by boats were met by increasing racism, but people seemed to care more about buying a washing machine for only three hundred euros than addressing the real world. And guessing its price right to gain some bucks too.

As soon as Drago approached her, Mom retreated to the opposite side of her chair. "Take it away. Take away this ugly beast!" she said with a shrill voice.

I restrained a confused Drago on his leash and pulled it back. "But Mom, you said you wanted to meet my dog. That's why I brought him along."

Mother looked at me puzzled. "This is Drago?" She seemed genuinely surprised, then embarrassed. "I thought it was another one of those strays you used to pick up on the street."

Her kind of apology—I was used to this after forty-three years as her daughter. I moved a few steps closer so that she could touch the dog.

"No, Mom. This is Drago, and you'd better apologize to him. He's very sensitive. Here. Give him one of his biscuits and make friends."

She tried to give the dog a treat but dropped it on the floor. As Drago picked it up, I grabbed a chair and sat close to her. I rummaged in my purse until I found a little plastic photo album. "I brought you the pictures."

Mother looked suddenly animated. I started flipping through it to show her different photos of Ondina in the new house. She fell oddly silent.

"Remember the antique desk you gave her for her fortieth birthday?" I pressed. "Doesn't it look good in that corner? And this is the patio with all the pots of flowers, so Ondina can smell them and get some fresh air. See how big and long it is? I plan on building a walking path with rails there. That way, Ondina will be able to work out more."

"But she can't even stand up."

"She will. They told us she was never going to open her left eye either, remember? And look here. Both her eyes are wide open."

"If you say so. To me, she looks like a fish. Fat, too. She's a monster!"

Mother threw all of Ondina's pictures on the floor. "Take them away. I don't want to look at them. And don't ever ask me to come see her."

I fell back on my chair. Drago immediately moved by me, protective. After all those years, my mother had found a breach in my supposedly 'tough skin.'

Wilma came in with tea and biscuits for Mom. I took the hint. I got up, gathered the photos, put Drago back on his leash and left in a huff.

Please, God, I prayed to a god I didn't believe in, *don't let me ever become like my mother. Just let me preserve generosity and empathy. I don't want to make it to old age if aches and pains make me become like my mother.*

It was a hard thing to think about but I couldn't bear the possibility. Why live so long if your days end in bitterness?

Chapter 37
CLAIRE

Sorisole, Fourth of July

The light of a bright afternoon sun played along the walls, painted in a delicate apricot and a marigold yellow just as at Ondina's former apartment. There weren't any fireworks planned for the evening; Italy's Liberation Day had been already celebrated on April 25.

On top of the electric bed, my sister lay on her back. I kneeled in front of her with her left leg on top of my shoulder, gently stretching it. One of the exercises the physical therapist taught me.

"The more, the better, Sis. At least there's one good thing that happened because of that damn baclofen pump that almost killed you. We can bend your legs now."

Ondina was physically alert, attentive to the new sensations in her limbs. She seemed to enjoy the exercises but she wasn't interested in me talking. I tried again. "Pretty soon we'll be able to plan your foot surgery."

She suddenly turned her head to the left, where the big

189

scar was now more a memory imbedded in her subconscious than a visible damage, hidden by the hair that had grown back enough to cover her skull with tiny coils of curls. But I knew she was listening.

"I know you don't like the idea, but we have to release the tendons so you can stand on the supports. Once you get back on your feet, pretty soon, you'll be walking."

Ondina looked at me but her eyes were now expressionless. She distrusted my enthusiasm, but one of us had to believe in miracles. I wanted us to be just that, a miracle.

July was merciless with its scorching light. I'd moved to the living room. Raissa wanted to talk. The antique dining table in the living room showed some signs of dullness, no matter how many times it was polished. But it was also four hundred years old. I traced the contour of the dull spots with my fingers, while listening to the caregiver hired only little over a month ago. We talked privately, while Ondina rested in her wheelchair on the patio, covered by a cotton blanket and a colorful Indian sari. In the shade, she was cold despite the summer heat. The swallows flew in and out of their nests, chirping.

"I'm sorry, Ms. Claire," Raissa added, clearly uncomfortable at my absence of reaction to what she just said. "I love it here and I couldn't ask for a better *signora* than you. But it just breaks my heart to see Ondina like that. Sometimes it seems to me like she's regressed. She looks so sad and helpless!"

She rushed the last sentence through a gasp, lowering her eyes. She tortured a handkerchief with her hands in her lap. "When you're not here, she looks at me with those big eyes. It seems like she's begging me to help her, but I can't do anything other than change her diapers. I can only give her medicines and blend fruit and veggies as you ordered, to feed her through her G.I. tube. I tried to give her a little bit of juice with a teaspoon this morning, and she almost choked. It was so scary! I had to aspirate the food out of the tracheostomy and after that, I was shaking so hard I had to go to my room and cry. I need to quit or I'll get sick myself. I've got a daughter I left behind in Ukraine to think about. I'm sorry, Ms. Claire."

The breeze brought in the kids' happy voices from the playground. They sounded like the chirping birds. A sharp contrast to Raissa's sobbing. Church bells rang the passing of another hour. I wanted to erase all those sounds, play a different soundtrack to help my sullen mood. In my mind, I heard the notes of "Little Talks," my favorite song from the band Of Monsters and Men. Their sound let me drift away to memories of when my sister and I were young and used to play outside, just like the kids in the playground. Racing on the swings for who'd go higher, dressed in matching outfits. Full of life and promise. How hard it was now to believe we really were, once, those happy kids.

Chapter 38
ONDINA

Sorisole, July 9

I do not know where I am. They call it home, but it isn't.

I prayed it was just a bad dream. But I'm still here, awake and sweating.

I remember my home. It's a high-rise that can be reached only by elevator. The electric car opens right next to my apartment. I remember watching down from my balcony at the plaza in the evening while tending my potted flowers after work. There is no balcony here.

There were soft pillows and a comfy couch to lie down on in my house. Here, I sit in a boxy, hard chair that somebody moves around through these odd rooms. Here, there is a dog. I hear him barking, and sometimes I feel his tail wagging when he comes close to the wheelchair, to sniff my legs.

There was a cat at my house. My beloved cat. Where is she now?

I know this is not the clinic. At least it's not that. The occasional call to physical therapy and a weekly bath, roughly *handled by nurses who couldn't care less to be delicate, respectful. That's all I got there.*

I'm thankful that's over. But what happened to me to take me there? It was either aneurysm, trauma, brain stroke or cancer that brought most of us to their doors. I don't know what was mine.

They left me for hours, wet and soiled in my bed. Nobody checked on the nurses. I once heard them playing strip poker in their station, while my neighbor was screaming in pain. Then I heard she was dead in the morning. I wish it was me instead of her, that gentle, white-haired lady who smelled like lavender. She was improving. But they came in one day at first light and moved her lifeless body out of the room on a gurney.

At least here, in this place that doesn't belong in my scattered recollection of memories, I'm cared for. A lady I like, about my age, who always smiles, acting as a nurse or caregiver. But I haven't seen her in days. Not since the day she had tears in her eyes. It was one of those rare days when I saw more than shadows.

She told me stories of her life, of her daughter, whom she had to leave behind in the place she came from, some old Soviet city with very cold winters that no fur coat or down jacket can defend you from. Some days, I could hear what she said. Some days, her words were undistinguishable beats of noise. Particularly when she forgot to speak to my right side where some of the nerves still function.

I sat next to her on the patio and we stared out at the greenery. Somebody planted jasmine and nandina bushes. I could smell them, not spot the flowers. My vision field is limited. Some lucky days, I can smell the cherry blossoms gracing the trees on the hills. Only my nose works like before 'the accident,' as everybody politely refers to what stole me away.

The lady, whose name I don't remember, talked a lot on the

*phone in her native language, when we were alone. I liked that.
I didn't feel neglected. She was there for me, attentive to my
needs, but she gave me space as well, to be by myself and cry.
Something my sister can't bear.*

We are so pathetic, my sister and I.

*She fights too hard not to show any pity in her eyes. She
does a good job of it, while others can't stand two minutes in
my company without starting to bawl. They are the honest
ones. My little, fearless, tough sis, going a little overboard to
sound positive and encouraging, edging toward nagging.
Better than dismayed, though.*

*Don't pity us, the wounded and disabled, because your pity
kills our fighting spirit. Your pity is like a grenade that
penetrates and nullifies the thick armor we've to wear to still
inhabit this world.*

But do I really want to fight? I'm not sure.

*I don't know what I should fight for. Me? Where is 'me?' I
barely recognize this woman who needs to be washed,
changed, dressed and fed. A creature. Unable to speak, to
express feelings in words. Unable to scratch her own nose, to
glance in the right direction, to taste.*

*I'm like an abnormally big baby, anything but cute at my
size.*

*I was gifted with an ability with words, I chose a career
where the right word could prompt cheering from thousands.
Hundreds of thousands when my copy ended up on national
television campaigns or my songs got clicked on YouTube. I
worshipped words, agonizing for hours over purple or lilac.*

*I have lost all my words. Forced into silence, as if life was
a never-ending silent meditation with my mind going wild. My
throat occupied by a foreign invader, its rubber tail sneaking
down my trachea to my lungs. There are days I dream not to
wake up, to no longer feel that thing scratching inside me,
making it hard to breathe.*

My sister and I.

I hate myself, and I hate her for pushing me so hard out to combat. What if I just want to stand back away from the trenches? Why can't she see that we're fighting in no-man's-land and it's full of booby traps out there?

I'd prefer just to be forgotten, a metal plaque on the memorial wall of those who used to know me for who I was. Not this... thing! All rigid and bent at the wrong angles. Salivating on the scarf that hides my hideous tracheostomy plug.

I could do it all, be the Phoenix and still find myself half blind and deaf. My body twisted, walking like a wooden puppet and giving off only cavernous sounds that some interpreting device connected to my throat would translate into readable words. Like Stephen Hawking without his genius.

Do you really want me to be this?

Is this for me, Sister? Or for you?

I'm sorry. I'm not that brave. I'm scared as hell of that possible outcome. Fifty-fifty would not be enough to convince me, and the figures are much less in our favor. I heard the doctors explaining it the day we left the clinic, while you thought I was asleep on my stretcher, ready to be uploaded into the ambulance.

I see you trying to breathe life into me, massaging me with such fondness, which I crave. I enjoy your touch, the light caress on my breasts, the warm pressure of your hand on the cold skin of my chest to call for my attention.

I'm always cold, little Sister. It feels unreal when the sun is shining outside and you're wearing t-shirt and shorts, your long thighs painted in gold by years of surfing with just a rash guard on.

I love the way you look at me, with such timid, affectionate grace. I don't take you for granted. I remember diving into your eyes when you were just a teen. Your brown irises speckled with purple, reflecting the excitement of the world you wanted to conquer.

My Warrior-Sis. Those purple specks in your brown eyes always made me wonder if Mom didn't have a secret lover. As if the iron maiden would have been as adventurous as that!

Your world is now confined inside the walls of this weird place that I can't remember or define. So is mine. A world for caged people, as we've never been.

I'm your porcelain doll. You tiptoe around me, afraid that I might break.

I'm a character in another one of your books. The one you'll be unable to shape to your liking. The book you will not write because somebody stole your magic pen.

You shuffle around me, afraid that I might break. But I'm already broken. I'm broken and the pieces are all scattered around. Some of them out of sight, too hard to recover.

Never give up, I know, we always reminded each other.

Don't take it personally if I do.

You did all you could, dressing me like a leftover hippy, wrapping me in tie dyes and precious Indian saris. A teen with a new life in front of me, and/or your beloved Barbie doll.

You are so transparent!

I heard the nurses telling you not to spend your money on nice clothes for me, bring in only worn out white t-shirts and old sneakers so that I, too, could become one of their asexual patients, so that the other patients' relatives would stop looking at me and murmur, "Such a pretty woman, what a tragedy!"

You give me love.

I should be grateful, but I'm not.

Forgive me for not trying. I just got so self-centered that I disdain myself. It's true, Sis. The more miserable you are, the more egotistical you become.

Always remember who you are, my invincible little one.

But choose your battles with a grain of salt, not only love. This battle could reveal impossible to win and I'm afraid you might break, if we are defeated.

I need you to keep whole. Wholehearted as you've always been, but also all in one piece.

Stand tall, resist. Never give up.

Promise me you'll go on, should I happen to fall again.

Chapter 39
CLAIRE

Sorisole, six months after the accident

I now slept in the caregiver's room adjacent to Ondina's bedroom instead of the sofa bed in the living room. Drago slept close by on the floor. *Sleeping* a very optimistic way to define another sweaty, unrestful night. Italian summers can be hot and humid as the tropics. But I had trouble leaving the damp sheet, getting ready to start another listless day. Ondina wasn't improving much and I worried about the months going by. I read that the longer a person remained in locked-in syndrome, the harder it'd become to break the glass.

A sudden disturbance alarmed me. Ondina's breathing sounded more like a rattle. I rushed to her bedside, clumsily banging into the metal rail of her bed.

"I'm here, Sis. What was it? A nightmare?"

A pained look in Ondina's eyes as she turned to me only for a second before her gaze started wandering about the room. I lifted the blankets and looked at her legs, clasped together on the left side of the bed as an indivisible item.

"You're all sweat. We better change you. Let me go get some warm water to wash you with a sponge. It will refresh you."

When I returned, I gently massaged Ondina's legs and thighs with the sponge. I couldn't help but admire them. She always had incredible legs.

"Look at these beauties! You are so damn gorgeous, Sis. Now we turn on the side to change your diaper."

I started the skillful maneuver I learned at the clinic to turn her, put baby cream on her genitals and butt with my gloved hand. I smiled at her back, spoke softly to distract her.

"Not many sisters get to see each other naked as adults, but look here. You don't have one gray hair yet!"

She didn't seem to care about my appreciation for her lustrous pubic hair. She kept exploring the junction of the walls and ceiling, rhythmically blinking, left to right. She'd retreated back into her hurt and I retreated into the other bedroom to avoid showing my distress. I'd hoped to achieve so much more improvement once she came home.

Chapter 40
CLAIRE

Sorisole, end of July

End of July in Northern Italy reminded me of October in Los Angeles, the hot Santa Anas making everyone miserable. In Lombardy, it was so hot we only dared to walk outside at the edges of the day. I longed for a hike to sweat away my concerns, finding peace in the automatic repetition of movements that my body executed without my mind's participation.

Filippo had invited me to take an evening walk in the woods, along a trail flanked by chestnut trees. Streaks of red and purple stained the evening sky. "Who's staying with Ondina now?" he asked, interrupting the silence of our soft steps.

"Giovanna came. She said she could stay until nine, and Ondina was already asleep."

I needed to get out for some air, clear my mind from all this endless second-guessing.

"You should take walks more often, or you'll get sick too."

"Yeah, but I can't. There were so many of Ondina's friends ready to help in the beginning. Now that Cristiana went back to Tuscany, it seems they're all gone except for you, Nicola, and Giovanna. Guilherme still comes around now and then but he can't cut work too often. And all of you have regular jobs, long hours."

"You can't do it all by yourself. Especially now, with her prescribed two months of physical therapy over."

Moltacci had kept his promise and sent a physical therapist to the house, but he could only prescribe a maximum of eight weeks. After that, I was on my own and it wasn't an easy task.

"I tried to enlist other therapists. But they change their mind when they see that it takes them too long to come from Bergamo. Few miles, but they can take forever with the traffic and—"

Filippo interrupted me, yanking my arm. He'd stopped and pointed in front of us.

"There. Look! *Lucciole.*"

I whispered through a smile. "Fireflies! They come to bring a message."

We stood motionless, captivated by the clusters of flickering light. After a few seconds, Filippo whispered back.

"So, what's the message? What is the firefly medicine?"

"Enlightenment."

The fireflies flew in different directions, away into the trees. Filippo turned toward the trailhead.

"Let's be enlightened then. We should start going back on the path. It will be dark in less than twenty minutes."

He took my hand as we headed back and it felt good, warm human contact. But my head kept turning. I couldn't see the light of the fireflies anymore but I felt their presence. Maybe they'd watch out for us, make sure we got back safe?

"Hey," I said when we made it out of the forest, in sight of the parking lot. "Could I borrow your bike?"

Filippo had this habit of carrying his bike on his car rack and that day was no exception. I felt like a bike ride.

While Filippo drove away in the direction of his house, I pedaled along a road snaking up and down the rolling hills, through a sequence of little towns. Where one ended, another started, as tight as pearls on a string. Unlike America, here there wasn't much open, unfenced space. Too many people, too many dwellings.

I glanced at the cherry trees on the hills, clusters of pale pink dancing in the wind, still visible despite the upcoming darkness, and at the few ancient architectural buildings on flat land.

I arrived at the city center, the historic stone city hall surrounded by ugly rows of modern two-story townhouses and tall buildings with flower and stationery shops, hair-salons and bars on their ground floors.

While Bergamo Alta is incredibly charming, the other part, Bergamo Bassa, is a vast flat of industrial neighborhoods with just few central streets that still offer a glimpse of its history and beauty.

I biked past the pedestrian street nicknamed *Il Sentierone*. Via Papa Giovanni XXIII brought up memories of *aperitivi* with my sister, a glass of Prosecco for Ondina and a non-alcoholic Crodino for me. Sitting at the bar tables placed under a pergola on the sidewalk, we snacked on olives and exquisite small tartines, catching up in person while locals pedaled around us.

The *bergamaschi* are outdoorsy, sporty people. Anyone under seventy has a mountain bike, a *rampichino,* to climb the surrounding mountains when they're not skiing down them. They are lean and trim.

As a kid, I built platforms on top of trees using plywood strips from fruit boxes, tied casters under big cardboard containers to turn them into cars, hammered any nail sticking out of fences or walls. Family and friends called me 'screw-driver,' referring both to my handy attitude and the fact that I was thin as a bamboo stalk. Ondina preferred to sit quietly and read a book.

I still liked to work with my hands and was able to fix things. I'd often been the handywoman at Ondina's home, mending her toaster or a broken windowsill for her. It felt good, being able to help. So, it was prosecco, then paintbrush and glue, then *spaghetti aglio e olio*, then crashing together in Ondina's big bed, the only one in the house.

This time, I'd skipped the household repairs. All my attention was pointed to a challenge much harder than replacing a defective outlet or unclogging a drain, and there was no *aperitivo* or belly laugh with my sister to lighten up the chore. Plus, I was losing my confidence that my sister's brain could really be brought back to acceptable conditions.

I kept pedaling up Via Vittorio Emanuele, aiming to arrive at the site of the old monastery turned into university and called 'La Fara,' a serene place with stone walls and meadows from where I'd see the city lights below, a view I'd always appreciated. My thoughts rolled at the same slow pace of the pedals and I started to realize what bothered me the most.

When I created Nails, I made her believe in a faith whose only commandment was *We can do it*. Like that old American wartime propaganda poster, Rosie the Riveter, a Michigander showing off her female factory worker bicep in a power flex. Nails was just like that, intensely convinced of her own power to face any enemy without a second thought. Brave to the verge of recklessness, like the Lakota warrior leader Crazy Horse, going into battle convinced that no bullet could kill him.

But I was disrobing my ghost shirt painted with its magic symbols, imbued with spiritual powers, like I had no more faith in my invincibility. Was I listening to Ondina? What she might say if her voice could be heard? Or was I avoiding it on purpose, filling the voids and silence with incessant action, afraid of what I might eventually perceive, coming from Ondina's own feelings?

I had put so much effort in making Ondina believe that everything was going to be okay. So fucking driven and... Bossy? Pushy? It made me ill to imagine Ondina might experience my insistence as a kind of cruelty, an expression of my ego.

What if Ondina's absence was her only defense? If that was her only way to escape the pain of being caged alive in an almost dead body?

These thoughts plunged me into a spiral, into a well of desperation. The place where my sister could not heal, that dark kingdom I had denied existence to, forbidding its shadows to penetrate the most hidden layers of my mind. Much worse than simply out of my comfort zone. Much bigger than the uneasy mental state provoked by second-guessing. I'd never thought panic attacks were real but there I was, panting for breath with an ache in my chest, the air choking out of my lungs.

My vision was foggy, blurred. It felt like a sword jabbed into my skull. I had to stop, put a leg down from the bike. I leaned on the handlebar, gasping, afraid I might puke.

When I came to my senses, I told myself, *you better fucking believe that she can make it*. Nobody else would.

Chapter 41
CLAIRE

San Giovanni Bianco, August 10

Weeks had gone by. On a beautiful, warm afternoon, Ondina sat in her wheelchair. I'd driven her to a small town in the high valley aboard the disability-friendly, used van I bought to transport her past the borders of her limited world.

I pushed the chair through the tree-lined path to the entrance of this other neuro rehab clinic, our reason for the trip. I was trying to enlist more cognitive therapies. The air smelled good. I took it in with a deep inhale.

Ondina looked alert. I wanted to explain how I believed she had a right to choose whether or not to participate in her recovery. "Can you smell the river, Ondina? You used to love this place. Having breakfast sitting in front of the running waters, just before hiking in the mountains. Well, they have one of the best rehab clinics here. It's not so far from our house and I bought the van so I can bring you here to do your exercises."

Ondina trained her eyes on me, but there was no evident reaction.

"We can drive here every day if they think it will help you recover faster," I corrected myself, "If you want to recover faster."

Ondina turned her head back to the Brembo River. I pushed the wheelchair toward the old building entrance.

The receptionist checked our appointment and directed us to a room on the first floor. A young woman with a stylish haircut came in, shook my hand and introduced herself as a resident neurologist, then turned to Ondina to administer the same old tests.

"Signora Ondina, look here at my index finger. Now I'll move it to the right, and I want you to follow it with your eyes."

Ondina didn't follow. Instead, she tried to look behind her left shoulder, searching for something or somebody only she knew. She looked terrified, the way her eyes rolled up. The neurologist wrote something on her notepad.

"Now I'm going to ask you to squeeze my hand. Can you do that, Signora Ondina?"

No response. The neurologist wrote some more. Then, without warning, she coldly grabbed hold of Ondina's bent right arm, and tried to stretch it. Ondina reacted like the doctor was hurting her, as she probably was. Then the neurologist tapped her other arm with a little wooden hammer. She was actually beating on Ondina's cast, under her long sleeve.

"No reflexes."

"Are you really using the reflex hammer on a cast? My sister just had botulinum injected in her left arm and hand to relax her spasticity. Her arm needs to be kept stretched, hence the cast."

The doctor went back behind her desk.

"Regardless, your sister is clearly still in a vegetative state. On my scale, I give her a grade four. Three is for deep coma. In order to enter our outpatient program, she'd need a six."

I glowered but kept my mouth shut, massaging my sister's shoulder to let her know I was on her side, an irritation mounting in my chest, climbing up to my throat, ready to erupt into words that I knew I couldn't speak.

"What do you suggest then? What can I do on my own? I can't find a physical therapist available to come to the house. They all say we live too far from town."

"Well, Ms. Strada. You can ask at the reception to put her on our waiting list to be admitted as an inpatient. In that case, she could have a program tailored to her needs. We have a few other patients here who're also vegetative."

Ondina shivered at this news, squeezing my hand with force.

"Well, that was a pretty strong reaction for a vegetative person, don't you think, Doctor? I guess she'd have to get up and walk from her wheelchair for you to change your mind. I've learned how these programs and clinics work. Thank you for your expertise."

I pushed Ondina's wheelchair out of the room, hurrying toward the elevator. As we waited in front of the still closed doors, I lowered my mouth to my sister's ear.

"If anyone's vegetative, it's her. We're out of here, babe."

Chapter 42
CLAIRE

Sorisole, seven months after the accident

Ondina sat by herself in the living room. A soft light came in from the window, creating a design on the floor through the plantation shutters. I entered the room with a small bowl of blended fruit on a tray. The strap that usually held her forehead up was nowhere in sight, but Ondina kept her head in the right position. I didn't remember not fastening it on her forehead when I wheeled her from her bedroom but I might have been wrong.

I witnessed the scene, holding my breath. Very slowly, she moved her head left to right, scanning her books on the shelves. Janis Joplin sang "Piece of My Heart" in the background.

Hours later, after successfully trying to swallow a few tiny spoons of my fruit concoction, my sister was still aware. Awake and aware.

I accompanied her back to bed to give her lower back some relief. Sitting for long hours in her chair was tiring—she couldn't adjust her position, not even incrementally. So I left her to rest with the iPod on low volume. Music filled the room. "I Might Be Wrong," by Radiohead. She seemed to be listening. Drago slept on the floor under the bed and my sister rhythmically blinked her eyelids.

A penny for your thoughts, I whispered to myself. Elated.

But it truly didn't matter if she couldn't tell me. I knew she was having fun discovering the lights switching back in the aisles of her brain, where they'd been dim and drab for too long.

Chapter 43
ONDINA

Sorisole, seven months after the accident

I... Might... Be... Wrong. Maybe I can make it after all. Maybe it's worth trying.

The look on Chiara's face when she watched from the doorway and saw me moving my neck, recognizing my books. I'd never known what the face of the truest love might be, and now I'd seen it.

She reminded me of my friend Giulia. She has a daughter with Down syndrome, Melissa. Melissa is thirteen. She has been through a lot. But she's fighting to have a life despite her disability. She's doing great, able to keep up in school. A good artist. The way Giulia showed me her paintings, explaining what feelings Melissa expressed with every stroke of color.

I am my sister's broken child.

Maybe her love will be my healer, after all.

I doubt that I can go all the way back to who I was. I don't remember myself.

But... it would be good to talk... to walk...

I didn't want to admit I'd slipped into oblivion, hoping to be forgotten. It was too painful. It still is.

I've been so depressed since I woke up from my coma.

First was the horror of realizing I was paralyzed. Disabled in this harsh, terrifying world, which is tough enough for a strong and intact person.

Then I discovered that I couldn't think straight. I didn't know where I was, who the people were. What did they want? I could barely hear their voices, trying to break through the glass bell from a thousand miles, that fishbowl I was given to inhabit as my new house.

But I could feel Chiara's hand on my skin. The gentle way she touches me, her strong hands kneading my spastic muscles. Her sweat when she'd go on for so many hours.

I wish I could tell her how she makes me feel.

All I ask for are two little syllables: 'me too.' When she tells me how much she loves me, so many times a day. Just two syllables would make her day.

Mine, as well.

But this knot in my throat distorts any sound. I've been so afraid to be responsive. I preferred to be passive. Resentful. Unable to yell out my fury. Anger, the emotion I felt most comfortable with, the emotion that saved me from any unwanted circumstance in life. But being angry requested too much energy, and depression crept in to take its place.

Chiara is so unable to deal with anyone who's depressed! She can't understand how anyone can't be willing to try. It isn't in her DNA. I thought it wasn't in mine either. But genetics played tricks on me, gifted me with this bubble in my brain. Doctors said it didn't have to blow up. It could have stayed there, unnoticed. I could have lived to ninety and died of other causes.

I feared I could inherit Father's cancer or Mother's Parkinson's disease, never imagined something could already be wrong. Something already there.

A sudden change in my blood pressure, I heard them say. That is what—rarely—causes these bubbles to burst.

Bubbles, like those in a glass of champagne. If I had a choice, I'd have skipped drinking from this glass. I woke up blind and almost deaf in a world of sharp noises and gray shadows. Damned to silence. What a joke for a talkative creature like me!

The worst was still to come. I picked up bronchitis in the hospital, they said. A fire inside me, a burning hell swallowing me up. At the same time, I felt so cold. Cold as I think only the dead can feel.

When I came back from there, I got ferried to shore by the devils of fate. "There goes the hearing!" "Let me take her speech."

When I came back the second time, it felt like someone else had taken up residence inside my skin. One who was numb to anything like life.

Numbness was my refuge. My respite from hell.

If I could talk, I could tell Chiara that I want my cat back. I don't care if cat dander can give me allergies.

Take that thing out of my throat—I'll deal with Belinda's fur.

I need to tell Chiara.

Tell her what I want.

But I'm tired now.

It has been a long day.

I'll tell her tomorrow.

Chapter 44
CLAIRE

Lake Como, August 22

I'd come to the clinic to talk to Moltacci. Reluctantly, but I knew that convincing him was my only hope. I sat in his office, on the opposite side of the desk. His eyes were a shade of aqua, maybe that meant a decent mood.

"You know it's a big risk, signora. I have never done this for any patient in your sister's shoes." He paused, then lowered his head mumbling a few more words. "By the way, you look very pale and thin. Did you lose more weight?"

I didn't confirm nor deny. "What can I do to convince you? My sister hates that thing in her throat. She's trying to speak, and all she gets out is a rasping sound."

I knew my way around Moltacci by now. Easier to make him sympathetic to Ondina's needs than arguing from a medical point of view. I liked that I could fish around for his empathy.

"I play songs from when Ondina was a songwriter. But she was twenty then, and her voice has grown lower and warmer with age. I want to hear my sister's voice. You got to help me, Doc. Or I won't be able to get Ondina accepted for pool rehab either. They won't take her if she still has an open wound with a cannula stuck in her throat."

"Pool? What a great idea! But are you sure you can handle that? I mean, putting a person who can't stand up in the water is no joke."

"In this Swiss clinic I found, they have the personnel and equipment to lower her safely into the water. They refused to take her when she came out of the Bergamo hospital the first time. That's how I landed in your clinic."

"Oh, we were a second choice then?"

Instead of taking the bait, I delivered a more detailed report of her progress and the fact that the clinic seemed open to an outpatient deal. I planned to take her there twice a week.

"My sister loves water. I have to show her that she can still enjoy life. It's one thing to be *partially* disabled and another totally. She needs to experience the possibility of recovering more of her abilities. Please! Help me make Ondina feel like her life isn't over."

Moltacci scanned my face, undecided. The tension between us sliced thick like we were in a wrestling match.

"I'll tell you what," he resolved. "Before you spend all your money on this private Swiss clinic, I'll take your sister in again for two weeks. She'll have the foot surgery we'd planned for down the road and the assistance and therapies needed during her downtime. If everything goes well, I will remove the cannula. After a week or two, I'll send her home with a customized stand to put her back in a vertical position. A lot of things can change when a patient regains vertical posture." He looked at me earnestly. "Deal?"

"Deal!" I could barely contain my joy. Of all the doctors I had to deal with, he'd been the absolute best.

"One more thing, Ms. Strada. I hope you don't take it as an

intrusion, but my nurses told me a secret. Is it true that you are Claire Waters, the American thriller writer?"

I had forgotten how much Italians love gossip. "I wonder how they learned that."

"Believe me, signora. Nobody can keep a secret in this place. In this case, I'm pleased at their indiscretion. My daughter has read everything you've written. She dreams of becoming a detective like your private eye, 'tougher than nails.' I've read a couple of your books myself and now that I've met you, I notice the similarities. I'll borrow some more from my daughter. I've always dreamed of becoming a writer."

Now I knew why Moltacci was so intrigued, and suddenly more helpful. Celebrity has no borders. And maybe knowing more about me helped to loosen him up. "You have a career more important than any author. You should be happy with it."

"I am, most of the time. But I'm always fighting this pachydermic bureaucracy and it gets stressful. Sometimes I wonder how my life would have been, had I answered my original calling."

I tried to imagine him as a writer. What would he write? What kind of stories stalked his consciousness? I couldn't conjure the opposite—my life without the whirlwind of stories blowing around in my brain, allowing them shape and life. But then, I realized, back here in Italy I'd become a powerful advocate.

I'd become my sister's keeper.

Chapter 45
CLAIRE

Lake Como, August 26

Ondina lay in her bed at the clinic with both her feet, and now her other arm, all in casts and bandages. She slept but she was clearly not at ease, biting her swollen lower lip.

My brother, Fabio, and his mother visited and were still in the room, one of those rare days when Fabio could cut work. They'd brought Ondina a present, an Anthurium plant with red flowers in the shape of hearts. My stepmother, Katarina, was standing at the bedside, leaning in for a kiss on Ondina's pale cheek. Fabio whispered to me as we stood at the footboard of her bed. "So, what did Moltacci say? How long is he going to keep her this time?"

"I hope to take her home next Monday. She didn't have any complications this time. No more surgeries. But first we need to get him to remove that." I pointed at Ondina's throat, right at the hollow where the tracheostomy still held the cannula.

"Did he measure if she can keep stable pressurization in her lungs?" Katarina asked. She knew medical terms, having had two open-heart surgeries herself.

"He's going to try it tonight after I'm gone. He wants to make sure she can breathe on her own without me 'clucking around like a hen with her chick.' That's how he put it."

Katarina kissed Ondina once more, then approached us. "I told Ondina to be good and breathe nice tonight so that she can go home. She doesn't like it here. She has the same face your father had when he was in the hospital with cancer. I wanted so badly to keep him home, but I was exhausted and couldn't keep going, with my heart problems. I still blame myself for letting him die in there, abandoned in the hands of strangers."

"We won't let that happen to Ondina. I mean, she will not die. Not now, for sure. But whenever that will happen, I promise, she won't die in a hospital. And she won't be alone." I paused, then added. "Dad was lucky to find you, Katarina. We surely suffered not to have him around when we were growing up, but were glad he'd found happiness with you."

"Your parents were always fighting. They hated each other so rabidly. He fell in love with me when you weren't even born, but I never imagined he'd abandon his children. You took it better than Ondina, but you never knew him to be in the house. He was there for the first three years of her life. She must have really missed him."

I knew my sister did, and I missed having a present father too, but didn't want to dwell on our sorrow. "Well, it's all water under the bridge. All we can do is care for her now."

Ondina slept. It was not a quiet sleep. When Fabio and Katarina left, I remained, watching over my sister as she shivered, chewing her already bitten lips.

When I finally arrived at what now was my Italian "home," I was exhausted but still couldn't find sleep. The house felt awfully empty without my sister's presence. My mind swirled with tornadoes of doubts, wondering what would happen when Moltacci removed her cannula.

Please, let Ondina breathe on her own, I prayed to whatever God might be listening. I decided to bring something to read in bed, no point in tossing and turning, churning over different possible scenarios in my mind.

Drago curled up on the rug, breathing quietly. I spread several notepads and scrapbooks filled with Ondina's small handwriting, pictures and travel memories, over the Lakota star blanket that I'd brought with me from my last visit to Bitten by The Snake. Inside one of them, I found a passage written by my sister. A letter to me, apparently, that was never sent:

Bergamo, 28 March, 2001

I dreamed about dad last night. For the first time since he left us, it was a good dream. He entered my house through the kitchen window on the ground floor, quick and agile. He looked beautiful. Thinner than I'd ever seen him. Happier, too.

It lasted only a second. Then, I remembered he was dead. The magic dissolved and I had no time to hug him before he left.

Maybe I should go to the cemetery, on that hill above the lake all covered in flowers. I couldn't do it when he died. I managed to show up at the memorial, but seeing him all pasty in that open casket made me lose my voice for days. I opened my mouth but no sound came out. My voice had taken flight together with his soul. His soul, thank goodness, was definitely not there, refusing to be buried.

You were not there either, gone back to the States after a month spent at his bedside. How jealous I'd been of your strength! Hospitals give me the chills. So do cemeteries. Maybe Father has a message to give me now, that he had no time to spell, while passing by into my hurried dream?

Remember that poem by Elizabeth Frye that I was supposed to read at his funeral? Maybe he just wanted to console me, let me know it didn't matter since he wasn't there.

That poem used to give me comfort, but what works one day, doesn't work another. Today it doesn't work at all.

I did not hear my wake-up call today and slept late. Giovanni was already gone, out in the woods camping with his fishing buddies this weekend. So, I lounge here with the cats. It isn't raining but the sky is that awful shade of dull gray that I resent so much. A weather for hot chocolate and homemade minestrone soup. I will postpone my shopping spree. But here's my list:

New tape recorder
More houseplants
Sporty shoes (sneakers, loafers, all sorts)
Dressy pants (cotton and silk)
Colorful t-shirts (not white or gray, I've had enough)

I miss shopping together, but when will you come next? Oh, right, you told me already, it'll still take a month.

Meanwhile, stay cheerful, write more stories, get more waves. Summer is just around the corner.

Your humble and tormented,
Sis

Chapter 46
ONDINA

Lake Como, August 27

They took it out!

That monstrosity, the snake that was climbing from my lungs to my throat, is gone. Gone! And it feels so good.

The doctors said that I don't even have too much phlegm, I heard them well.

One thing you still need to know about me—I might be brain-damaged but I'm not absent.

I can't express myself. I can't react as I wish I could to the neurological tests when they march into my room. A squad of doctors always going too fast, never giving me the time to gather the images in my brain.

I don't think like they do. Like you do and like I used to. Not anymore. I lost my ability to think in a linear way.

I've discovered truths about the brain that none of these big-shot neurologists can imagine. They didn't experience what I did.

One day, I might be able to tell my story and show how

wonderful our right brain can be. What miracles it can convey that science could never perform.

And if my story might lift the veil of some mysteries of our brains, my suffering might not have been in vain. Because I have been suffering, for as long as I can remember!

Next step, I want these casts gone. Claire said that without them and with my straightened feet, I'll be able to stand. And I heard the doctors talking to her and saying that getting back in a vertical position should waken more neurons in my brain.

I'm scared to hope, but what would it be like to spell out a few words? To see my sister at eye level, standing on my own?

I don't want to hope, but I can't help it.

Chapter 47
CLAIRE

Marina di Pietrasanta, September 4

"Song to the Siren" flooded the van. Tim Buckley's lyrics resonated in the van with the soulful voice of Elizabeth Fraser. Filippo was driving and I sat in the back, close to Ondina, fastened in her wheelchair. Drago lay at her feet.

"Almost there," said Filippo, turning back toward us. "Ondina is going to the beach."

"Right," I echoed. "Ondina's going to the beach. Who said she couldn't travel?" My sister moved her head toward the sound of my voice. "Travel is what you like, travel is what you'll get. See? Wheelchair and all."

Ondina stayed silent but she looked comfortable despite the bumps. She was definitely aware, moving her head to look out of the window. Out to the view of the Tuscany coast. And I felt grateful that Filippo joined us in this adventure, which wouldn't have been possible without another person's help. He was such a great sport. I liked that. I'd started to see why my sister considered him her best friend.

I hadn't shared my intention with anybody else, to avoid being called reckless and irresponsible. If it was up to them, Ondina would have just survived in her electric bed and wheelchair pushed as far as the porch. And how could Ondina wish to go on, then?

We arrived at the beach in the afternoon and lowered Ondina with her wheelchair to the ground. I wheeled the chair along the path of wooden boards and parked it on the shore.

My sister watched the ripples in the seawater with great interest.

"Come on, Filippo. Give me a hand. She wants to go into the water."

The mechanics of lifting her up were no different than what I did at home to put her on her stand, which had already proved to be a big help for prompting more awareness. And now I had help, so the maneuver should turn out even easier. I was determined to show Ondina that life could still give her some pleasure.

"One, two, three, and we lift her on her feet," I instructed Filippo. "Then you go behind Ondina while I hold her up, help her move her feet forward, one at a time. Ready?"

Filippo hesitated just a second, then moved to the other side of the wheelchair.

Ondina seemed scared but also interested. The tracheostomy hole was almost completely healed after the cannula had been removed, but we had to be careful not to let any water contaminate the wound. Her curls had grown back. Her face had regained mobility and expression, losing the frozen look that was the fabric of my nightmares. But, due to the lack of exercise of all the previous months, she weighed more than I did. Hoisting her up and then lowering her down to the water level was going to be complicated, despite my show of confidence.

"One, two, three, UP!"

We lifted her up and took one full step forward. As soon as we recovered from the effort, I stepped in front to hold her against my chest and shoulders, hugging her with both arms. I had to use all my strength to support her standing.

Filippo quickly pushed the chair away and went to support Ondina from behind. He knew we had to be quick.

"Now, one, two, three, MARCH."

We moved forward like a giant crab. Three people wrapped in an embrace that made it impossible to distinguish who was who. After a few steps, we slowly entered the water with our feet, Ondina's face registering the change of temperature with attention. We lowered her into the inflatable chair, letting ourselves drop in the shallow water on each side of the float, splashing and laughing. Inebriated by our success, which wasn't at all guaranteed when we started.

Ondina's feet dangled in the water. She lay on her back in her floating lounge. Her stomach faced up, and her head was on the blow-up headrest. Filippo grabbed one of her hands and delicately brought it down to touch the water. Ondina inclined her head to look at her fingers brush the small ripples. Then she lifted her eyes to Filippo and smiled. A timid smile but it was there. Definitely there!

I felt like crying, but knew I mustn't let her see that. She'd had her share of people crying in her presence, lately. Instead, I looked at her in awe. Music played in my mind. The perfect soundtrack for this: "Sæglopur," by Icelandic band Sigur Ros. A lost seafarer, alive, returning home.

Ondina was far more alive than I'd seen her in the past seven months. I breathed deep and easy for the first time since January.

Chapter 48
CLAIRE

Sorisole, eight months after the accident

Our Tuscany vacation was everything I'd hoped for. Now we were back, and I felt energized and ready to push forward.

I sat next to Ondina's wheelchair in the living room. In front of us, taped on the TV screen, there was a giant letter. An "A" that I'd drawn with markers on a piece of paper.

"Let's try again, Ondina. AAAAAAAAAAA...."

"a—a—a."

"That's just great, Sis. One more time."

I had not heard her voice since January. The rasping sounds that came together with the attempted letters were nothing like the velvety tone that made her voice so precious. I was overjoyed just as well. But Ondina didn't seem to share my enthusiasm. She looked puzzled, maybe a little disgusted. She turned her head toward the back of her left shoulder, as she used to do months before. Maybe, caught in my excitement, I hadn't realized that I was putting her through more than she could handle.

"You're probably right, Sis. It must be exhausting. You're not a baby. You're a grown woman. You know things. At least, you used to know them. I'm sure it must be so frustrating not knowing how to begin bringing down this damn glass wall all around you, separating you from the rest of the world."

She turned toward me with two big tears rolling down her cheeks. I crouched in front of her chair to wipe them away. "Don't cry. You'll get everything back." I wasn't sure that my prediction would prove true, but I couldn't bear to see her cry. "I can reinvent the alphabet for you. We can invent our own code to communicate. A secret one just for us like when we were little, remember? We didn't want Grandpa and Grandma to know what we were talking about, so we used the silent alphabet behind their backs. Remember?"

I stepped in front of her wheelchair. "Watch!"

I painted silent letters with my hands in the air.

"This is an E. And this one a B. And this, remember this other one? This is an A, just like the one on the wall. AAAAAAAAAAA." I stuck my tongue out to the sign that hung on the TV. "Take that, stupid alphabet!"

Ondina smiled.

"Aha! I made you smile, I saw you! You want to create the secret code? Blink your eyes once for yes. Keep them open and still for no."

Ondina blinked her eyes slowly and deliberately, leaving no doubt. I grabbed Ondina's hand and kissed it, then rolled my eyes to the ceiling like Paradise really existed there.

"Thank you, God!" It slipped off my lips like a typo from fingers on the keyboard. Instinctively, I brought my hands to my mouth to stop the sentence there. It was a ridiculous reaction, so I added, more lightly: "Whoever and wherever you are. You're listening to our prayers!"

Somebody—call it God, Tunkashila, Shiva, Allah, Yahweh,

Brahman, Odin or someone else—had listened. And in that moment, I didn't feel the need to question their name or their existence.

Chapter 49
CLAIRE

Milan, seven months after the accident

The day after, Giovanna came to visit, allowing me to leave my sister in good hands for a few hours. I took the train to visit my mom, a thing that had become hard to do now that I was Ondina's primary caregiver.

Mother was in her usual spot, in her chairlift in front of the TV. I lowered the volume and pulled a dining chair close to hers. With stars in my eyes, I told her of our breakthroughs.

"Did she really say, AAAAAAAAAA?"

"You should have been there! She hasn't heard her own voice for so long, she must have forgotten how it sounded. I certainly had."

My mother smiled, genuinely touched. She put her hand on top of mine, a rare gesture of affection.

"You've been so good to your sister. You're so brave. I was too, once. Now I'm a coward. I was scared, Chiara. I still am. I try not to think about Ondina because I cannot bear the pain."

"I know, Mom. Don't apologize. You felt hopeless, but now

you have reason to feel a bit encouraged. Mamacita, hope! Let's hope for the best. We need to believe in more miracles."

Again, the news covered the endless debate on the comatose Eluana Englara. Her father had won the right to stop feeding and hydration. The right wing was trying to reverse the court's decision supporting the father's rights. I found it terrible that the only way in which the Catholic church and court system would grant the father's wish was by letting her die of hunger and thirst. But I was glad that Eluana's father won his battle to save his daughter from a future of needless suffering.

The news switched to another topic. Thank goodness, Mother hadn't paid too much attention to the story of Eluana's struggle, distracted by Ondina's news. I kissed Mom's fingers one by one. Then, I brought her hand to my own cheek.

"I need you to hope. Ondina needs you too."

She looked into my eyes.

"I'll be gone soon. You know that. My time is coming, fast. I will be gone by Christmas. Just a couple of months away. But don't be sad. I want to go. This is not the life I've wanted to live. I've already endured it for too long. I just don't want Ondina to be stuck in a wheelchair like me. But you are the one who's in charge. I'm so glad she has you."

My phone vibrated in my jacket pocket. I took it out and saw a message from Giovanna. I immediately clicked on it. *San Giovanni Bianco called. They have a spot. They'll take Ondina in for a period of intensive rehab, but they need an answer ASAP.*

I told my mom I had to go to the bathroom and closed myself in there to call the clinic in San Giovanni Bianco. I could hardly contain my excitement for that opportunity. More therapies could help Ondina take a big step forward. I just had to find a way to make her accept going back to another clinic, reassure her it'd be only a temporary stay to recover her abilities faster.

Will I be able to convince her?

I had to. The alternative, the status quo or a very slow progression, was no longer enough.

Chapter 50
CLAIRE

Sorisole, October 15

The weather had changed. Chilly morning and nights, pale light when there was a hint of sun in the middle of the day. The autumn foliage already fallen from the trees, which now sported more bare branches. The wispy grass had turned a straw color and the rains had intensified. So, it was harder to keep Ondina outside on the patio for fresh air. No matter how many blankets I wrapped her in, her cheeks and hands felt cold to my touch.

At least this new clinic's in-patient stay, planned for a couple of weeks down the road, would happen at a time when being outdoors was less of an option for my sister. It was a meager consolation, but I hung on to that.

Ondina rested in her bed after our long physical therapy session. She was awake, though, and didn't look as exhausted as she usually had after such effort. I was nervous about bringing it up again with her, but I had to try. The first time I spoke about it, she didn't seem to have registered the information.

But now I had to make her accept the new clinic stay as a necessary step on her road to recovery.

I spoke softly into her better ear. "It's only a matter of a couple of weeks, Sis. You'll go to the clinic where you'll make more progress. Filippo will be there with you while I'll go back and vote in the U.S. elections. You won't even notice I'm gone."

Ondina rolled her eyes to my face, clearly alarmed.

"We need you to progress more so that next time I go to America, we'll go together. I'm going to take you with me to the States, Sis."

She kept looking at me with dilated pupils, scared eyes. She didn't like America, but I thought it was the best choice. Guilherme had finally moved on, allowing Beatriz to come back. Her friends were no longer the tight circle she'd relied on. And there was nobody else who could assist her.

"They've better doctors there. New stem cell therapy. I'm going to meet a doctor in Tijuana who has this state-of-the-art day clinic. Tijuana's about a three-hour drive from L.A. We'll go there just for the therapy sessions, then we'll go back home. And there will be no more hospital or clinics stays, I promise."

Ondina looked straight into my eyes. She had not blinked once.

"You'll love it there, Sis. You've seen only pictures of my place in the hills. Your last visit happened when I was still living in Venice. Then, you said 'I've seen enough of the U.S., and the world still holds more promise in countries I haven't visited yet. I'll see you when you come to Italy.'" I chuckled, but Ondina was squeezing my hand hard, alarm all over her face. "Next time, we'll go together," I reinforced. "You'll like the trees in the big garden, the sun shining, the wildlife visiting every day. And it will never be cold like here. But first you should focus all your energy to get the best out of this little stay in San Giovanni Bianco. Promise me, Ondina."

I held her stare, puzzled by her reaction. I'd hoped to detect a hint of excitement. I didn't know how to interpret Ondina's lack of response. Maybe I was afraid to.

Chapter 51
CLAIRE

Los Angeles, November 9

Filippo woke me up early on the morning after Obama had become the first Black President of the United States. Other people would have chosen not to call, knowing I'd been up most of the night, but I'd made him promise to report the truth. His tone eclipsed the echo of the epic moment when Obama's victory was announced live on TV.

He'd just left the clinic, after a doctor's visit. "The doctor said Ondina's fever is rising." The day before it was just a cold and a cough. *What was happening?* "They have to give her stronger antibiotics because high fever can affect the brain, and her brain is already damaged."

When Filippo asked the doctor what went wrong since she was perfectly fine when she arrived at the clinic, the doctor added, "Vegetative patients don't tell you what's wrong. We can only guess."

I didn't expect this turn of events when I left Italy, just a week before. Ondina was in good health and more aware than ever. She'd reacted well to the first days of therapy. I'd felt relaxed, able to enjoy my brief permanence and get things done. I had a good meeting with the doctor in Tijuana. I'd met my renters and we'd agreed on a month notice when I'd have more clarity about when I'd come back to stay, this time with my sister. Things were finally looking up. The only disappointment had been not seeing Xavier, who was held up at the reservation. His uncle was sick. He even canceled his show for two weeks, fearing Bitten by The Snake's health could deteriorate more. *And now, this?*

Filippo told me how Ondina shivered and moaned. He'd taken her hand and tried to comfort her, silently communicating not to pay attention to the doctor's rudeness. "So, what's your guess?" he'd asked the doctor, trying to remain calm. "We could go through the whole medical encyclopedia and never find out," the doctor had answered, not showing any sympathy for Ondina's suffering. "As she's not telling us anything, we can only rely on tests. Blood work says she has no pneumonia, bronchial or urinary infections, which are the most likely cause for a high fever. So, we're stuck with the mystery."

Filippo also relayed how the doctor had left the room without touching Ondina nor lifting the sheet to visually examine her. "I'm going on vacation tomorrow," he'd concluded. "My colleague will check on her again tomorrow evening. If the fever doesn't go down, we'll have to transfer her to the hospital. We are a rehab clinic. We don't have the structure to deal with this."

No way my sister was going back to that hospital where they'd done everything wrong! I'd hoped her stay in the clinic could be a big step forward, not back.

I dropped the call with Filippo and dialed Air France to change my reservation to the first flight to Italy out of LAX.

Memories of another rushed flight to Italy months before

bubbled up my throat, mixed with bile. A thousand wings fluttered in my stomach, an icy wind rattling my ribcage.

What the hell was happening? And why? I had no answer to any question breaking into my mind.

All I knew was my sister needed me. *What was I thinking, leaving her alone?*

Chapter 52
CLAIRE

San Giovanni Bianco, November 10

I rushed up the stairway of the clinic, two steps at a time, toward my sister's room. I stopped in front of the door to compose myself. Ondina didn't need to see me worried.

I found her alone in the room, the other bed empty. She lay with her left arm out of the covers, two IVs poked into her skin. She looked delirious in her sleep. Her eyes were half open, like the upper eyelids couldn't make it all the way down. She was sweating, her cheeks bright red, her lips bitten through and bleeding. Her body had an angular shape under the bedsheets.

Delicately, I lifted what covered her. She was contracted in a spastic, defensive pose. Her arms were bent at the elbows and her hands turned inwards and cradled at shoulder height. Her legs were clamped together, turned on one side. I was in shock, in disbelief. It was a flashback to the terror experienced when I saw her at the hospital, still in a coma. A whisper escaped my lips. "Oh my! What happened? What did they do to you?"

I believed she couldn't hear me. But she opened her eyes, looked agitated. Her mouth was now open. She was desperately trying to speak but there wasn't any sound. I kissed her cheek and put my right hand on her heart, which was racing.

"Hush, baby, hush. I'm here now. We overcame the other difficulties. We'll deal with this too. But first let me change your diaper. Evidently, they don't even do that in this place."

I turned her on her right side, as I did at home, to refresh and change her. Ondina resisted me, though, trying to keep on her back, complaining with her body in her own peculiar way. Something must have been deeply wrong. I let Ondina return supine and checked her tummy where the baclofen pump was inserted under the skin. "What happened, Sis? It's hurting, isn't it?"

She jumped when I touched the spot, biting her lip more. At that same moment, the door opened and a nurse pushed in a wheelchair with an ancient woman lolling in it.

I greeted the nurse and the lady and asked to call for a doctor. "My sister is clearly distressed. I think the pain is localized on the right side of her stomach. Has anybody noted that? Has this been reported to a doctor?"

"We haven't noticed anything. Only that she's so contracted that washing and dressing her is a pain in the neck."

"Please call a doctor?"

"You can go look for the doctor—I have no time. But let me tell you, there is only one on shift now, a substitute to the doctor who's on vacation, and he's doing his evening rounds. He'll get here later anyhow."

The nurse didn't show much interest in my concern, as if Ondina's sufferance did not have any weight. She helped the lady off her wheelchair, sat her on her bed and left the room. When we were left alone, the lady spoke out.

"They leave her in bed all day without turning her over. They know she can't do it by herself. I would have helped if I could, but I can't stand without support. I can't say anything or they'd throw me out. My daughter begged to get me in here. She needed a rest. It's so hard on her to take care of me at home, working all day at the bank."

I smiled and went over to shake her hand. She looked fragile, with feathery white hair neatly combed behind her ears and pale-veined skin on her arms and forehead, but her mind sounded sharp. She told me that her name was Dora, like her mother's.

I knew going after the only doctor on shift wouldn't do any good, so I focused on making the wait more bearable.

"Nice to meet you, Dora. Do you mind if I read out loud to my sister? She's an avid reader. When I read to her, she relaxes."

"I would love to listen to your story, too," she said.

"Well, this isn't just a story."

I took out of my tote a scrapbook with a magenta cover that I'd brought with me. "Ondina wrote it herself. She has a way with words. I found a bunch of her journals when I packed up her stuff before moving to another apartment. She's a reader and a traveler. But she also wrote diaries and scrapbooks while globetrotting. Her storytelling makes you see with her eyes, transforming you into an invisible bird on her shoulder, watching what she describes."

Ondina's eyes flickered with attention. She turned her head towards me. *Progress?* I vowed to believe it, despite the unsettling feeling of seeing my sister in such a regression. I moved a chair close to her bed, took her hand and started reading.

Laos to Cambodia. August 2002

July 31-August 1. The flight is never ending. From Milan to Rome first, then to Amman, then to Doha and then to Bangkok.

Here, we find a railway station right in front of the airport, and we take a train with air conditioning and comfortable beds—what a luxury for $30!! —that will take us to the border with Laos. It leaves at 9:30 p.m.

We kill time going to an early dinner at a restaurant nearby. From my Tom Yang Kung soup emerges a cockroach. Too bad. It was so tasty.

Jet-lagged, my eyelids were getting heavy but I heard Dora chuckle. Her giggling brought me back. As I read on, I could *hear* Ondina's silvery voice telling the story, sounding as cheerful as it used to. I could *see* Ondina transported in the tuk-tuk. Exploring temples hidden in the forest, negotiating prices at street markets. I was so tired, but I could see every scene, rolling like a movie while I read to my sister and her roommate.

Ondina in my dreamy mind, standing on a street of Vientiane, with a group of six other people, four women and two men, riding in different tuk-tuks on a busy street, brown waters of a river in the background. I read on.

August 2. We got some sleep despite the bumps on the road. Breakfast was delicious, with hot tea bought on the train and cookies brought from Bangkok.

We apply for our Laotian visas in a local office in Vientiane and are surprised by how fast we get them. Then we board a tuk-tuk to the Soradith Guest House to leave our baggage.

I never thought I would join an organized trip, but divorce plays weird tricks on you. I realized that I didn't want to go on a solo adventure. I needed company and reassurance. My travel companions, though, don't seem to be all that interesting, so far. Or maybe it's me. Maybe I am less available than usual.

Oh, well! I'm eager to see the wats, the Buddhist temples.

I imagined Ondina walking inside, admiring statues and paintings, crossing paths with some monks clothed in their traditional orange dress.

The atmosphere here is peaceful more than spiritual. These wats look to me more like museums than active temples. Not bad, though. Tomorrow I think we'll fly to Luang Prebang and see the resplendent roofs of the stupa poking through the greenery of the hills when the plane lands. I heard it is one of those sights one can never forget. Plane tickets cost six-hundred-thousand kips each, but the kip is worth almost nothing, ten thousand against a dollar at the airport exchange rate.

There was a one-thousand kip bill glued to the page there, at the end of the passage. The next was from the following day.

August 3. Luang Prabang is gorgeous and impressive. Zero traffic, lots of temples, deeply green, trailed by two rivers, the Mekong and another one, I forgot its name. Not so easy to distinguish one pagoda from the other. But the peace, silence and colors are priceless.

More than anything, I liked the statue of a reclining Buddha who softly rested his hand between his cheek and the pillow. Sweet! I painted it in my pad in watercolors.

Last night, I had a dream about Giovanni. He was here. There was no group, just him and me, as in the best part of our long relationship. As a travel companion, he gave his best. In some way, it felt good to dream about him this way. I think I'm making peace with how it went. I'm past the mourning and definitely past the anger. Even if anger—I can see it clearly now—is what kept me going most of my life, the fuel that carbureted my delayed decisions. Not very Buddhist, I know, but I'm only an amateur on this new spiritual path.

Traveling must be my own medicine. That put me in the same category of some of my idols, like Bruce Chatwin and Tiziano Terzani, whose travel reportages made me dream of unknown countries and people long before I could meet them in person.

The sound of a door opening and slamming interrupted

the dreamy images. It brought me back to the grim setting of Ondina's room. The doctor had arrived, finally, followed by a male nurse. I jumped to my feet.

"I understand you are Ms. Strada's sister and that you want to speak to me." He was tall, clean-shaved, with pale skin. He was young but looked at me from above his eye-glasses, worn halfway on the bridge of his nose like old people did. He held himself straight, opening his chest as he believed it to be handsome, but he looked oddly ugly. Something in his posture made me want to back away from him, and I had to resist the impulse when he moved toward Ondina's bed.

"My sister is in pain. I believe the cause is in her stomach, but I don't think she has been checked for that."

"Let's see."

The nurse pulled the bedsheets down and the doctor approached, still not touching her. He pointed to the spot where the baclofen pump was inserted with the penlight he took from the chest pocket of his white coat.

"What is that?"

"A pump," the nurse informed him. "It's listed on her chart. It releases the medicine to alleviate spasticity, but judging from how rigid she has become, it might have stopped working."

How could he not know any of that? He was a substitute, sure, but shouldn't he be informed of the condition of the patients left in his care?

The doctor pushed on that spot with his gloved hand, and Ondina jumped as if electrically shocked, biting down hard on her lip. His lack of care matched his disinformation and it was shocking.

"Or it might have infected the tissue around it," the doctor guessed, speaking to the nurse, not to me. "It could also be appendicitis. Or liver stones. I see here on her chart that she's been administered medicines that have liver stones listed as a side effect."

"What medicine?" I interrupted.

The doctor handed me the chart, clearly bothered by my request.

"This prescription wasn't in her daily chart when she entered this clinic," I said after scanning the chart. "I don't know who prescribed it or why, without checking with my sister's physician. But now we have a problem and need to deal with it. Are you going to prescribe an ultrasound of her abdomen?"

"Good idea, *signora*. I can schedule it for tomorrow morning. When we see the results, we'll know more of what's going on with this patient."

This patient.

The doctor turned to the nurse while they hurried out of the room and spoke in low tones. Not low enough, though. "I wish they wouldn't take in vegetatives. Too many problems with them."

I gazed at Dora in disbelief. She'd heard it, too. Not only he was wrong calling Ondina 'vegetative,' since she'd entered the clinic in an aware state and able to perform tasks a vegetative patient couldn't do, but he also acted rude and unprofessional, uncaring as I never expected a doctor to be.

"*Good idea, signora?*" I imitated. "I thought they were supposed to have doctors here. I thought it was *their* duty to prescribe the right tests to determine why patients are in pain. They let my sister suffer, prescribed medicines for conditions she didn't have."

"Mah!" sighed Dora. "It used to be different. A mission. Now it's just a job like any other. I wonder why they chose medical school."

Chapter 53
CLAIRE

Sorisole, November 11

The fog was thick and wet in the morning. Impossible to see much of the Mura but I still ran the path around them, clad in warm sweatpants and a heavy hoodie. My breath, a puff of white smoke in the cold air. My phone rang in my jacket pocket. I stopped to answer, panting. It wasn't a call that I wanted.

"I will be there in less than an hour," I murmured at the end. I didn't have time to change clothes or shower, just ran back to the car and drove to Milan at high speed.

I arrived at the hospital in record time. My mother had been admitted to room 233. The door of the room swung open and Wilma came out. Her nose was red, she was sobbing.

"Wilma, what happened?"

"I didn't want to call you but Doctor said I should... Mama no recognize me... She didn't want to wake up. I was scared... Called the ambulance."

"Is she awake now?"

"Awake but no talk to me... No look."

"Oh! Let me go in and see. You go get some water. Some coffee and breakfast, okay? Here." I gave her twenty euros. The hallway filled with her weeping as she walked away.

Inside the room, Mom was sitting in her wheelchair staring out of the window. Absent, not really looking at anything. I approached her slowly and sat on the bed. "Mom?"

No answer.

I took her hand in mine. Her fingers were boney, deformed by arthritis. I felt perplexed that I'd never noticed this before. I used to admire those hands. The oval nails perfectly filed and painted with pearly beige polish. 'Red is so tacky, not for a lady's hand,' she used to say, a covert reference to Katarina's bold color preference.

Ondina had taken after Mom, had the same lovely, elongated hand shape with the slim palm, soft skin and lean fingers. I might have gone the same route, but hours of carpentry, woodcutting and martial arts to make my fingers strong as weapons had changed their genetic imprint. I had my own breed of hands, wide and capable, not even square with short pulpy fingers like our father's. They've served me well but have never been as charming as Ondina's or the one that I held now.

"Mom?" I tried again but she didn't turn or give any sign of acknowledgment. I let silence fill the space between us. I didn't want to prod her but I worried about my sister too. I wasn't sure how I could handle two people who could no longer talk.

"Mom, I have to go to Ondina now but I'll come back. I'll talk to the doctors and see if you can go home, see what they think. Don't worry, Mom. You're going to be okay."

Mom didn't seem to register my words, but when I rose from the bed and started for the door, I heard her voice. "I don't want to go home with that witch."

Shocked, I turned around and knelt close to her chair. "Wilma? Why, Mom? What happened?"

"She was out partying with her men last night. I woke up alone in the house. I called and called, but no answer. I had to go to the bathroom, so I got up by myself. I almost made it to the toilet leaning on the walls and moving slow. But then I bumped into something and fell. I must have hit my head on the bathtub." Her voice croaked, turned to a whine. "I woke up in a puddle of my own piss, and she still wasn't there, that *strega*!"

We heard the door opening and Wilma came in, taking in the scene. "She talks?"

"She did talk. Now she's tired. I need to go. Ondina isn't doing good, and I have an appointment with the doctor to look at her test results. I'll be back this evening."

I turned toward my mother. "Okay, Mom? I'll be back soon." But Mother had already retreated into her silence, staring back at the gray sky out the window. When I kissed her cheek, she grasped my hand and gave it a squeeze. I squeezed hers back.

"I'll talk to the doctor," I addressed Wilma this time. "If Mom can't be discharged by tonight, I'll stay with her. So, you go home and rest, Wilma. She'll be alright waiting for me. Come back tomorrow morning when I'll have to go back to Ondina's clinic.

I drove back through pouring rain. The road had become slippery and dangerous. I was speeding, way above the limit, blasting my iPod, drumming my fingers on the wheel to the notes of "Black" by Pearl Jam. I was upset and confused. My world had turned black.

The doctor had told me that my mother was going downhill fast, no matter if the caregiver was a witch. I knew my mother wouldn't have made all that up. But even if Wilma's red nose wasn't from crying, but from drinking the night before, Wilma wasn't the cause of my mother's deterioration.

Mom scored very low on her cognitive test and her neurological response was delayed, often missing. Parkinson's disease is an ugly beast. "It won't be long," the doctor's verdict was. "She's winding down and will extinguish like a wax candle."

It had only been days since the last time she'd told me she was ready. "By Christmas..." And now, it was happening. All the times I'd scolded her for being so pessimistic, so unwilling to fight. "You're making things worse, Mom, always projecting negative thoughts," I'd told her whenever she turned the conversation to her 'imminent' funeral.

We were so opposite, my mother and I. Our physical resemblance deceiving. You couldn't find two temperaments further apart. I liked bright red, she, powder blue. I saw rainbows after a storm. She saw floods, dams unable to contain the swollen rivers, houses washed away by the muddy avalanche. I was excited by the unknown; she, terrified. And when I told her I believed in the old saying that when there's a will there's a way, she scorned at me, bitterly. "You always thought you were Wonder Woman."

Ondina always resented our mom's pessimism more than I did. It really enraged her. I tried to feel compassion—it had to be hard to live in fear, seeing black on the horizon spreading like a vampire's cape. But there was a time when Mom was different. She was a brave woman in many ways, raising two girls as a single parent by choice in Catholic Italy in the sixties. She went out and found a job to support us, to give us more than the basics that child support from our father could provide.

Father was bread and tap water, Mom, Perrier and *petit fromage de chèvre au poivre*. Father was vanilla pudding for dessert, Mom, a *Saint Honoré* cake with tiny beignets filled with chocolate and whipped cream.

She may have been strict in terms of buying clothes and toys or material things, but she had a longing for traveling and exposed us to far-flung countries and cultures when we were young. For that, I'll always be grateful.

She felt we should know what went on at the Folies Bergère in Paris, that we should admire the paintings of Botero at the Prado in Madrid, that this would help us more than ballet classes and art lessons. And it did!

Our adventures with Mom skyrocketed our imagination and created a new sense of wonder, a gift I could never thank her enough for. Other kids lived on a planet defined by fancy new cars and big-screen televisions. We lived surrounded by tales of Spanish Islands where gorgeous women with red, luscious lips would dance flamenco and tango into the wee hours of the night, smiling out at us seductively from the travel brochures that Mom collected. We tasted pâté de foie gras when we were only seven and ten. Raw oysters, *ugh,* slid into our mouths directly from their shells, wrapped in newspaper and bought at a cart parked on the Croisette in Cannes, France.

Who cared if she made me wear my sister's hand-me-downs and we had to endure the same shoes every year on our growing feet? She made us wait, Christmas to Christmas, before finding a replacement pair under the sad fake tree she bought at Metro Wholesale with the membership card lent by her sister, our aunt, who owned a bait & tackle shop. But it didn't matter. She gave us so much more than clothes and shoes.

Mom loved us, as long as she could shape us. She wanted us to have not only her long legs and noticeable cleavage, which, luckily, we both inherited, but also her view of the world. She wanted us to be fascinated by ancient languages like Greek, appreciate exotic culinary delicacies without indulging in too much food. "You'll get fat like your father." She was flattered by the attention we started getting growing up as long as we didn't fall for any man—an unforgivable sin, almost worse than being fat.

She was in love with us until we were impossible to control. I suspect that was how it was with anybody and anything. Losing control made her insecure, disoriented. Now, it was killing her. When we started claiming our own opinions, our right to decide on our own, the honeymoon was over.

She resented our artistic inclinations and tried to push us toward what looked to her like a more solid future. "A singer and a writer? How about making a decent living instead? How about law school or psychology? How about a teaching career?"

I kept scribbling on every kind of paper I could find. Supermarket receipts, ice cream napkins, toilet paper. Fairy tales, little notes, dialogues between my imaginary friends. Words came to me, springing in my mind like a mountain creek, a waterfall in Yosemite Park. I'd sit on top of a tree with pen and paper, look at the clouds and the birds, and write. I'd touch the sky with my little finger, creating worlds different from the one below me, down there on Earth.

Ondina loved to write as well, but she was more introspective. She liked to search her soul and feelings in poems that would take up a new life when her fingers switched to her guitar. She sang her emotions with a nightingale voice.

It was painful not having my mother's support but I didn't need her to stand on my own. I left home at sixteen. Ondina stayed. In the same house with Mom until she turned twenty-three, depending on mother's approval, letting her influence her choices. She put her foot down only to pursue her singing, but soon she gave it up to use her talent for writing in advertising, following Mom's advice.

While I rebelled full force, Ondina was still on the merry-go-round with Mother. She never got to vent and rant, all of that swallowed. When Mom got sick and I was already gone to my new life in the U.S., Ondina had to care for her, igniting a smoldering battle of tempers and wills.

The view outside the car window called me back to the suburbs of Milan blended in with the villages of the *bassa bergamasca*, one exit of the highway after another. Agrate, Pioltello, Trezzo d'Adda, Dalmine, Capriate. They came and went in gray procession.

I ached for the blue California sky, pristine even in winter, the colorful buildings of Los Feliz, East Los Angeles, Highland Park, Silverlake, Frogtown. Bright-painted houses, walls adorned with murals and tags.

Here, the ugly towns looked identical, made out of the same shapes like steel-colored sandcastles, cut in halves by the railway line and its parallel highway. The busy route that Ondina refused to drive every day to go to work: "I'd rather take the train, have time to read and write instead of spending two hours a day fighting traffic and getting cranky at the wheel."

I could see her point.

Truth to be told, she hated to drive. Her driving license must have been delivered by magic, bestowed from the clouds. She never told a soul she was studying for her license, long after kids usually do that. One day, she came back home to Giovanni, showing off a plastic card with her picture, and triumphantly announced, "I passed!"

She took the wheel once, the day after, on the wings of enthusiasm. She went half a mile in a straight line on an alternated-license-plate-Sunday with half the traffic on city streets. She switched gear only once and sweated gallons, then floored the brake pedal. "I drove enough." And that was it for the next fifteen years.

Loud music and family memories took over my mind, carrying me away from the uncomfortable reality I had to deal with. I was a master at living in the present, leading my life as if there was no tomorrow. Yesterday is history, tomorrow we don't know, today is a present, yada, yada, yada. But what a grim present I was gifted today! Fifty shades of gray and beyond. Beyond, no rainbow in sight. Only black, the dull black waters of... nothingness?

I tried to paw my way from under those heavy clouds. By instinct, like a blind animal, I felt the cliff nearby. If I allowed myself to be frightened by what would be the future of my vanishing family, I'd fall into that nothingness. Not a bright present full of unexpected and exciting surprises. A dull black sea populated by monstrous creatures that would dine on my fear.

I had to rise up, ride this wave on its crest, all the way to shore. All the way to safety.

I remembered the day Xavier and I were surfing and saw the fin of a great white, just a few waves behind. The tension on Xavier's face, suddenly twisting his head and looking at me for directions, copying my every move in silent agreement. No screaming, no fear. Only speed and focus. Get to the beach fast, get to safety. The shark followed us for another fifty feet, his long and scary shadow barely visible under the murky water. Suddenly, its fin popped up. A change of direction, probably after realizing we weren't the seals he expected to lunch on.

I landed from my daydream just in time to avoid a big semi-trailer that almost cut me off. I was traveling at one hundred miles an hour. It suddenly hit me, together with the rush of adrenaline. The way I'd always felt, until now. Always been uncomfortable dwelling in the past, as much as I didn't like obsessing about the future. My present was the life I created for myself, as snug as a neoprene wetsuit. I didn't need to escape it, projecting back or forth. Ondina was the historian, the keeper of the winter count, as Xavier called it, the Lakota pictorial calendars histories painted on buffalo hides. Ondina filled piles of scrapbooks with our family history.

I didn't feel the need to photograph or write to remember. If I wanted to remember, I remembered. Mostly, I preferred to remove memories to make space for imagination. I longed for a clear mind, almost as unachievable as a blank canvas but I never stopped trying. I could always throw the fishnet in the memory archives when I'd need to recover the important things. They'd still be there. My mind had to be free to focus on the present, the hours of the day, the minutes in that hour.

But in this moment, I admitted with surprise, I drove too fast to avoid the present, my mind gloomy as the jaundiced industrial towns.

"Hurt," by Johnny Cash, came up on the playlist blasting from the car speakers and I sang along, in tears. I was still singing when I swerved into the driveway leading into the parking lot of the clinic. Neurological Rehabilitation Center, the sign read. My singing stopped at once.

In my sister's case, this clinic had become her very own Dante's *girone dell'Inferno*. A spiral of horrors with smooth, slippery walls that proved impossible to climb. I'd come to that epiphany the night before, leaving the clinic. No matter what the ultrasounds will show, Ondina was not up to try again. She was exhausted, tired of all those ups and downs. Tired of being trapped, locked-in. She didn't want to suffer any longer.

I made myself get out of the car, to enter the revolving door. "Abandon all hope, ye who enter here!" Dante reminded me.

But I was here, regardless, dragging myself toward a soupcon of hope beyond hope. Still reluctant to admit my denial.

Chapter 54
CLAIRE

San Giovanni Bianco, November 11

My appointment was at 3 p.m. The doctor's desk was covered in charts and compact discs of test results. My sister's destiny in a flash drive. The room was small and bare, furnished with cheap metal chairs and a desk lamp that didn't work well. The light was faint and dingy despite it being afternoon. The small window panes thick with dirt.

The doctor looked at the papers. His hands moved fast and nervously. His eyes kept low, focused on the records. "Your suspicions proved right, Ms. Strada. Your sister has a gall-bladder full of stones. Some are in her liver too."

"And that is the explanation for her high fevers, right?" I managed my question in a polite tone, despite my anger.

"Correct."

"What's next, then?"

The doctor lifted his eyes up to meet mine, pursing his lips. He looked almost surprised by my question. "I'm afraid there is not much left that we can do here. We need to move her to the Bergamo hospital. She needs surgery. Her gallbladder has to be removed. Her liver..." He paused for a second, like he was thinking of something else, distracted from the routine task of informing me. "They can try to dissolve the bigger stones with ultrasound, see how she responds to medications. In her condition though, nothing can be assured. Before they can consider surgery, the fever needs to go down. She's not responding to antibiotics. I switched to a more specific drug this morning after seeing the test results, but for the moment, her fever is still high."

He started gathering the results to put them back into a folder. "I guess they'll take care of that in the hospital. I already called to arrange transportation. So, if you sign this authorization..." He started pushing a document toward me. "The ambulance will come to pick her up tomorrow morning."

I glared at him but he tried to avoid my eye contact. I struggled to keep from shouting. "So, you're washing your hands of her?"

"I've tried my best."

My best! Fucking bastard. He hadn't even lifted the sheet to check on her swollen belly! Afraid to touch my sister, as if she might infect him with her disability. I cursed myself for believing this place was a good choice, for being so naive. All this place did was to obliterate her newly found will to fight, while I wasn't here to shield her.

I pushed the unsigned paper back to him. "I don't think so, doctor. The only kind of transportation I'll arrange is to take my sister home. Away from the likes of you and your hospitals."

He squirmed in his chair, a metallic squeak underlining his disapproval. His domed white forehead turning red with anger. "You don't know what you're talking about. The director would never authorize that. That's... It's... Reckless!"

"Reckless would be leaving her another minute in any

hospital, especially your *model* clinic." My voice sounded uncannily low. When I get mad, I don't yell. I hiss. I don't get red faced.

I got up from my chair. This place was Dante's hell.

"No more surgeries," I sibilated at his indignant face. "No more hospitals. She's coming home with me. And regarding your boss's authorization, I have no doubts he'll gladly sign after I tell him about the complaint I can file for the way my sister was treated."

I turned and started for the door. "Have a wonderful evening, doctor," I said, razor blades in my tone.

Chapter 55
CLAIRE

Sorisole, November 11

I called Filippo from the parking lot. I explained what happened and asked him the huge favor of going to visit my mom at the hospital in Milan, giving me a few hours to regroup. I wasn't in a good mental state and didn't trust my driving in those conditions. He'd met Mom before, with Ondina. I was convinced she'd accept his company, better than waiting for me alone since I'd told Wilma to pack her bags and leave, not to return to the hospital. Her severance pay was already on its way. Mom didn't want to see her anymore.

The deserted house was humid. Gloomy just like the weather. I'd tried to go straight to bed to catch some rest but sleep eluded me, dark thoughts swirling inside my restless mind like chocolate syrup on ice cream.

I stood in front of the dinner table where I'd spread a bunch of family pictures, taken out of albums my sister had religiously catalogued. Black and white prints and color Polaroids of when we were small, and Mom was still gorgeous, her elegant willowy figure towering over us. Portraits of us at different ages. Shots of places we'd visited with her, Pisa, Paris, Salzburg. One showed the three of us standing with Mom's arms around our shoulders. We were smiling wide with the future laid at our feet. The present warmed with each other's presence. Carefree times.

My hand moved to cover Ondina and Mom, to focus only on myself. Trying to imagine a world without them, where I would truly be alone. Would I still come back here? Or would I avoid all thoughts of Italy, remembering these hellhole last months I spent in my home country? A still life of frozen emotions instead of the land of sun and green meadows, an espresso and croissant for breakfast standing at the counter with the barista calling you by your first name, warm Mediterranean Sea of the Tuscany coast and pizza still done right.

Would I ever feel whole, legitimate, in a world without them, where I was the last one of my family, the last of the Mohicans?

Would I still enjoy being alive?

Would I make any sense?

Fuck memories! I brushed the pictures off the table, let them fall on the Kilim rug where Drago slumbered. At least I had him.

I breathed in deeply, counted to four while exhaling. I had to stop this horseshit. Stop this useless wondering and take action.

I knew what had to be done. I might have known before, but it was too painful to acknowledge. But here it was, that awkward moment when the naked, unpleasant truth of it roared at me like a giant wave. Ripping me out of my denial, my cotton-padded limbo. Slamming me onto the hard, wet sand.

I pumped myself with resolution.

Peel it off. Not just your wetsuit. Peel your skin. Tear your flesh, shed your blood if you have to.

I knew nobody else would or could do that for her. I knew nobody'd help me do it. And I wouldn't let them anyhow.

I would act alone. I wasn't afraid.

"Prepare for battle," I told myself, letting the words escape my mouth, their sound echoing through the thick walls. "Transform yourself into Nails."

Chapter 56
CLAIRE

Milano, November 11

When I entered her hospital room at 8 p.m., Mom lay in her narrow bed, breathing loud as a buffalo. Buffaloes breathe that way when the herd moves fast to take the calves away from a place that smells of danger. I once heard them when I found myself surrounded while cruising a back road in Custer State Park, in South Dakota.

Filippo held her hand. Fingers laced together, sitting on the side of the bed and praying with a *mala*, the Buddhist rosary. I thanked him and let him go. It was going to be a long night. Most likely, my mother's last. I knew she'd chosen to die in the hospital, away from 'that witch'—I didn't need to check the bottle of sleeping pills in her drawer to know that. Maybe she'd taken some already.

I talked softly. I assured her she'd see Ondina soon, both of them free and healthy again. She didn't talk but opened her eyes briefly, gifted me with a tender smile. And she squeezed my hand. It was as if I'd given her permission, as if she'd waited for me.

She was dead by early morning, her limp hand still in mine. So small in her hospital bed. So lifeless. I bent over the bed to kiss her cold lips. A whiff of the *Miss Dior* perfume. I hadn't seen the bottle anywhere in this room, but I smelled it on her. She'd wear it when she went out in the evening with one of her admirers. Clad in a soft black otter fur and smelling heavenly. In my four-year-old mind, that was the smell of mystery and adventure. I couldn't wait to be an adult to go out with mysterious men, wrapped in soft layers of silk and wool, surrounded by a subtle perfumed cloud.

I was crushed, despite knowing she wanted to die for a long time. *No more pain*, I kept repeating, but the knot in my throat kept tightening as I signed medical papers in the administrative office. When I got back to Mom's room, the funeral home staff was already there to show me pictures of different kinds of caskets. I signed the papers and gave them back to the undertaker.

When they left, I took hold of my mother's hand again. Cold, but not rigid yet. "Finally, we can talk about your funeral, Mom. Your favorite topic for these last ten years." My attempt at humor felt cynical without her scorn in return. But I couldn't endure just staying there with the pain—my sister was right.

I knew Mom's will from memory. She wrote it years earlier and made sure to give copies to both daughters. She wanted to be cremated, her ashes spread on common ground: "Don't keep any and don't have a public ceremony. I was alone in life, so I'll stay alone in death."

She was precise to the last detail: "Don't let the jackals fool you, those who will want to make money off your sorrow. No expensive casket. No crimson velvet padding. No embalming since I will rot anyway. The dead don't care for velvet. I won't need a zinc casket to feel your love. Choose the cheapest. It will burn, so who cares?"

So, yes, they could have her corpse, burn it in the cheapest casket, as she wished.

I drove back to San Giovanni Bianco and Ondina. I felt drunk without having touched a drop of alcohol. Cotton balls floating into my head, the sounds of traffic muffled despite the window being open.

I had to focus, stay calm. Assess the situation, plan a single action, commit entirely. That was what I had learned made all the difference before pulling the trigger at the shooting range while working on Nails' character. Battles are won one maneuver at a time.

But my mind was stuck in a loop—my mother dead in that hospital bed. Her mouth slack, no matter how many times I tried to close it. The mortician suggested putting the Bible under her chin to stop her jaw from falling open. Deep trenches dug a spider web of wrinkles at the corners of her mouth and eyes. Her skin no longer stretched and smooth on her sleek swimmer muscles, all gone slack with Parkinson's.

The most beautiful among us are still reduced to a sack of bones draped in loose flesh, pasty yellow pallor and stiff limbs. Rigor mortis freezing our last expression, surprise or relief, as the last breath escapes our mouths. Life is over, and if there was suffering, peace is finally back. Then comes the time for the last goodbyes of those who'll remain for a while longer. But there was only me there when she went. And I was grateful for it. Ondina had been spared. She didn't need more sorrow.

Our mother's life was over, hopefully now in peace. Peace

wasn't a wish I'd be granted for a long while, I felt certain of that.

I was the one who'd have to stay. Me, the one who'd always been the first to leave.

Like I needed another fucking life lesson.

Chapter 57
CLAIRE

Sorisole, November 12

Surrounded by the darkness of my grief and of the moonless night, I was glued to my laptop, surfing the web for 'painless methods to commit suicide.'

I hadn't told my sister that our mother died when I visited her in the afternoon at the clinic. I hadn't told her I was researching methods to end one's life.

"Are you looking for a painless method to end your life? A quick way to commit suicide and/or a clean way to die? If so, you have come to the right place! Methods like slitting wrists, cutting throat, poisons, suffocation, jumping off a cliff or tall building are not painless methods of suicide. Nor is inhaling carbon monoxide. Why? Because the real pain comes after death, being burnt eternally in hell."

Holy shit! I really didn't need all this. I was quick to refine my search. Different key words led to more results. Information implied between lines since nobody was willing to give out a plain recipe, not risking responsibility. Odd. One could find every kind of detailed instruction on how to build a homemade bomb, a device that can kill thousands used by terrorists, but it was hard to dig out anything on how to take your own life, or a loved one's who wanted to die, not harming anybody else.

If you're good at surfing the web, you could get it, though. And I was a good surfer, of both waves and the web. Soon, I realized I'd best focus on morphine. How much was needed for my sister's bodyweight? Inject it in a vein or administer it under the tongue? What if Ondina couldn't swallow, now that she was one hundred and eighty degrees back into regression?

I researched silently, grateful for technology. At least, I didn't have to stand in line at some library and ask for 'everything you have about painless ways to end one's life?' Or, 'is it better to use Nembutal or another barbiturate first to avoid feeling the stomach burn?'

I remembered a day in Los Angeles when I had to put down Conan, a ragged stray dog that I'd named after picking him up from the street where he was bleeding to death, a bunch of broken bones probably caused by dragging him tied to the bumper of a running car. The vet said there was no way Conan could heal from the multiple fractures human cruelty had caused.

When they gave him the final shot, they told me his effort to get up and run was only muscle spasm, but nobody could convince me that the dog didn't feel anything. An acrid smell emanated from his body as I held him in my arms. Animals can't talk, that's what vets rely on to convince owners to put an end to their suffering. But *painless death*? The desperate look in that sweet dog's eyes was sculpted in my mind. I didn't want Ondina looking at me that way, to feel that way.

I found the Hospice Patients Association webpage.

"One method of hastening death used by physicians, nurses and family members is to administer overly high dosages of narcotics, sedatives or antidepressants when the patient has no need for them. Giving high doses of narcotics when the patient is not in pain or does not have a symptom requiring the use of that narcotic is inappropriate and may cause death. The most serious adverse effect of giving inappropriately high doses of narcotics, sedatives and antidepressants is 'respiratory depression.' Respiratory depression can be so severe that breathing stops altogether resulting in death. Families need to ask questions and know exactly why medications are given and to be especially aware of rationales for increasing a dose. Morphine is commonly given for severe pain in terminal illnesses, especially from cancer pain. In the case of severe pain, extremely high doses of morphine or other narcotics may be necessary to control that pain."

Reverse information, but also something else in between the lines: "A patient's family is their only advocate if the patients cannot longer speak for themselves."

Apparently, there were physicians and nurses who believed in administering high doses when the patient was not aware. I wished I could find one of those rare physicians in my Catholic country, but I didn't have time to go on that uncertain hunt. The wait was over. Ondina couldn't wait any longer, I felt it in my skin. The stagnant, swampy waters of forced nonaction were finally retreating. A swell was mounting, powerful like the roaring waves of the Pacific Ocean, rescuing my mind to clarity.

"The world was divided between hunters and growers," Ondina, historian-in-the- making, once explained to me when we were girls, pretending we were the last of a lost civilization. "Our world will divide into dreamers and hunters. Let's pretend that I was the dreamer, staying home and writing the futures that the spirits whispered in my vision quests. You were the hunter, going out to fight the dragons to get our dinner."

I had been both Dreamer and Stalker. Peaceful like a monk or savage like a warrior, depending. My new hunting season had just started. I would go out, chase and trap what I was after.

Here I go, I mentally told my sister, *out to get you your last supper. Here I go, and the dragons will let me pass. Because I'm one of them.*

Chapter 58
CLAIRE

Milan, November 14

The evening fog circled trees and benches, hiding them from sight. I was back in Milan. I accompanied my mother on her last trip to the Lambrate Cemetery, where her body was cremated in the afternoon, and I found myself hoping her spirit would rise from her ashes, transformed and rejuvenated by the fire like the Phoenix.

But now I walked toward Parco Sempione, after driving across the city. I needed to score on the black market. You don't buy morphine at the grocery. *A pound of ham and three ounces of morphine, thank you very much.* I walked along the gravel path wrapped in mist, half an hour before the gates would be locked for the night. Despite the locks, I knew there were still ways to access the grounds for the creepy creatures who take over after dark.

My contact had given me an appointment at a time when many people were still around, crossing the park on their way home from work. But when I arrived at the spot, a warped wooden bench with chipped hunter green paint, nobody was there yet.

I walked to the nearby trash bin to discard a tissue—the dampness made me sneeze—and checked the time on my phone. I raised the lapels of my jacket to protect my neck. I could smell rain in the air. A storm on its way.

I scanned the grounds. Woman with a dog. Bearded man walking in the opposite direction. Kids, three. Two on skateboards. Dogs, farther away. Barking, not in sight. Three girls and two boys. Chatting, loudly. Grouping around another bench. Guy in his forties, approaching. Balding, lanky. Him.

I started back toward the designated bench. We arrived at the same moment and stopped in front of each other. The man extended his hand to shake mine, adjusting his glasses. "Chiara? It's been so long. Nobody ever saw you after high school."

"I know. My kid, and trying to make a living. Not much time for high school reunions." We sat on the wet bench. "How have you been, Alfonso?"

"Not that good. I quit medical school during the third year. I'm sure Maurizio told you when he gave you my number. My father died the same year my mother got sick. The student life couldn't go on. I worked odd jobs. But in the end, I went back to what I was good at in high school."

"Getting stoned and smuggling?" It just came out of my mouth, before I realized how hurtful that could be. Alfonso looked at me sideways, milky eyes behind the glasses. Hunched shoulders, chest hollow under the heavy waterproof coat that he had on. "I didn't mean to offend you. I'm sorry."

"It's alright." A flick of his hand in the air to wave away my need for an apology. "It's the truth. That's what I do. A stash of cash for a stash of drugs, that's my specialty," he sighed. "I hardly sell to kids, though. My clients are professionals, adults with their full ability to choose. Mostly cocaine, some hash. It helps to round my earnings. I have a small business online. I sell computer parts for fixers. People who dare to repair their own electronics."

"Sounds good."

"It is. But not enough. I can't live off it yet."

Hence, the drugs. Which was the reason I was freezing my ass on a bench. Talking to a guy I never liked. He was listless already at sixteen, go figure. But I'd have more than kissed a toad for my sister.

"So, were you able to score it?"

"Sure did. But this isn't my usual gig. It's going to cost you a chunk. I needed to pay people who needed to pay people on the inside to get your stuff."

"Name your price. I need it fast."

"I have it. Don't worry. I won't ask you why. But, please, make sure that what you told me is what you need. You said that you wanted both, injectable and oral, correct?"

"Both. How much?"

Alfonso calculated in his mind and told me it was two grand, what I'd expected. I checked around to be sure no one was watching, then grabbed the thick envelope of cash I held under my jacket, slid it into Alfonso's.

"Okay, Chiara. Now, let's stand up and hug."

The unspoken code of street dealing.

I raised my arms to reluctantly hug Alfonso, who had a few inches above my height. His quick hand went under my jacket to plant a small envelope in the back of my belt, hidden by the coat. The pressure of the package on the small of my back felt warm and reassuring.

I walked away from him fast, through this park I used to love when Alessandro was four years old and we'd come every day after preschool to play in the gardens of the Sforza Castle. We pretended to be armored warriors of the Middle Age, defending our fort against the descendants of the Barbarians.

Guess the Barbarians won after we left.

I made it out just before the security guard locked the gates. *As if those locks could resist the Barbarians!*

Chapter 59
CLAIRE

San Giovanni Bianco, November 15

The ambulance stood by in the parking lot of the clinic. The EMs were up in her room putting my sister on the stretcher. A task that apparently required privacy since they asked me to wait downstairs. I didn't object; the sooner we'd get out of there, the better.

The doctor tailed me out to the parking lot, mumbling his litany. "You don't know what you're getting yourself into. Please, be reasonable. You won't be able to manage. You will exhaust yourself!"

I didn't care to answer his objections. He didn't deserve even a curt comment. I opened my van's door, sat at the wheel and started the engine. Readied myself to follow the ambulance. The doctor faded away.

About an hour later, the church bell ringing noon, Ondina was home. In her own bed, in her room with the faint winter light dancing on the apricot walls.

She was awake but still looked absent. Far away from

where her body lay. I put a hand on her forehead. It was sizzling. I placed a small damp towel on her brow, hoped it might give her some relief. Her limbs were contracted. Her fingers clamped into fists. I knew in my bones there was no return from this last ailment. She'd already endured too much.

"Rest, my love. I promise I will let you go. I will set you free."

Ondina turned her head towards my whispering, tears filled her eyes. For the first time since I came back from the States, she looked into my eyes. I had to keep that little window of attention open, tell her what I longed to say.

"I was so presumptuous, Sis. I believed I could save you. My mistake, I guess, was not remembering whether anybody can ever save anybody else. Can anybody be so foolish and arrogant to think that they know best?"

Her eyes glistened. She was alert, listening.

"I was layered with so much grief and guilt, I couldn't accept reality. I believed we could still escape it, make it *our* reality. The doctors said one in a thousand. I wanted us to be the miracle, as if believing it enough could make it happen. Remember, Sis, when we were little? Our magic trick box? It'd take us hours to get that card deck to open at the right spot, to get that paper dove out of the hat, but we did it!

"I wanted to yell: we did it. Against the stormy skies, we did it! Me and you, my beautiful sister that fussy gods dared to try turning into a bougainvillea plant. We did it! We shook off the spell of the gods, jerked it with a shake of our salsa-dancing hips, beating the maracas to the punch of our throbbing hearts. What kind of god could ever plan such destiny for a human being who never hurt a soul?

"But the gods fucked us over. I couldn't save you. And the thing I curse myself for is not the failure, since we were against such powerful foes. It's the forgetfulness. I can't forgive myself for betraying your confidence. The pact we sealed: don't let me live if anything really bad happens... I was blind with love and I was so scared of losing you. I forgot or chose not to remember. I'm not sure. I was so crazy, trying to convince you that *this* wasn't bad enough, that we could still succeed. You should have slapped me across the face. I know you'd have if your brain still commanded your hands. I was selfish."

Ondina drank in my words, rarely blinking. An array of emotions moved across her face, her lips sometimes quivering like she wished to interrupt my monologue with her own words. I paused to give her space for words of her own but nothing came from her. Instead, she moved her eyes up and down my face. As if I *owed* her more.

It'd taken a lot of effort to be so naked, so... truthful? Honest? To say those things that had churned inside my mind for days but that I didn't want to spell out loud. I couldn't stop now.

"I put you through misery and pain with senseless surgeries and exercises that could kill a horse. I closed my eyes when you were speaking without words. It was so clear. You wrapped yourself inside, cradling your fists on your chest and tightening your legs together, turning your head to the back and the left, to the spot where true life ended and hell began. Refusing to answer my calls, my invitations to fight. Couldn't be clearer, had I only had the humbleness to listen."

My throat chocked my voice, giving it a raspy tone. Tears I'd pushed away made their way back to my eyes.

"I've been a fool. Worse, an abuser, too. I know it wasn't just the hospitals, the nurses and doctors. But me. I don't ask your forgiveness. I had my lesson and I should treasure it. I learned that love counts more than courage sometimes. And if love wasn't enough to heal you, I can still entertain the possibility that it warmed you up. Blowing on your cold, still limbs in the winter nights. Holding your hand in your dreams, where you'd run and jump and feel the moist sand under your bare, perfectly working feet."

I sighed. I hadn't seen her so intent and aware since 2007. It was heartbreaking and beautiful at the same time.

"I love you, Sis. My love couldn't heal you, and now I'm late, I know. I thought I'd never be, fixated on punctuality like an Amtrak train. But here I am, finally ready to honor our pact. I love you so much I'm ready to let you go. Don't worry about a thing. I will…"

It was so hard to say it.

"I will make you go. With a little push to prompt your launch. With a backpack full of sweet Mary Jane. I went searching for Sugar Man in Milan, baby. I can make you go, sticking your fingers in a jar of jam."

The notes of "Just Breathe" by Pearl Jam started playing in my mind, and I mindlessly hummed the lyrics. I started singing, trying hard to believe that every life must end.

At the sound of my singing, Ondina switched to resting mode. She turned her face away from mine and closed her eyes, as if she agreed with the lyrics. She retreated into her own world where light came only in bursts, and darkness wrapped the rest of the day.

Coming clean had wiped away all my resolve. I let my head slowly fall on my sister's chest and closed my eyes, listening to her uneven heartbeat.

Chapter 60
ONDINA

Sorisole, November 15

She admitted it! She knew it all along. My brave little sister, the most decisive and resolute person I ever met, who had become someone else entirely: a woman who preferred irrational hope to science. Who let love blind her and her emotions rule.

We're not that, Chiara. Remember? We were warriors!

I had hoped so much that you'd come to your senses. To listen to ME. Not to all those stupid doctors who don't have the guts.

But why are we talking about this now? What did you say that we were going to do?

No. Not us. You. You said you were going to?

Aarrrgh! I hate this fog inside my mind. I can never follow a rational line of thought for more than a couple of minutes. Then everything gets blurred and confused, and I don't remember what was so urgent a second ago.

It's the fever, they say. Yeah, right! Like in other moments

I can think straight.

This is what drives me crazy. And I pray it will end soon. This dullness. Losing my mind is a torture I can no longer bear. So many empty spaces between one thought and the other. So difficult to remember who I am. Who I was.

I'm always cold. Then, suddenly hot. Shivers and sweat. Each time I close my eyes, I pray not to open them again. To be gone in my sleep. That would be such a gift.

My calves cramp, twitch so bad but all I can do is... take it. Try to ignore the hitch and the pain by leaving my body. I retreat into the shadow realm.

This is not life. I'm glad Chiara finally said the words.

But what else did she say?

It was so important, and now I can't recall it. I'm too tired, I need some sleep now. And if it was so important, she'd tell me again, won't she?

Yes. Yes. She will.

Sleep now. Wish I could sleep forever.

Chapter 61
CLAIRE

Sorisole, November 16

Not much had changed in the past two days. Ondina was still feverish. Pained expression, eyes shut. Bitten and swollen lower lip.

On either side of her bed, Filippo and Nicola caressed her hands. Rattling the window panes, the sputtering noise of a rough lawnmower. Dark gray clouds gathered in the evening sky, the promise of more rain. The sky willing to match the mood in the room. November weather creeping inside my mind.

I tried to keep my cool, be like a samurai. I wore my jeans and boots, a t-shirt and a flannel. My battle armor. I entered the room to send Filippo and Nicola home.

"Ondina needs her rest now. And I do too. You guys can go. We'll be fine."

Filippo looked at me, his face like a question mark. I ignored him. I wouldn't let him stay.

"I'll leave my phone on," he said. "You know you can call

me at any moment, right?"

"Yeah. Everything's going to be alright."

Nicola kissed Ondina on her cheek.

I just wanted to get them out the door. We hugged but I was already somewhere else. In a place where the only emotion allowed was... no emotion. I'd been there before. In some odd way, it felt almost familiar. This time felt harder, though.

As I shut the door behind them, I exhaled. Finally, alone. Ready to get ready.

I moved to the kitchen and took out some bread and eggplant leftovers from the fridge. I put two slices in the toaster oven I'd bought to make myself a sandwich. My sister never felt the need to have a toaster. Fresh bread is tastier and she could buy it every day at the bakery in front of her old apartment. Or maybe just because it was 'too American.' But the new house in the countryside was far away from any store, hence the sliced bread in the fridge. "Bleah!" Ondina would comment. "I'd rather eat no bread at all." But I couldn't stomach cooking those days, and small mechanical actions like toasting the bread felt reassuring.

I carried the plate to the yellow Formica table that I'd moved from Ondina's old apartment. She was so proud of her yellow kitchen. I sat and looked at the plate. Mustard dripped out the sides and the sandwich no longer looked appealing. I forced myself to take a bite. The bread was stale and the filling tasteless. I chewed the food but there was no way I could swallow it. I spat it in the trash. Same destiny for the rest of the uneaten sandwich. Who could eat on a night like that?

In the bathroom, I brushed my teeth, washed my hands. Drying them, I glimpsed my reflection in the mirror. More lines around my eyes than cracks in the dirt of Death Valley at the end of summer. I aged ten years in a matter of months. My hair was limp. It used to be as lustrous and soft as the fur on a golden retriever. My back was constantly hurting. All the strain from lifting Ondina to her feet and making her stand up to regain consciousness and function of the nervous system had taken a toll on my body. And yet, I treasured the lines, the aches that left a mark on my skin and limbs—they were a roadmap, a tattoo of my days here. Together. Ondina and me.

I'd lost my proud, fast stride, and a few of my beliefs, but I'd gained something like wisdom. I learned things about the world and myself, surrendering to the truth that I might not be invincible after all.

My childhood dream was to make a difference. To save the world, make everybody free. My idea of happiness was freedom. My ideal world was populated by happy people who believed in their willpower and pursued their dreams, convinced that they had all it took to make them happen. But Italy didn't fit this bill. That's why I left it behind. This country of artists and talent was paralyzed by its attitudes. So afraid of change, poets at heart walked with the heavy pace of somebody who put up with the idea that their destiny was written in the tracks of their disdainful routine. They resented it, complained but didn't fight, expected someone else to take charge of their happiness while they burrowed in their dens. Many Italians lacked the pioneer gene that has you believe in dreams, long for unexplored lands. They lack daring.

Too many Italians also have a snobbish attitude toward Americans. They criticize not only their bread habits. They consider them superficial, deprived of culture rooted deep in history. They think that the ancient walls protecting their Middle Age cities, like here in Bergamo the Mura of Città Alta, were erected to protect their superior bloodline, enriched by more intellectual genes. But what is culture if it doesn't grow corn? If it does not allow you to change the things you can't enjoy?

That's what I believed. And yet, I realized not everybody

wanted to be happy my way. I had to learn to respect *their* idea of freedom, admitting they might make different choices. And their different choices didn't necessarily mean that they're cowards, less brave. I had to learn that everybody's threshold was different, the amount of pain and suffering they can stand, their way to react to it.

Truth is never only one thing. A revelation for Claire Waters, The Invincible. The enemy I faced, much more powerful than all my foes, was my ego. That's why it took me so long to learn that my sister's freedom of choice belonged to her. I interrogated myself. I had to challenge my beliefs. How could I give my sister her life back if she didn't want to live? How could I be so sure that my sister would heal if she didn't believe it?

Can anybody really free somebody else?

I plummeted into the unknown world of doubt, had to peel off all my assumptions. I scraped away the layers of certainties that I built over the course of my life with a butcher knife. Convictions that made me feel like a savior, a warrior at the service of change. My self-mythology, I realized, was the flattering idea that I was the designated helper for whomever intended to take fate in their hands.

I had this effect on people. I was charged like a neutron bomb, propelling them toward a different mindset. Up to them to pursue their dreams but, in my mind, I was the trigger entrusted by high powers to spark them off.

Sometimes, though, fire weapons backfire. And the recoil can be so powerful and strong as to jerk you backward into the dirt, unable to get up one more time. Sometimes, wounds are too deep for anybody to lick and heal them. Some awful times, your trusted mate, your companion, your child, the love of your life, bleeds to death on the battleground in your powerless arms. At times, you have to shoot the wounded to end their suffering.

This turn of events that started in January had changed me forever. I could never imagine more unbearable pain, a worse duty. And yet, I thanked all the gods who gave me such strength.

The iPod standing on the bathroom sink's tiled counter that I'd switched on stole me from my thoughts, calling me back with a song from the soundtrack of *The Phantom of the Opera*.

Time to play my part. Angel of Death. Granter of wishes.

I looked at myself in the mirror one last time, wiped the tears from my face. I opened a drawer of the vanity. Inside, pushed all the way to the back, was the envelope.

Seven p.m. Time to measure morphine.

Chapter 62
CLAIRE

Sorisole, November 16

The longest night of my life had started. I wiped pearls of sweat from Ondina's forehead with a clean washcloth. Her breath was painfully labored. Raucous. Slow. The first dosage of morphine I gave her had started to work already. Her eyes were open, watching me tending to her, gazing back into my eyes.

"Sweet Child O'Mine" by Guns N' Roses played at low volume. My music, not hers. If it were up to Ondina, she'd have probably chosen *Carmen* by Bizet, or *Carmina Burana*. Something ironic, dramatic. But the words of this song fitted my mood.

"Wherever you go, Ondina, I hope it's a place where no pain exists. I hope you can breathe long and easy there, walk and run and sing. And that I can hear your voice again."

I hadn't dared to leave my chair pulled close to her bed. I removed a damp curl from Ondina's forehead. She had finally closed her eyes.

"Sleep, sweet sister of mine. Breathe. Each of these painful breaths is taking you one step forward to your destination. A place in the middle of nowhere, my favorite kind. A place of freedom. I will help you get there. I would go with you if I didn't know the pain that my departure would cause to Alessandro. My son, Ondina, your nephew. He hasn't visited you since your accident. He couldn't, or he'd have risked losing his job. He loves you so much. I told him you might leave today and asked if he can stay tuned. So he's here with us, meditating, praying, thinking of you. Sending you energy since you need a ton to fuel your purpose."

Ondina's jaw hung open, probably to grasp more air.

"Don't worry, though. Don't be scared."

I took both of her hands in mine. They were icy. A shiver ran up my spine and I felt the urge to move. I put down the washcloth and stood. I turned Ondina on her side. "Is that better?"

I looked at my brave sister who'd asked the unthinkable from me. The thing she could have never asked of anybody else. I injected more morphine into Ondina's IV line. I moved around the bed and slipped inside the blankets with her. It was pitch dark out. I had kept open the curtains of the window facing the patio but couldn't see much through the finger-print-covered windowpanes. The room felt chillier than usual, maybe it was me.

"I'm going to hold you, hug you. Try to warm you up. Here, my sweetie. In my arms. Where you belong." I wrapped around her. A tapping on the terrazzo tiles outside. "Hear the rain? The sky is opening to welcome you. "November Rain." It's really a Guns N' Roses' night."

I was guns, Ondina, roses. I hummed the song into Ondina's hair. I stayed silent a few long minutes, paid attention to her breath. It was changing, heavier now.

I picked up the lyrics. Nothing lasts forever, it was true.

Not even the freezing November rain.

I put my left cheek to her upper back, listening. She was having longer apneas, her heavily labored breathing paused. But now the dense silence was lasting too long.

Alarmed, I held the air down in my lungs, to catch the next of Ondina's breaths. Which didn't come.

"Sister?"

No answer. I lifted myself up on my left elbow, pulled at Ondina's nightgown.

Nothing.

I straightened myself up, pushing on my arms to check Ondina's face. She seemed asleep but when I put a small mirror I grabbed from the nightstand in front of her mouth, it didn't fog.

I hastily jumped out of bed, my heart racing at an impossible pace. I hurried to the cabinet where I kept all her medical aids and pulled out the blood pressure monitor. Then I changed my mind, put it back. I checked for a pulse with two fingers on Ondina's carotid artery, instead. My hands were shaking and I was talking loudly to myself.

"Oh my! Oh my! Is this how it all ends? One last breath, and she's gone? One last breath and she will never be with me again?"

No pulse. No heartbeat.

I rushed out of the room. I didn't want Ondina to feel my despair, in case she could still feel emotions. I knew I was close to breaking down.

My legs collapsed as soon as I braved to get out of the bed. I crawled out of the room. I made it to the hallway, just outside Ondina's room. I hugged my knees and muffled my sobs in my sleeves, rocking myself back and forth, murmuring.

"I know it's right. It's what she wanted," I repeated it like a mantra until I'd quieted down enough. I was screaming, but only inside my chest.

Wiping tears, I tried to stand and when my legs felt stable, I walked to the bathroom. On the way, I saw the house telephone sitting on the antique console. I yanked it off the plug and threw it on the rug. And I was bawling again.

Inside the bathroom, I grabbed the brush I'd used to comb Ondina's hair, and threw it in the bathtub. I scanned the objects on the vanity looking for the softer ones, those that would not make so much noise when I smashed them. Just in case Ondina could still hear. I threw the bundle of multi-colored hair-ties on the floor. The box of tissues. The cotton wads. The syringe used for the morphine and its wrapper. The spare toilet paper roll. The adult Pampers bag. I pulled the towel off the rack and threw it. Then I spotted the empty plastic container of the nasty liquid formula used to feed by G.I. tube and directed all my fury against it. I smashed it with my feet on the bottom of the bathtub. I twirled and ripped the shower curtain off the rings that hooked it to the upper bar. I spun and wrapped myself in the torn fabric.

Exhausted, I dropped to the bottom of the tub. Sobbing inside the white plastic printed with yellow sunflowers. I rocked and rocked. Transformed into an alien caterpillar inside its polypropylene cocoon.

Chapter 63
CLAIRE

Sorisole, November 17

Sunrise brought some relief. There were things that needed to be done, people to be informed. That helped me to get back into my familiar doer mode. It fit me as an old favorite sweater, smelling like my previous life. It was a meager consolation, but I didn't know other ways to cope with the black hole of despair that was spreading inside me.

At first light, I stepped out onto the patio, clad in a down jacket and wool beanie to shield myself from the fog and drizzle. I sat at the teakwood table, in front of the greenery that Filippo had placed in big planters the previous spring to screen Ondina from curious passersby. Dry branches, no more flowers. They were sad, too. But I was grateful to this house for allowing me a few months with my sister away from hospitals and clinics.

I typed on my phone.

"She's gone. She is no longer in pain."

A group message to those who deserved to know. I clicked

off the phone and switched to my laptop. I wrote a post in the blog. The *Road to Recovery* title was hard to swallow but my fingers typed fast, without giving much thought.

November 17, 2008

It was the thing she loved most, traveling. And now she's free to... run, laugh, sing, all things forbidden in the hell she lived in these last ten months.

4:45 a.m., this morning. In her bed. In my arms. What more could a fierce woman like her ask for? She wanted to go. Her departure may have been caused by a series of medical mistakes and dire circumstances, but she ultimately chose when and how. She waited for me to come back from L.A. and rescue her from the last miserable clinic. She wanted to be away from any hospital environment to take flight in beauty.

I never met anybody braver than my sister.

I love you, Sis, and will always remember your courage, dignity and strength.

RIP now. You deserve it.

Not much and not great for a writer, but style wasn't on my mind, only duty. My job was to inform. It was the right thing to do despite the fact I'd not have wanted to talk with anybody. Nobody, but her.

I went back inside her room, took her hand in mine. "I will put you in a beautiful dress. Purple. Or red. Maybe that gorgeous gown that you wore that time on stage. You looked like a blooming rose."

I could see the scene like it was happening in that moment, right in front of me.

Ondina in her twenties. A spotlight bathing her in a circle of brightness. A complete dark background. Ondina folded over herself, hiding in the layers of red velvet. Kneeling with her head down. Sitting on her heels and hugging her calves. After a few moments, she started singing softly, raising her head and extending her arms like petals of a budding rose.

Let me part
Let me part
Let me paaaart
That's what I do best.

I will still dance in the rain
Our love won't have been in vain
But I need to fly now
Leave the nest of your love
Got too sticky somehow
I'm no longer your dove.

Then she stood up, sang louder, marching on stage, crossing left to right and back, dropping on her knees and jumping up. She kicked off her shoes and shook her dark curls. She danced wildly.

A force of nature. A gypsy. A savage. And I remember how proud I'd been for being her sister, watching her in awe from the audience.

Let me part
I have dreamed of this time
Change my route
On the drop of a dime
Change my heart
Clean it out of all lime
And soar free like an eagle.

Let me part
I won't forget
Your hands warming my cheeks
Chinese food with chopsticks
On the snowy mountains, the Alps
Where we smoked our love
White forbidding the dove

Let me paaart
That's what I do best.
Can't give up on the zest
How excited I am
That I'm finally leaving.

I will gather my things
Give away to my flings
A whole line of new boys
I can choose from more toys
I can go and ignore
Turn away with a snore
And just soar like an eagle.

Let me part.
Let me pa-a-a-a-rt.

Let me part.
Open your hands
Let the dove
Follow her heart
That's what she does
Best

Let me pa-a-a-a-art!

On the last note, she'd dropped to her knees, panting hard and red-faced. She lowered her head, chin on her chest, sat back on her heels, wrapped herself in the crimson velvet. She'd turned back into a rose.

I looked at my dead sister with moist eyes. That song was our inside joke. Since she chose to hold onto the notion of a perfect, faithful love. *Due cuori e una capanna.* A home with a fireplace and a cat purring on the couch. A solid man who'd never leave her side.

I, on the other hand, would have happily lived my life in

hotels. Room service as my motto, if it wasn't for Alessandro. Kids need stability, and my son was the only reason to compromise my dream of a nomadic life. Happily and willingly, not feeling sacrificed.

"I was the one who never bought the fairytale. I chose my own line of defense. I didn't allow anybody to leave me, I'd always leave first."

But here I was, forced to stay while she'd already left. How ironic!

I looked closely at her face. Was she smirking, or had the corners of her mouth involuntarily twitched up?

Chapter 64
CLAIRE

Sorisole, November 18

The house was overcrowded with friends. Some had to wait on the patio for their turn to come in, bundled up in jackets and hats to handle the morning chill. Ondina was laid out on her bed in a light purple sundress with matching sandals. Her arms and legs were bare. She couldn't feel the cold that had plagued her for the past almost ten months. I'd clipped my favorite earrings on her, those silver hoops I wore day and night, and an amethyst and silver necklace. Also, three different rings on her hands, and an Indian silver anklet. It looked like she was ready to go to a summer party.

Her face muscles were relaxed. Her eyes slightly open, just a tiny slit under her lowered lids. Her mouth still sported that smirk. It was not agape like Mom's was, which had made me so uncomfortable.

Friends alternated at her bedside, paying their last respects after my brother and stepmom were done. When the last friend left her bedroom to join the others gathering in the living room, I moved the chair closer to my sister. The seat was still warm from the last occupant. The French doors to the patio were open to air the room. I could see the funeral workers lined up, waiting to carry the casket inside. My last minutes with her.

"They all came," I whispered, convinced that she could hear me and she needed me to say those words. "They didn't forget. Filippo, of course. Guilherme, Giovanni, Paolo, Fabrizio... all the men who loved you. Giovanni and Guilherme holding up, their arms on each other's shoulders and backs, trying to push back tears. Cristiana, who never abandoned us and, like Giovanna, was there until the end. And Paola, Lucia, Nicoletta, Giulia, Chicca... The women who went missing lately but had been your friends, your confidants and comrades. They all showed up in the end, lined up for you. I'm the only one not crying. I have no tears left."

I cried a river already, early in the morning before dawn. I cried the night before when I was in her bed, hugging her from behind and trying to warm her up. I cried when my ears registered a suspicious silence. An interruption, all of a sudden, in her fatigued breath.

I believed I was prepared. I was so wrong. Death strikes you in a way you can't prepare for, no matter how confident you think you are. I knew every sound, every image, every moment of the night my sister died would remain sculpted in my memory, whether I liked it or not. I just hoped to forget the scent of decay. But I knew it would chase me in my dreams, that unforgettable smell, so unlike any other, that announces the immutable end.

I'd kept opened all the windows, despite the cold. Nobody else should remember that smell. I wanted her friends to think of Ondina smelling of citrus and amber, her favorite perfume. I'd try to remember her smelling the white camellias that Grandma had planted in the garden of the lake house to celebrate her first granddaughter, when Ondina was born.

Grandma's magic was powerful but she, too, had to surrender. I remembered when our Uncle Claudio got sick with cancer at twenty-eight. She had trouble accepting that magic couldn't cure him. He was her baby. He was also my absolute hero. He taught me how to drive his red Porsche when I was nine, how to shoot a rifle. Like me, he couldn't stay still for two minutes. He was very physical. A handsome man with plenty of girlfriends. Grandma hated them all. He finally got married, a year before succumbing to cancer. Uncle Claudio was in the hospital for five months. He shrank to wren size and became weak to the point he couldn't turn his head. But he had a miraculous burst of energy toward the end.

I happened to be there that day. Ondina had chosen to remain home with Mom. Hospitals scared the hell out of her, and seeing her uncle so sick made her depressed.

Uncle Claudio didn't know that he had cancer and was going to die. Grandma had decided to keep it from him. I was convinced that he should know the truth but I was only ten and wouldn't dare to cross Grandma's orders.

Uncle Claudio sat up in bed, propped up on the pillows, hugging his knees. He called for his wife. "I feel good today. I want to go shopping. Call the nurse and take this stuff out." He had various needles stuck in his veins, pumping chemicals into his blood. He wanted to go out and enjoy the spring sun, drive his red Porsche around town. He wanted to go to a good restaurant and have a decent meal. But the doctors didn't care about his wishes. They didn't want to take responsibility for allowing him to leave the hospital and maybe die on the street. That's what the hospital director tried to tell Grandma, when she pleaded for her son's temporary freedom.

"Young man," Grandma told the doctor, about fifty years old and gray-haired. "My son was under my responsibility much longer than yours and he still is. I decide what's best for him. If he says he wants to go out, he'll go out. The only thing I can do for you is promise that I'll have him back here tonight, safe and sound, so that you'll keep your job."

My father left the hospital to fetch the red Porsche. He offered to drive and my uncle allowed him. They went out shopping, had lunch at a fancy *ristorante*.

I stayed at the hospital with Grandma, awaiting their return. The whole time, Grandma remained quietly seated with her eyes closed, mumbling, a rosary in her hands. She imagined her son healthy, vibrant and lively as he'd always been, before getting sick. She told me this in a rare moment of closeness, after his return. But despite her will and her prayers, Uncle Claudio died two days later. It was a terrible blow. I'd believed that Grandma had the power to heal him. "I was not strong enough to beat such an advanced cancer," she admitted. "But I could at least give him some relief. I could still make my baby-son happy for one day."

I landed back in the room with my dead sister. "I called for Grandma and she came, Ondina," I felt like telling my sister while suddenly remembering a dream I had many years before, in which Grandma explained why she'd always seemed so angry with me. "I had to harden you. I needed to prepare you for what was going to come." I never knew what she meant but I knew now. And I wish I never had to.

She did prepare me, with her scolding and neglect. She made me strong, able to endure even this crushing pain. Dreams tell the truth. But it can take decades to finally understand their meaning.

We were alone in the house, finally. Just me and Ondina after everybody else left, getting into their cars, ready to follow the funeral hearse to the cemetery. Only the undertakers stood by, outside on the patio, waiting for me to leave so they could put Ondina in the casket. But I wasn't ready.

I stood up from the chair and looked at my sister on her

deathbed, surrounded by the rose petals that I spread on the bedsheet. Beautiful again, shining in her purple gown. And I heard her in my mind, singing the notes from "Don't Cry For Me Argentina," the version she adapted for me when I left home, teasing me by singing it to me at the airport, *Don't cry for me, sorellina.* To say goodbye to her younger sister, me, her grown up "sorellina" leaving Italy to placate her thirst for new horizons.

I smiled at the memory and the way it had surfaced to my mind exactly in this moment. Ondina's present for me to help me let her go. Which was the hardest thing I'd ever done in my life.

I glanced at the funeral people, reminding me of big ravens all dressed in black. They waited to come in and seal my sister in her wood casket. The baclofen pump prevented cremation, since it was still running and could explode in the oven. "Can you imagine?" I teased Ondina. "Going away with a loud boom like a firecracker?"

The smirk on Ondina's lips seemed to deepen, the corners of her mouth lifted a tad more. Or maybe I was just imagining, but it still felt good.

I was ready. Or, to say it as it is, I was as ready as I could ever be. Which was not ready at all.

Chapter 65
CLAIRE

Sorisole, December 21 - Eleven months after the accident

My suitcase and carry-on were already out on the doormat. Drago was guarding them, waiting for me to step out. I puffed small white clouds with each breath, dressed in the same ankle-long black coat I wore when I arrived in January, and a multicolored Pashmina scarf, gray mittens and a black beanie hat. It had taken weeks and more tears to empty both houses, Mom's and Ondina's.

I'd always loved empty houses, as they meant a blank canvas. A new place to make yours when you move. The beginning of a new adventure. But emptying their apartments felt conclusive and sad. The end of them, truly. Places I'd never go back to when I'd travel to my birth country again. But would I?

It would never be the same, without my mom and sister there. I still had my brother, whom I loved to pieces. His mom, my Aunt Marilde and her son Stefano, Uncle Giorgio and my cousin Manuela. All of them were part of my Italian childhood.

All that was left of my once-big family. But it was my mom and Ondina who'd shared my daily life, my happiness and sorrows, my conquests and falls. Their absence left a void. A heavy knot of emptiness, as if a golf ball had been placed in between my throat and my lungs.

When you lose loved ones, people tell you they'll live in your heart. I hoped my sister wouldn't. My heart was a jigsaw puzzle trailed by deep scars and angry welts, a bad place to inhabit. I hoped her spirit would run free around the world instead, visiting all the places she'd never been yet and the ones she'd loved.

I'd already closed all the shutters, the *persiane* that Italians use to block the light and sleep in total darkness, locking them from the inside also for security, when they go on vacation or leave an apartment vacant. One of those things like the *bidet,* that gave points to Italy in my perpetual comparison to the American way of life.

I locked the front door and grabbed the suitcase with one hand, the handle of the carry-on with the other. I crossed the courtyard, walking toward the wooden door that opens to the street. I stopped under the arches in front of the mailbox slots and dropped the keys of the apartment in number 12, as instructed. Then I pushed the button to release the very small pedestrian door cut inside the bigger one, and stepped outside.

The cab was already there, engine idling. A sign on the windshield said TRANSFERS FROM/TO MILAN MALPENSA. The driver got out to take my luggage, put it in the trunk. I opened the passenger door in the back, let Drago in and dumped myself on the seat.

As we drove, I looked at what felt like my last glimpse of Italy. The acacias and oaks had lost all their leaves. The pomegranate trees were still green but no longer adorned with ripe red-purple fruit. Maples and sorbus trees had changed foliage and wore a symphony of yellow and orange. Rows of cottonwoods with silver leaves bordered the road, thick bushes growing at their feet. Honeysuckle. Philadelphus. Non-native Japonica with dangerously poisonous flowers. Hawthorn, with its small red berries. Elderberry, that Italians use to make the aromatic liqueur Sambuca, a great digestive served at the end of a feast. Red, white and pink geraniums that were common on the balconies of apartment buildings until only a month earlier, when they had been replaced by pots of winter camellias, mauve-colored heather, white narcissus, arbutus with orange and red fruit, pansies, solanum, calycanthus.

I wanted to remember them all. The colors of the Italian fall. The last season I lived with my sister.

Epilogue
CLAIRE

Los Angeles, 12 March, 2013

The evening breeze gently pushed away the few remaining clouds in the darkening sunset sky. It carried the fragrance of California poppies and hummingbird sage, the first wildflowers to bloom in Griffith Park that clothed the hillsides with a shawl woven in bright orange blended with hot pink.

A crowd stood in line outside the entrance of Skylight Books on Vermont Street, my favorite independent bookstore. Backpacks, boots and clogs, colorful sweaters and cargo pants, but also more formal attire. Locals from Los Feliz and the neighboring Silverlake and Hollywood, but also fans from Venice, Santa Monica, Long Beach. Girls and women wearing red skirts, purple blouses or scarves, fresh flowers in their hair. Some of the guys held a red rose in their hands or had a twig of purple bougainvillea fastened to the lapel of their jackets.

Posters on the store windows showed the photo of a book cover with the silhouette of a woman branching into a bougainvillea plant. It read: "Claire Water's new book. *Bougain-*

villea Sister - A memoir. Join us at 7 p.m. for the book signing. Please, wear something red or purple if you can." My agent had suggested it, and I'd liked her idea.

Inside the store, I hid in the office upstairs. I wore a spaghetti-strapped, form-fitting dark red dress and heels. My hair was pinned in a high bun decorated with purple bougain-villea blooms.

I sneaked a peek when the door opened. Two-by-two, people came in past the front desk covered with piles of my book ready to be sold and signed. But the crowd was too big for the number of seats, for the small room. I retreated into the shadows and looked for tissues in my purse. My armpits, neck and cleavage were beaded with sweat.

"It must be the outfit. It's been so long since I dressed up."

"You'll do great. You've done many things you didn't use to," Filippo said, winking. And he was right. I wasn't used to love. I couldn't contemplate that togetherness with a man was possible. It was nice, for once, to be wrong. I always teased my sister, and now I felt like a teenager in love for the first time. Ondina's last gift. This man, her friend. He'd come all this way, leaving behind his life. And we'd come a long way. We'd shared tragedy but also beauty. And now intimacy and knowing.

The microphone blared, then a clear voice announced: "We're ready to begin and welcome Claire Waters. Back from hell, as she writes in the foreword, and from a long hiatus. Five years since her last thriller, and this new book is a first for her in many ways." He crescendo-ed like a circus host. "Ladies and gentlemen, please give a big welcome to Claire Waters and her just-released, *Bougainvillea Sister*!"

I smoothed my dress, moved a curl away from my damp forehead and readied myself. Filippo gave me a thumbs up. I walked down the stairs toward the podium and the micro-phone nodding at the applauding audience, shook the present-er's hand. Clearing my throat, I opened the copy in my hand

and read from the preface. I felt flushed and my voice had a quiver in those first words.

"I've killed lots of people in my life. Always on paper, though. Then came 2008, the Year of The Rat. That year, I was transmuted. I'm no longer the mystery writer, creating and destroying hardcore killers."

I looked up from the book, at the audience. I spotted my agent, who'd encouraged me to take the plunge and write this intimate story, so different from my others. Alessandro sat with Filippo and several of his friends. Xavier stood in the back. He winked and raised his palm in greeting when my eyes found him. My Mount Washington neighbors, who were also my friends, had conquered the first row of seats.

I'd prepared more paragraphs to read, but now it felt wrong. There was a different thing I wanted to say. I closed the book. "There's somebody else here with us. My sister, Ondina. This book is dedicated to her and it's titled like one of her songs. She was a singer/songwriter. She also was the bravest person I ever met."

I had to pause and breathe. Five years later, I still had trouble talking about her, but I had to go on.

"She lost her ability to move, eat and talk because of a brain stroke. Some said she was in a vegetative state. But those were people with no imagination."

I didn't need to read from the book to spell the words now crowding in my throat. I wanted to share what I discovered, all that I learned in my journey. I didn't want others to find themselves unprepared as I was. I didn't want to see pity in people's eyes when facing somebody carrying a disability.

"There is much to learn from those who have limitations in their abilities, who have differing abilities. We're limited in our left-dominated vision. We are brought up to primarily use the left part of our brain, the rational side that informs our linear thinking, our decision-making. We lose access to a whole world of wonder experienced by kids, artists and monks but we, too, can achieve deep states of relaxation through meditation. It's the great challenge of our lives to open the door into stillness."

I paused and searched again the faces in the audience, silent and attentive. Everyone was there for me. For Ondina. And our story.

"My bougainvillea sister took me there. It was a journey of transformation and I came back a different woman. In this book, I share the beauty of our journey into another world, while fighting against the odds in this one. It was no bed of roses. It was harsh. Sometimes, horrifying. It took me three years to gather the courage to look back. I was afraid of reliving an unbearable pain."

I was surprised to find myself sharing my feelings so openly with the audience. I didn't feel the need to hide my emotions, as I'd been doing for such a long time.

"I was afraid, but inside me there was a desire much stronger than pain. My sister kept talking to me. I could hear her in my dreams but I couldn't quite get what she said. But finally, I heard her voice. *Her* beautiful voice. Singing. Laughing. Whispering in the wind. And I let her tell her side of the story."

I turned the book I still held in my hands and showed the audience the cover.

"So, here it is. My sister's story. Something I thought I could never write."

I set the microphone back on its stand, walked behind the desk. The notes of "Bougainvillea Sister" filled the room together with the clapping of hands. Filippo had planned for the song to play at the end, without my input. His gift.

I signed a lot of books and shook many hands, grateful for the show of support received despite my years of absence from the bookshelves. Years I spent first grieving, then listening to my sister's voice, whispering the right words for me to heal, writing her story.

Xavier had remained in the store, hanging by the exit. He signaled me to reach him in the parking lot in the back. I wondered if that meant he had to leave in a rush. He lived in New Mexico now. I didn't know if he'd planned to remain in town for the evening or drive straight back. But when I stepped into the lot, another surprise welcomed me. Bitten by The Snake stood by a truck. In his arms a beautiful boy with long, straight black hair and chocolate brown eyes. Noah, Xavier's three-year-old son, his reason to remain at his reservation. I'd only seen the boy in photos so far. Holding him in my arms brought an unstoppable surge of emotion, joyful tears flooding my eyes.

The evening breeze blew in from the hillside and Drago suddenly halted, his nose raised high to sniff the intangible whiff of a new fragrance in the air. That's when I smelled it. Amber, citrus and woody notes blended with white flowers. My sister's scent. Drago knew it, and I knew it too.

Acknowledgments

I have a huge debt of gratitude to many people who helped me along the way on this nine-year-long journey, often interrupted when I couldn't bear the pain of writing something so close to my personal experience, something I'd never tried before.

First and foremost, to my friend and critique partner, author Litty Mathew, and twelve-year old Isabella Han-Bolelli, a great writer herself and an avid reader of my work: without you two, this book would have never seen the light of day. Thanks for never giving up, submitting yourself to review my many revisions of this story and surprising me with strokes of pure writing genius. Thank you to Isabella also for putting my lyrics to music with the help of Jude Rega. If you follow me on Instagram, you'll have the pleasure of listening to this talented duo playing the songs included in the book.

To my alpha and beta readers, particularly my son, "History on Fire" podcaster Daniele Bolelli, his writer father Franco Bolelli, Danny Guerrero, Jeannie Winston, Arianna Dagnino, Margaret Arana, and Anne Stockwell, who provided valuable feedback on my first draft. To Laura Drake and David Francis for offering their expert editing help. To my dialogue critique group: Tanya Oplanic, Linda Moore, Dennis Cusack, Loraine Shields and Janine Weyers. To my writing teachers at Community of Writers and particularly to author Janet Fitch, who never fails to inspire me: your generosity, constructive criticism and sound advice made me a much better fiction writer than I was when I enrolled in the first of your awesome workshops. To the whole team at Atmosphere Press, especially to Trista Edwards, who immediately clicked with my story, and Megan Turner for editing my mistakes.

To the Women's Fiction Writers Association, where I found my online community of sister authors whom I can always ask for advice, opinions, encouragement, support, and celebration of each other's success. To artist Maria Loor, for creating a beautiful cover that reflected my view of Ondina's and Claire's story. To Cataldo Dino Meo, whose raw and beautiful poetry inspired me every day when I read it before writing a new page. To my friend Luciana Daniotti, also a friend like no others.

To the French Association ALIS, for providing great insight into the many ramifications of locked-in syndrome. To the American organization Compassionate Choice, for defending everyone's right to die with dignity. To my Dakota family and my Lakota friends in South Dakota for their love and trust in sharing their ancestors' ways and traditional knowledge with me. To all the caregivers out there, to those families who don't abandon their own, to the sisters, the mothers, the daughters, the brothers, the sons and the fathers of severely disabled people. I know what it takes and immensely appreciate your generosity and dedication.

Last but not least, to my husband, Federico Giordano, whose infinite patience, true independence, and self-reliance has allowed me to live in my own fictional world surrounded by these characters who were struggling to share their voices until I could hear them loud and clear. Thank you for allowing me total freedom, for not feeling abandoned and for your terrible boiled zucchini when I was stuck for long hours buried under deadlines, unable even to cook.

Book Club
Discussion Questions

If you'd like Gloria to speak to your book club, either in person or via zoom, you can contact her through her website:

www.GloriaMattioni.com

She's always glad to connect also with readers who might want to ask her questions regarding her work using the same form.

1.   How does Claire's personality change during the course of the story? How do her values? Why do these changes occur? And what happens to Ondina, when she wakes up trapped in a body no longer responding with a mind that works only intermittently and along other parameters than the linear thinking she was used to? How does she change while the story develops?

2.   Claire is the narrator in *California Sister* but Ondina's voice, despite her being speechless, is expressed through letters, journal entries, lyrics she wrote in the past and fragments

of her thoughts after waking up from her coma. Which voice is more resonant and powerful for you? And why?

3. This story has a strong sense of place. Part of the book is set in Los Angeles and part in Northern Italy. Do you agree with Joan Didion, who wrote: "A place belongs forever to whoever claims it hardest, remembers it most obsessively, wrenches it from itself, shapes it, renders it, loves it so radically that he remakes it in his own image"? How is this description reflecting Claire's relationship with the city she chose when she left Italy?

4. Italy and Los Angeles 'speak' along the novel almost like two other main characters, with their own distinct "voices". Do you think they represent Claire and Ondina? Are they a metaphor for the more yin-oriented, reflective Ondina and the yang action-driven Claire?

5. Los Angeles is described by Claire as a place for wanderers where no one really fits in; a perfect landing for her rootless, nomadic spirit. What are the other characteristics of the city that are present in the book?

6. Claire turns to the outdoors for reprieve. Walking is her medicine. However, she also has a strong passion for surfing. Water and earth. To which element do you think Claire is more connected to? And Ondina?

7. When Claire is first introduced to yoga, she does not have the best experience. Why do you think that is? Why do you think she is so independent and generally unwilling to give up control? Could her childhood have something to do with that?

8. Claire and Ondina have a different relationship with their mother. In which way? And why?

9.   Their Parkinson-ravaged mother is fragile and powerless in her old age but sometimes hard and strong-willed, still trying to exercise authority and control over her daughters like she used to do when they were young. Why? Do you know anybody with these characteristics? How did you react to this character?

10.   Ondina has many friends who initially surround her with great love but most of them disappear during the course of her illness. Why do you think they abandon her? Does Ondina suffer their abandonment? Would you have reacted the same way or stick around like Filippo, Nicola, Cristiana and Giovanna?

11.   Doctors seem to think Ondina is in a vegetative state although she's in locked-in syndrome. Do you know the difference between these two neurological conditions? Why does Ondina let only Claire know that she can understand and feel emotion while she retreats into herself with the doctors?

12.   When the doctor in charge of Ondina's first rehab clinic tells Claire that he'll dismiss Ondina, Claire refuses to put her sister in long term care and instead takes her home with her. How did you feel about Claire's decision?

13.   After a long battle, Claire can no longer ignore the pact she stipulated with her sister when they were little girls and feels more determined to abide by Ondina's wishes, helping her die. Why do you think it took Claire so long to come to this decision?

14.   The right to die with dignity is a hot topic worldwide and is the subject of books, movies, documentaries, and podcasts. It is also a controversial issue with specific sets of rules in

different countries and states. Are you aware of the laws in your state? What obstacles does Claire meet in Italy when she finally recognizes Ondina's right to choose for herself? What does she have to do to help her and why?

15. There are some important male characters in the book. What did you think of Xavier? And of his relationship with Claire? Were you hoping they'd go back together in the end?

16. Filippo is Ondina's friend but proves himself as the most reliable support for Claire during Ondina's ordeal. He seems to be the polar opposite of Claire's personality but Claire, so protective of her sister and also so guarded of herself, lets him in more than others. Why do you think that happens?

17. Aside from the trust and friendship developed between him and Claire in 2008, Filippo makes a surprise entrance in 2013 at the very end of the novel when Claire launches her new book, a memoir of the events of that year. We come to know that he is now Claire's partner. Did you suspect Claire and Filippo would eventually get together? If so, when did you realize it? Do you prefer Claire and Xavier or Claire and Filippo? Do you believe that opposites truly attract? Why or why not? Aside from Claire and Filippo, what are some other examples found in the story?

18. Along with the outdoors and walking, music is another form of comfort for Claire and a recurrent theme in the book. Ondina used to be a singer and songwriter in her youth. How important is music in your life? Do you have a favorite genre?

19. Ondina used to express herself in music and words. She's always been very talkative and wrote beautiful lyrics, letters, and travel diaries. Now speechless, she cannot commu-

nicate her wishes with words. Not even with Claire. Her hearing has also been damaged, so Claire tries to enhance communication through gentle touch and physical contact. Did you ever experience non-verbal communication with an adult? If so, how did it feel? Was it difficult or natural?

20.   Claire has a special connection with animals, who are naturally attracted to her. She also seems to have a kind of animal instinct for danger and her sense of smell is as fine as Drago's, the rescue dog that will accompany her to Italy and will be her best friend during the long year of Ondina's ordeal. Have you ever had that kind of relationship with an animal? Is smell an important sense for you too or are you more visual or auditive?

About Atmosphere Press

Atmosphere Press is an independent, full-service publisher for excellent books in all genres and for all audiences. Learn more about what we do at atmospherepress.com.

We encourage you to check out some of Atmosphere's latest releases, which are available at Amazon.com and via order from your local bookstore:

Tsunami, a novel by Paul Flentge

Tubes, a novel by Penny Skillman

Skylark Dancing, a novel by Olivia Godat

ALT, a novel by Aleksandar Nedeljkovic

The Bonds Between Us, a novel by Emily Ruhl

Dancing with David, a novel by Siegfried Johnson

The Friendship Quilts, a novel by June Calender

My Significant Nobody, a novel by Stevie D. Parker

Nine Days, a novel by Judy Lannon

Shining New Testament: The Cloning of Jay Christ, a novel by Cliff Williamson

Shadows of Robyst, a novel by K. E. Maroudas

Home Within a Landscape, a novel by Alexey L. Kovalev

Motherhood, a novel by Siamak Vakili

Death, The Pharmacist, a novel by D. Ike Horst

Mystery of the Lost Years, a novel by Bobby J. Bixler

Bone Deep Bonds, a novel by B. G. Arnold

Terriers in the Jungle, a novel by Georja Umano

About the Author

Gloria Mattioni is the author of several books and a long-time magazine contributor. She has been a storyteller since she learned to form complete sentences and became a professional writer at eighteen. Raised in Milan, Italy, she moved to Los Angeles in 1992. She shares her home with her husband, a skittish rescue dog and the occasional strays she picks up to find them a forever home. She's a proud member of the Authors' Guild and a volunteer with the Women's Fiction Writers Association. She's also an avid hiker who finds her solace in nature, a worshipper of waves and Italian cooking.

Website: www.GloriaMattioni.com

CPSIA information can be obtained
at www.ICGtesting.com
Printed in the USA
BVHW040616060622
638842BV00003B/12